LAMB'S CREEK

A Tennessee Community that Spurned Slavery
and Survived the Bloodshed of the Civil War

DON MILLER

This book is a work of fiction. Names, characters, places, and incidents either are the product of the author's imagination or are used fictitiously. Any resemblance to actual events or locales or persons, living or dead, is entirely coincidental.

LAMB'S CREEK, A Tennessee Community that Spurned Slavery and Survived the Bloodshed of the Civil War

Dog Pound Press Paperback Edition / September 2014

All Rights Reserved
Copyright © 2014 Don Miller

This book or any portion thereof may not be reproduced or used in any manner whatsoever without the express written permission of the publisher.

For information contact Dog Pound Press at
www.DonMillerWriter.com

Dog Pound Press
ISBN-13: 978-0615891156
ISBN-10: 0615891152

Lamb's Creek was written by Don Miller with advice and review provided by Paula Miller and Cindy Taylor

Cover design by MillerLine Design and Webtegrity, Copyright © 2014

Author Photo by Webster Miller, Copyright © 2011

Photo of the old oak tree in Cayucos, CA, by Jan Moore used on the cover design with permission, see www.ArtbyJanMoore.com

To My Family

PROLOGUE

God divided the light from the darkness. And God called the light Day, and the darkness He called Night. And the evening and the morning were the first day. Genesis 1:4-6

Stories are to be told and shared with others so who better than one that was witness to the happenings. I will introduce myself only as Time though I have been called by many names and described in many ways - a short Time, long Time, slow and fast Time, bedtime, daytime...well, you get the picture.

I am not the Creator although I was the first creation. All others came after me and I witnessed them all. I have many stories to tell but decided on this one about a young boy born into slavery and how he transcended those bonds to become part of a very special community. In order for me to tell and you to experience the story, we have to travel through a most perplexing era of time. This is not only a story but for me an opportunity to reveal myself a little more. This part of my story began in the fall of 1825 in two unique places each with their own circumstances, comings and goings, though in time you will see how the happenings are related.

A beautiful two hundred-year old chestnut oak stood proud at the entrance of a lovely valley in Tennessee that ran north and south between two tree-covered ridges. The valley opened to a grassy meadow about two miles long and one mile broad at its widest. A large creek ran through the valley with smaller tributaries feeding it, supplying water to the entire valley and making the soil rich and fertile.

On a stormy night in September, lightning flashing, the old tree seemed to guard the little valley from danger when one very large bolt of lightning struck the heart of the old oak splitting it asunder. The next morning the sun was shining bright and nature was at peace as if there had not been a storm at all. The only evidence remaining from the storm was a full, fast running creek next to the large chestnut oak that now lay in two pieces on the ground. The old tree had retired its position as sentinel, never to stand guard over the entrance of the valley again.

Deer were feeding on the leaves and acorns of the chestnut oak. A red squirrel grabbed an acorn from its little crown where it had grown to maturity. Deciding not to eat it, the squirrel scampered across the ground, buried its discovery but never unearthed it later as little creatures often do. The acorn would one day take the place of its parent tree at the entrance of the valley. This is the way of nature.

Two hundred miles away in South Carolina on the same night in a small shack a little boy was born to a sixteen-year-old slave girl. When she looked at the tiny newborn, she cried to her mother, "Mam, I don't wants that baby. Give him away to somebody."

"Mable, hush up. You don't know what you sayin'. Jus' hush

up. You'll feel different later. Now let 'im suck some milk. It'll make you love him. Jus' wait till tomorrow," Hattie said as she held the baby out to Mable.

The next day Mable did not like the baby any more than when it was born and refused to hold it other than to allow the baby to suckle. The act caused her pain in many ways.

"Child, I sure don't understand you. Ain't right not to love your baby. What's got into you? It jus' ain't natural."

"Mam, I love you and I love Daddy, but I just don't love that baby. I don't know why." Two weeks later, Mable was gone. No one saw her go and no one tried to find her.

"Did Mable say where she might go?" Hattie's husband, Samuel, asked.

"No, Samuel, she don't say nothin' about leavin'. She's jus' gone. I guess we got another baby to raise. What we gonna call him? I say we name him Samuel like you."

The little boy was named Samuel. Sammy is what everyone called him.

PART I
The Beginning

CHAPTER ONE

Sammy set the basket of hen eggs inside the back door. Hattie smiled at him and said, "You run out to the road and see if yo Pap is comin' home for dinner. He oughta be close enough for you to see 'im comin'."

"Okay Mam, but can I have a biscuit till it's time to eat?" Hattie scooped a hot biscuit from the black iron skillet and handed it to Sammy.

Before he made it down the wooden steps leading from the back door, Sammy had a mouthful of hot biscuit. He shifted the biscuit back and forth between his little hands, blowing the heat out as he chewed, thinking, *Pap shouldn't be far down the road.*

Just as he pushed through the wooden gate from the yard and set small bare feet to a smooth dirt path, Sammy noticed something shiny, *a coin, money!* He bent over to pick it up and said quietly to himself, "Real money! What I gonna do? If I show Mam, she probably makes me give it up." But show Hattie was exactly what he had to do right away. He turned back toward the house forgetting the errand to which he had been charged.

Sammy swung the screen door open shouting, "Mam, Mam, look what I found! Money, real money! Can I keep it? I bet it ain't nobody's. How much is it? Let's don't tell nobody I found it. Just let me keep it, please Mam."

"Sammy, that's a dime, ten cents. Where you find it?"

"In the road, Mam. Please, can I keep it?"

"Well, tell yo Pap and see what he say. Was he comin' up the road?" Hattie asked.

"Aw Mam, I forgot to look, but I'll go see right now. I won't forget this time."

Hattie smiled and watched Sammy turn, move again down the steps, through the gate and out to the road. She thought about herself at Sammy's age. *I was jus' a little younger than Sammy, was it five or six, when they took mama away?* Hattie couldn't recall her exact age, but recollected like it was yesterday the incident of being held back by her old Granny while her mother was dragged to the wagon that would take her to auction.

Hattie heard someone say, *"Too old to bear more children and too crippled to do a day's work,"* as she watched her mother and several other frail women shoved into the wagon. *"Costs too much to feed them when they get in such shape."*

Hearing those terrible words, Hattie pulled away from old Granny and ran after the wagon. Unable to catch up and blinded by tears, Hattie tripped, fell and lay paralyzed by the horror that she may never see her mother again. As the wagon rounded a bend in the road and rolled out of Hattie's sight, she had the sensation of being lifted up from the earth. That sense of lightness was disrupted by the reality that she had indeed been physically hoisted up and carried by two strong arms. Samuel gently delivered her to Granny's cabin.

Samuel, twelve years old and *big as an ox* as the white folks described him, had no trouble carrying Hattie to Granny. "I'll take care of my lil' girl and ain't nobody goin' to hurt you," Samuel had said to comfort her.

Samuel seemed to appear each time she needed a hand. Hattie always felt safe when Samuel was next to her, and the bond between them grew stronger as they grew older. It was the day her mother was taken that Hattie knew she and Samuel were supposed to be together always.

Hattie, small, spry and spunky, was a chatterbox. Samuel, big, strong and silent, was slow to anger. The two made a striking contrast. The South Carolina plantation owners and the small slave community respected Samuel. There was no question of Samuel's intent to marry Hattie.

Two weeks before her fifteenth birthday, Samuel asked the Master if he could marry Hattie. He was given permission and a wedding was planned. The Master insisted there be a ceremony, "Samuel and Hattie, not only do I give you permission to marry, but we'll have a ceremony and celebration. Samuel, you do the work of three men, never complain, never cause trouble and never ask for anything. This is something I can do for you."

Later, Hattie claimed, "Samuel, the Massa is puttin' on a show." She felt certain such an extravagant event was the Master's way of easing his conscious for selling her mother. Samuel found a way to console her. He reminded her that most of the slaves allowed to marry simply moved into a cabin together.

"Our weddin'," Samuel told Hattie, "will have a preacher presidin', makin' it a legal bound union."

Hattie had heard about slaves jumping the broom, but she had never witnessed it and certainly had never thought she would experience it for herself. Once she and Samuel were pronounced husband and wife, they were led to two brooms laid under the large oak tree nearest the front porch of the plantation. They jumped lightly over separate brooms to join hands and lives. Hattie could not have imagined then that she and Samuel would be blessed to have a grandchild like Sammy.

Right now, Hattie thought, *Sammy is probably going on and on to Samuel about the coin he found.* The thought made Hattie smile. She loved Sammy as much as she had loved her only child, Mable.

Washing the last of the dirty dishes, Hattie said aloud to herself, "I sure do hope that little Sammy gets to see his mama again. I sure woulda' liked to see my own."

Sammy, seeing Pap not a stone's throw away, picked up his pace. Working hard to hold his tongue, thinking it would not be a good idea to say anything about the dime that someone might overhear, Sammy grabbed Pap's hand and gave three quick pulls, signifying he had something very important to say. Samuel smiled, nodded his head at Sammy and stooped down to appease the child.

"Pap, Pap, can I keep it, can I?" Sammy spoke fast and hushed.

"Keep what? What you talkin' 'bout keepin'?"

"A dime, Pap, a real dime. I found it in the road. It's a lot of money I know, but can I keep it, please?"

"What do Mam say 'bout it?"

"Mam say to ask you, Pap."

"Well, Sammy, you just hold on to the dime, and we see if somebody mentions losin' a dime. If they do, you gotta return it to whoever lose it."

"Bet nobody round here lose it," Sammy replied quietly as he entered the house underneath Pap's outstretched, knotted arm holding the back door open.

"Mam, Pap say I can keep the money if no one say they lose it. I'm gonna get me a nail and hammer and make a little hole in this dime so it don't get mixed up with other dimes I get. Mam, do this dime make me rich? How much candy can I buy with it? Pap, do you know any nine year ole boy with so much money?" Sammy thought to himself about how careful he needed to be not to lose the dime.

Hattie and Samuel smiled at one another. Sammy could ask a series of questions faster than anyone could gather them up to give answers. Pap answered simply, "Sammy you go outside and make a little hole in yo dime. I need to talk to yo Mam a few minutes."

Hattie could see in Samuel's smile that something was weighing on his mind. "What's on yo mind? You look a little worried."

"Well, since ole Massa Roads pass on last year, the Missus looks to be gettin' worse. Her mind seems to be leavin' her. Young Massa Roads wants us to move up to the big house so we can help out and keep an eye on his mama," Samuel replied.

"We can do that, but I kinda worried 'bout Little Sammy. What's gonna happen to us if the Missus pass on? I hope young

Massa's not thinkin' on sellin' us. You and I be gettin' old Pap, and little Sammy bein' our granchild might not mean much to Massa Roads. We got to show him he needs us around."

"Massa Roads is a good man, Hattie. He ain't like the Massa who sold yo mama, but I do know you worries."

There was more bothering Samuel than moving up to the big house. He was hesitant, however, to share it with Hattie. Hattie could worry on a thing whether it was something out of her control or something with a simple solution. Thinking about Hattie's needless worrying gave Samuel the perspective he needed to keep his concerns about working with Mr. Sims tomorrow to himself.

Sims rented pastureland for his sheep from Eli Roads, and they had an agreement that Samuel would help bring the sheep in for lambing. Roads paid Samuel a quarter a day for the work. While the work was something Samuel enjoyed, seeing new birth in the spring, *Sims,* Samuel thought, *is just about the meanest, crooked as a snake fellow as I'd ever known.*

Samuel had helped Sims with the lambing for three years, and this would be the first year Sammy would go along to help. Samuel thought it would be good to have the boy's help and to give Hattie a break. The child's energy could be draining. While Hattie agreed to the arrangement, she had cautioned Samuel, "You know he be a notional child and no tellin' what he might say or do."

"He be alright, Hattie," Samuel had assured. "He just full of bein' a boy."

The morning the lambing was to start, Sammy woke up

excited, thinking about how he would be working with Pap and doing a grown up job.

The pastureland was about a half a mile from the house that Samuel, Hattie and Sammy called home. The morning walk gave Samuel time to reflect on the beauty of the landscape. He and Sammy traversed past a low-lying, brackish pond and up through an inclined thicket of trees to arrive at an open meadow. The pastureland was surrounded by gently sloping hills and gray rock. The meadow was one of two pastures that Sims rotated the ewes between to avoid overgrazing. This particular pasture housed a small structure with eight stalls for the sheep and was enclosed by a low fence.

The land also provided the hay needed for the ewes during sheltering and birthing. Sims had a herd of about one hundred Southdown sheep that were bred in the fall and collected in the early spring for lambing. The Southdowns were a hearty breed, and there were always a few ewes that gave birth early, prior to sheltering.

"Pap, how many sheep we help get here the last few days?" Sammy asked on the final day of work.

"Sammy, we got in more than a hundred sheep. Remember, the mama sheep be called ewes and the babies lambs."

"These lambs 'bout the sweetest babies I ever see. Pap, I see a mama sheep, a ewe, in the bushes over behind the rocks. Let's go see," Sammy said pointing to the north corner of the pasture.

"You go see if she got a lamb, Sammy. I'm gonna sit here on this rock for just a minute to rest. Go on and see. I'll be watchin' for you."

Sammy ran toward the sheep and once over a small rise, slowed his pace to quietly approach the sheep. The ewe had a lamb. Motioning for Samuel to come his way, Sammy cried "Pap, Pap, come quick! Hurry Pap, I ain't never seen the likes of this lamb."

Samuel, having only had time for a sip of cool water, rose from the rock and made his way toward the chatter. "Pap, it's a black, baby lamb. Is it one of them miracles the preacher talks 'bout in church? Maybe the first ever born. Pap, what we gonna do?"

As Samuel reached down to pick up the lamb, Sims shouted, "Hey you two, you trying to hide in the bushes? Get back to work or I'll take some hide off. You don't put in a full day's work and I don't pay Roads one nickel for today."

"Missa Sims, sir, we workin'," Sammy replied excitedly, not understanding the meanness in Sims' tone or words. "Just found another mama and baby. A little black lamb, Missa Sims, and you ain't never seen a more pretty lamb. He could be worth a lot of money."

"Black sheep ain't worth ten cent boy." Sims barked. "Billy, come over here and club the black one. We don't want it to get in with the others. Likely to cause them to have black babies if we don't get rid of it now."

Billy, Sims' son, all too eager to gain the approval of his father, asked, "Daddy, which black one you want me to club, the boy or the lamb? You say to club the black one, and I just wanna make sure I get the right one." Billy laughed hysterically, pointing at Sammy.

Sammy looked at Sims and said, "Missa Sims, please don't kill the black lamb. You say he ain't worth ten cents. I got a dime I give you for 'im. Please don't club 'im."

"Where'd you get a dime anyhow, boy?" Billy asked. Surprised to see Sammy holding up a dime he turned back to Sims, "It's a real dime, Daddy. I expect he stole it. You know how these little niggers are. The dime has a hole in it, probably ain't worth nothin' no way."

"Is too still worth a dime," Sammy said.

Samuel put his big hand on Sammy's shoulder signaling with his grip for the boy to pipe down. Samuel knew no good would come of any words with Sims.

"That's enough, Sammy," said Samuel. "We know it's yo lucky dime, yo first dime. The hole you put in it I reckon' don't lessen its worth none."

Stepping between Sammy and Sims, Samuel said, "Seems the boy made you a fine offer for that lamb, Missa Sims. What you say you make 'im a deal?"

"Billy, bring me that dime, and boy you get that black lamb off this place now. You better not be gone long. All you want to do is loaf and take advantage of folks' kindness. Now take that lamb and then you get yourself right back here to work."

"Yessa, Missa Sims," Samuel nodded in agreement. "Sammy, you go put that lamb in the barn stall and come right on back like Missa Sims say."

Recognizing the seriousness in Samuel's eyes and hard squeeze to his shoulder, Sammy knew it was time to take care of business and get back to work. This was one of those times he thought, *Mam would say hush up now and be excited later.*

The adrenaline from the excitement of discovering the lamb and the thought that he might have been clubbed gave Sammy the strength to carry the little creature home.

Sammy passed Hattie hanging clothes on the line on his way to the barn.

Hattie, humming a hymn and pinning sweet smelling laundry to the line, thought she was seeing things as the bed sheet, caught by a wisp of wind, blew away just enough to catch a glimpse of a black lamb. The lamb seemed to be suspended, and the sight confused and startled Hattie. "Lord, Lord," Hattie said excitedly as she moved the sheet to reveal Sammy carrying a little lamb.

"Sammy, what you doin'? You 'bout scared me to death. I thought you was helpin' Pap today? And, what you doin' with that lamb?"

"I am helpin', Mam. I can't talk now, got to go back to help Pap. Tell you all 'bout it tonight. Keep an eye on my lamb till I get back, please Mam. I'm gonna leave him in the barn stall. That's what Pap say to do. I gotta go back quick. Pap's waitin'."

The rest of the day Sammy was quiet, working alongside Samuel. He had little to say on the walk home. Samuel thought the silence was just as well, since he was struggling with his own thoughts.

Seeing Sammy be so bold with Mr. Sims concerned Samuel with the boy knowing his place. As they neared the house, the distinct smell of salt pork and cornbread filled the air. Sammy was in a full run to the barn as Samuel called for him to look in on the lamb, wash up and come in to help Hattie with setting the table for supper.

"Samuel, what happened today?" Hattie asked. "Sammy come home in such a hurry with that little black lamb and then jus' rush away."

"Sammy bought that lamb with his dime."

"I can't believe Sammy give up his dime," Hattie said as she took a skillet of cornbread from the oven to the warmer. Steam rose from the hot iron.

"Well, when he see Missa Sims gonna have that boy a his club that innocent creature, he woulda give a bag a dimes to save it. You know how soft his little heart be. I never see a boy like 'im. Just hope the lamb like cow's milk 'cause it's all we got."

"In all the commotion 'bout that lamb I almost forgot, Massa Roads came by and say he want to see you when you come in today. I hope it's nothin' bad. I be prayin' it's good. I'll have supper on when you come back. I'll help Sammy feed the lamb a bottle a cow's milk," Hattie said.

Samuel walked the short distance to the Roads home, wondering what was on Master Eli Roads' mind. Samuel knew that Sammy had over stepped his bounds as far as Sims was concerned. *Had Sims complained about the day's events?* He also knew that Eli was a fair man. Samuel felt that he and Hattie had been blessed by the debt that their former Master owed to Eli Roads. It was because of that debt they had moved from plantation work in the rice fields to working for Roads, whose family owned the only general store for miles around.

"Evenin', Massa Roads," Samuel said as he removed his hat and tipped his head. "Hattie say you wanna see me. I just got in from work with Missa Sims. We done with gatherin' the sheep. Don't know if you heard, but Sammy bought a little black lamb from Missa Sims today. He bought it with a dime he found aside the road. Hope you don't mind."

"That's all quite fine, Samuel. Here's two dollars for the five days you worked for Sims. It's a little more than our agreement, but I expect after five days with Sims, you certainly earned the extra. You know you don't have to work for him again, but that's not really what I wanted to see you about."

Samuel felt relieved.

"You're aware that I've been down to Charleston the last couple of weeks. I'm happy to say that I've been spending my time with a Miss Lizzie, a lady I've known for quite some time." Eli moved around the desk, perched on the edge, placed his hand on Samuel's shoulder and said, "Samuel, I plan to marry Miss Lizzie in two days."

Samuel replied, "Well, that's right nice, Massa Eli."

"The ceremony will be at ten o'clock in the morning on Saturday, here at the house. I expect we'll need you and Hattie early to help with the preparations. I would like for you, Hattie and Sammy to stay for the wedding ceremony. That'll be all for now, Samuel. Be sure to tell Hattie what we talked about."

"Yes sir, Massa Eli. Hattie will be some excited," Samuel smiled.

"Oh, and Samuel, the day Miss Lizzie and I marry, I have a good surprise planned for you, Hattie and Sammy," Eli said with almost as much excitement as the announcement of his wedding.

"Yes sir, Massa Eli. If yo daddy was still with us the news

would make him right happy. I'm sure Missus Roads is happy. Good evenin' to you, Massa Roads. I wish happiness on you and the new Missus."

Samuel left the house of Eli Roads relieved that the situation with Sims had not been the reason he had been called. He was pleased that Eli would marry and wondered what he meant by a good surprise.

Samuel couldn't imagine what a good surprise might be or recall a time he may have had one. *What in heaven's name could Massa Roads mean by a good surprise?*

Samuel didn't want to worry Hattie when the first question she asked as he entered the back door was, "Samuel, what do Massa Roads want? Hope it be good."

"Massa give me the money for the work with Missa Sims. He say I don't need to work for Sims again. He also gonna get his self married in two days. We'll have to be there early Saturday morning to help get ready for the weddin'. Say he wants you, me and Sammy to come to the weddin'. He say he got a good surprise for us that day."

"Surprise? For us? What you think it be? Puzzlin' is what it be. Two days you say? Two days a lot a time to wonder on a thing."

"He say it be a good surprise," Samuel repeated.

Before Hattie could say anything else, Sammy bolted through the back door, all smiles, mimicking every sound and each move the lamb made. He had put together a bed of hay for the lamb and decided to call him Blackie.

Samuel told Sammy about the upcoming nuptials.

"Mam, you hear what Pap say? Massa gonna jump da broom

with a lady name Miss Lizzie."

"That's right, Sammy. Massa Roads gettin' married, but white folk do it different than me and Pap. Miss Lizzie gonna be Mrs. Lizzie Roads."

"Tell me somethin' Mam, why do white folk have more names than me?"

"Well, Sammy, the first name tells who they is and the last name is the family name. And, most got a name in the middle. Lots of foolishness if you ask me."

"Mam, why I got just one name?"

"What difference do it make if you got one, two or ten names? Everybody knows you is Sammy."

"I really wish my last name could be Lamb," Sammy said as he set down for supper.

"Sammy, you is a lucky boy. Not everybody gets to pick their own last name. I think the name Sammy Lamb fits you jus' fine, jus' fine," Hattie said placing tin plates on the table.

CHAPTER TWO

It was entirely dark when Samuel left Eli's house that evening. Eli could hardly believe that Lizzie would be arriving on the stage tomorrow. He felt excitement about both seeing Lizzie and the surprise he had for Samuel, Hattie and Sammy.

Starting up the stairs to his bedroom, Eli realized that the Roads family had never thought of Samuel and Hattie as slaves. They were paid for their work, though not much, all their needs were taken care of, but they were not free. Eli's daddy had talked about freedom papers but never got around to getting them. *Well, that's been taken care of now. After the wedding, I'll give them the papers.*

Eli knew that while he and his family had not thought of Samuel and Hattie as slaves, their families had been torn apart by slavery. As far back as Eli could recollect, Samuel told him stories of his childhood, about how his mama was taken away one morning. Samuel never saw her again. "Don't know why they do that to a mama 'n child," Samuel lamented. "Some say the Massa need some money so he ups and sells my mama. Another woman took me in and tol' me I would forget Mama in time. It's been a whole lotta time and I still think about her every day. Yo GranPap buy me and Hattie when the Massa was goin' to sell us at the auction. He give us this little house to stay in and we just work 'round the place." Eli couldn't imagine what it would have been like to be taken away from his own mother and father.

Eli smiled as he thought about Lizzie and how she had reacted at his news about the freedom papers. He told Lizzie about Samuel, Hattie and Sammy. "They are part of the family, and I hope you'll love them. They will be so excited about the freedom papers, especially Hattie."

"And just think," Eli said aloud as he pulled the covers back to get into bed, "if I had not gone to file the papers with the county deed's officer that very day, I would not have run into Lizzie and there would not be a wedding." *Funny how things happen, just one good deed and my life will never be the same again.*

The next morning Eli was up early. *I have a lot to do today*, he thought as he hurriedly dressed. *I hope Samuel comes to the store early today. Since he has been helping Sims with the lambing, the work at the mercantile is piling up.*

As he descended the stairs, Eli heard his mother call, "E.Z., oh Eli, I'm sorry. I forget you don't like to be called E.Z."

"That's all right, Mama. You and Daddy have always called me E.Z. It's just that I was teased so much about the name E.Z. Roads, and I don't know why Daddy thought it was so clever to label me with that name. If ever I have a son he will not be named Eli Zebulin Roads. Eli Roads will be sufficient."

"Eli, what I wanted to ask is if you and Lizzie will be taking a honeymoon after the wedding?"

"No. I've been gone for two weeks to Charleston and have neglected the store. Getting to know Lizzie again, going to the Governor's Ball and just passing time during our walks was like a honeymoon."

"Well, I do hope Lizzie won't be disappointed," Mrs. Roads replied.

"We talked about it and both agreed that just being together is all we need now. I do appreciate you keeping the store in order while I was gone, Mama. You know Lizzie's father ran a mercantile in Charleston for years but had to retire two years ago because of a weak heart. Lizzie says she's looking forward to working in the store."

"It will be nice for all of us to have the extra help," Mrs. Roads said.

"Because you and Samuel were so helpful, I was able to attend to some business while I was in Charleston. I had the freedom papers drafted and filed for Samuel, Hattie and Sammy. I intend to give them their papers after the wedding. I mentioned to Samuel I have a good surprise for them on the day of the wedding, but they'll never guess what I've planned."

"I am so proud of you. That's something your father intended to do. I bet Hattie is beside herself to guess what surprise you have in store. You know that curiosity has consumed her if Samuel mentioned a surprise. How about I invite the store customers to the wedding?"

"No. Lizzie and I want it to be a small affair – just you, Hattie, Samuel, Sammy and of course the Reverend and his wife. I expect

Mrs. Barbara has no intention of Reverend Downey presiding alone. I sure hope we're not doing wrong by such a fast courtship, but Lizzie and I both feel like it's meant to be this way. How long did you and Daddy court before you got married?"

"Four days, Eli, a wonderful four days. I knew immediately that he was the one for me. I was unaware when your daddy first noticed me. The first time he saw me I appeared to be wearing a wedding dress. He said he had been thinking on having a wife and family and seeing me in what seemed to be a wedding dress, well he took that as an omen that I was the one. What your daddy didn't know is that I really did have a wedding dress on. I was in Lucy's Cloth and Seamstress Storehouse getting the dress fitted for my best friend, Rose, who was getting married. She was sick that day and couldn't make her fitting. We were the same size, so I went to the fitting for her. When Lucy saw your daddy looking in the window, she closed the curtains. Of course I left the store in my own clothes, and he was outside waiting for me. Four days later we were married. Neither of us ever regretted our quick courtship. Some months later I told him the truth about that wedding dress. He said it mattered not for whom the dress was meant, it was the sign he needed. Eli, for forty-one years we enjoyed as good a marriage as ever was, and I hope you and Lizzie have the same."

"Mama, that's a great story." Eli continued, "You know, I thought I'd be up before you this morning, but I guess that'll never happen. I can only imagine what time Hattie got here. I hear her in the kitchen banging pots and pans. Guess we all have lots to do today with the wedding tomorrow. Lizzie will be here on the two o'clock stage. My plan is to bring her to the house straight away. I just know you'll love her. She's a loving, caring person. I'll be so lucky to have her as my wife."

"And she, my son, will be lucky to have you as a husband. I have so much I need to do. I must get in the kitchen and help Hattie. Make sure you eat something before you go to work."

"I'll eat something at the store, and I'll see you this afternoon when Lizzie arrives."

Eli put on his hat and walked over to Roads Mercantile, the store that had been in the family for generations. *I wonder if my son, if Lizzie and I have a son, will want to work in a store. He may want to be a doctor, teacher or maybe President. Well, first things first and that is marrying Lizzie.*

Samuel was sweeping out the store when Eli walked inside. "Mr. Ed White just got two sacks a cow feed, Massa Eli. He said put it on his ticket," Samuel said.

"All right, Samuel. Has anyone else been in?"

"No sir, Massa Eli, nobody else."

"Samuel, I've told you before that you don't have to call me Master Eli, just Eli will do."

"Yes sir, Massa Eli. I just can't remember, and it just don't seem fittin'."

"Samuel, is Sammy coming in to help this morning?"

"Yes sir, Massa. He be comin' in a little while. You need him now?"

"Whenever he arrives is fine. I want him to make the weekly delivery to Mrs. Jackson. When he comes in have him see me and I'll set him up to deliver."

Eli put a few coins in the cash register and began writing orders for supplies he had sold out of the past few days. *Business has been great* he thought to himself. *Surely Lizzie will be a great help, with her already knowing the business. Maybe things will be easier for Mama now that Lizzie will be here to help.*

Eli heard Sammy approaching the store giving Blackie orders to stay outside.

"Now Blackie, you gonna have to stay outside whiles I go see what Massa Eli wants. Don't go get yoself in no mischief now. I be right back." Pushing open the screen door to the mercantile, Sammy said, "Massa Eli, I's here. You needs me?"

It was easy to recognize Sammy's short quick steps and *a wonder how someone so small could make such noise,* Eli thought. "Yes, Sammy. Get the little delivery wagon, and I'll put in the flour I need you to deliver to Mrs. Jackson. And Sammy, I have a couple things for you to do today so don't dawdle."

"Yes sir, Massa Eli. Is drinkin' milk and eatin' cookies dawdlin'? She always makes me do it. And sometime she gives me a penny. I gots me seventeen cents saved up. I kinda rich now, huh, Massa Eli?"

"I guess that's not considered dawdling, Sammy. It's alright to have your milk and cookies, and saving your coins will certainly add up in the long run."

"She gives Blackie a cookie, too. Most everybody wants to talk to us when we go out. Is that dawdlin'?"

"As long as you don't talk too long, Sammy, it is not dawdling. It's important to politely speak to people when they inquire as to how you and Blackie are doing." Eli put the five-pound sack of flour in the little wooden wagon and Sammy went off with the delivery, Blackie following at his heels.

Watching Sammy and Blackie walking away from the store reminded Eli of the childhood rhyme "Mary had a Little Lamb." *It sure follows him everywhere he goes. Everyone for miles around knows about Sammy and his little black lamb.*

This day, the day Lizzie would arrive, seemed to be the day everyone in town decided to buy groceries and supplies. Eli was busy with customers the entire morning. He took a quick break around one o'clock to have a sandwich and sarsaparilla.

"Samuel, the stage with Lizzie on it will be here in a few minutes and Mama is busy. Can you work the store by yourself?"

"Yes sir, I can. Not as good as you, Massa Eli, but I can remember what people gets for you to write up the tickets."

After eating, Eli left Samuel to tend the store. He hurriedly walked down to the stage depot to await Lizzie's arrival. *Don't know what I would do without Samuel and Hattie. Little Sammy is also starting to be a big help. Ole Samuel, boy I wish I could remember like he remembers. He knows everyone that shops with us, and can tell me without error what and how much they buy even if he can't read or write. Now that's something we can correct with Sammy. Lizzie and I will make sure he gets his schooling. I agree with Lizzie that it's a lot of nonsense that blacks shouldn't be educated.*

The stagecoach was three minutes early and Lizzie was the only passenger. The stage stopped in a cloud of dust because of a four-month drought. As the stage pulled to a stop, Eli quickly opened the door and lifted Lizzie to the ground. "My, Lizzie, how can you look so beautiful and fresh after riding two days in a dust-covered coach?"

As Lizzie's feet softly touched the ground, she looked up and down the street taking in the buildings and the townspeople. *I want to always remember this day,* she thought as she turned to look at Eli.

"Lizzie, the house is just half a block down the street from here. We can be there in just moments. You can meet Mama and then you can rest from your travels."

"You look so handsome in your work clothes with your sleeves rolled up. The store, Eli, is that it across the street? I just have to see it after we meet your mama. Do you think I can call her Mama?"

"You would make her happy if you did, Lizzie."

"This is a day I will always remember. Seems like forever since we were together in Charleston."

As they approached the house surrounded by a low, white-picket fence lined with roses and lilacs along the path to the front door, Lizzie's eyes began to tear. She stopped at the gate overwhelmed by the beautiful two-story, pale green, clapboard house. Its trim was a darker shade of green and a gallery with round fluted columns stretched the length of the house. The porch swing and rockers were the finishing touches to welcome one. Lizzie looked at Eli and said, "This is lovelier than you described. I can't believe this will be our home. I feel as if I'm the most blessed girl in the world."

Eli put his arms around Lizzie and kissed her forehead. "We are both blessed my love, because we have each other."

As they approached the house, Eli opened the door for Lizzie and called out, "We're home, Mama. Come meet your new daughter."

Mrs. Roads came out of the kitchen wiping her hands on the apron still tied around her waist. Untying the apron and laying it across the back of a low tapestry chair, Mrs. Roads extended her arms to embrace her soon-to-be daughter-in-law.

Lizzie said, "I am so glad that I'm finally here to meet you, Mrs. Roads. Eli has told me so much about you and the family. It's like I've known you all my life. Your home is lovely and grand. I am just so excited."

"We are excited as well, dear. Eli failed to tell me just how beautiful you are. You two sit in the parlor. I'll get Hattie to bring us some lemonade. And dear, please call me Mama."

A few minutes later Mrs. Roads and Hattie came into the parlor and Eli introduced Lizzie to Hattie. "Hattie has been with our family since before I was born, Lizzie. Sometimes I think she and Samuel run this family. You will soon see what I mean."

Eli turned to Hattie and said, "Hattie, this is Miss Lizzie."

"Massa Eli, I think the Missus is mos' lovely. Can she cook?"

"Well, Hattie, I don't really know. I've never had her cook for me. We'll have to see, won't we?"

Lizzie moved closer to Hattie and said, "I can do a few simple things in the kitchen, but I'm sure my skills are not up to par with yours. In fact, I am going to rely on you to teach me how to cook, so I can prepare some of Eli's favorite dishes. Can you do that, Hattie?"

"Yes Missus. I know all Massa Eli's favorites." Hattie relieved, nodded her head, turned and walked back to the kitchen.

After talking a while and drinking lemonade, Lizzie asked Eli if they could go and visit at the store. As Eli opened the gate for her, they exchanged smiles and when they neared the store, Lizzie, looking up at the sign uttered softly, "Roads Mercantile." She held her hands to her cheeks and thought of working in the Charleston store with her father. "Oh Eli, what a beautiful building. I didn't give much thought as to how grand it would be."

"I'll admit that it certainly has a bit of character. Grandfather always had a lot of pride in everything he did and this store was no exception," Eli replied. "The two large store-front windows flanking the entrance is what he liked best, but I'm partial to the porch columns and gingerbread work."

Eli and Lizzie walked across the street, up the wide steps and into the store.

"Samuel, this is Miss Lizzie. She wanted to come over, see the store and meet you. Lizzie, this is the one and only Samuel or Pap as Sammy calls him."

Lizzie walked up to Samuel and took him by the hand and said, "Samuel, I think that I'm going to like it here. I am so glad to meet you." Lizzie turned to the small head peering over the counter, "And, this must be Sammy. Come here, Sammy, and let me see how big you are."

Sammy felt shy and wanted to hide, but curiosity pulled him from behind the counter to meet the woman that Hattie and Samuel said would be Mrs. Eli Roads, the Missus of the big house. He slowly walked from his hiding place to where Lizzie stood looking at him.

Lizzie knelt down on the floor and held a hand out to Sammy,

"Well, Sammy, you are a handsome young man. You are going to be as big as your Pap when you grow up. Will you introduce me to Blackie? I want to meet your lamb that I've heard so much about." She let Sammy take her by the hand and lead her out the back door where Blackie was nibbling on grass growing through the fence.

"Blackie, this be Miss Lizzie. She comes from a long ways to meet you. Miss Lizzie, this be Blackie, my own lamb that I bought with my own money. He cost me a dime. Miss Jackson give us a cookie this mornin', even to Blackie, everybody likes Blackie."

"I can see why. He is so adorable. Will he let me pet him?" Lizzie waited for Sammy's reply and then stroked the lamb along his side. She turned to Sammy and said, "It is clear that you are taking good care of your lamb, Sammy. He's so soft and shiny."

Lizzie had made four new friends in less than two hours' time, and thought, *this is going to be a wonderful place to live*. She sat next to Eli as he made entries in his charge book for the store. Samuel and Sammy said their goodbyes and went home to do their evening chores.

"Eli, I can't wait to start working here and meet the town's people. I know we are going to be happy together, and I just love your entire family."

"I'm so glad your first impression is a good one and you feel like you'll be at home here, love. You've already won them over, even Blackie. I'm going to close up the store now. We can go home and have supper. I'm famished and you must be exhausted."

Eli and Lizzie sat down to a bountiful supper of salad, potatoes and gravy, roast pork, lima beans, cornbread, slices of lemon pie topped with two inches of browned meringue and glasses of cold, fresh cow's milk.

"My, my, Mama, what a fine meal you and Hattie fixed for our supper. I don't think I can get out of my chair," Eli said.

Lizzie insisted on helping with the dishes so Eli volunteered to help as well.

Mrs. Roads was clearly tired and thankful for the help. *Now that Lizzie is here,* she thought, *I'll have more time to do some of the things I've put off because of work in the store. I will be able to visit friends and spend more time in my garden.* She said good night and went to her room.

After doing the dishes, Eli and Lizzie said goodnight to one another and went upstairs to their rooms. "I can't wait to see you in the morning, love. This will be the last night we will have to sleep apart," Eli said as he kissed Lizzie good night.

Lizzie felt a slight blush and replied, "Good night, Eli. I am more tired than I thought. My excitement has kept me going, but now I look forward to that soft feather mattress I saw earlier. I will see you in the morning."

The next morning Eli awoke, dressed and quietly made his way down the stairs. He poured himself a cup of steaming coffee, and making his way to the parlor saw Lizzie descending the stairs, "Good morning, Lizzie."

CHAPTER THREE

"Samuel, I could hardly sleep last night thinkin' what Massa Roads got on his mind. I been worryin' my head till I can't think no more about the surprise."

"Hattie, it wouldn't be a surprise if we knows what it be. Just got a wait a little while longer and we'll see. You about to go to help Mrs. Roads with the weddin' dinner?"

"I done baked a big chocolate cake for the weddin'. You know how Massa Roads takes to chocolate. We'll be cookin' a mess of food all morning. The weddin' be at ten o'clock, so we startin' early. Wish I know what the surprise be. Reckon I can wait a few more hours."

"We'll know soon enough," Samuel replied.

"This Miss Lizzie the Massa marryin' seems nice, but I wonder if she like black folks. Be jus' our luck she don't."

"Now Hattie, don't go makin' troubles for yoself. The Massa wouldn't marry nobody that wasn't kind. He a good man and we need to thank the Lord for that."

Samuel, hoping he could get Hattie's mind off the new Mrs. Roads asked, "Where Sammy been all morning?"

"He foolin' with that sheep again. They together all the time. You see one and you see the other. They sleep in the same bed if we let 'em," Hattie replied shaking her head.

"I best be gettin' out and find that boy to see what he up to," Samuel said as he walked out the back door.

"Sammy, where you be?"

"Over here, Pap," Sammy called out from Blackie's favorite grazing place, "helpin' Blackie find some good grass. He eats all the time. He sure gonna get fat."

"Sammy, bring Blackie along so we can finish up our chores and then dress for the weddin'. You can feed the chickens and pick up the eggs while I milk ole Betsy."

Lizzie woke early and quickly dressed to the sounds of kitchen work. She was eager to see what Mrs. Roads and Hattie were doing in the kitchen. Most of all she was anxious to see Eli.

Eli was at the bottom of the stairs. The smile on his face widened when he saw Lizzie. "Good morning love. You sure are beautiful," Eli beamed. "I feel I am the luckiest man in all of God's creation. It seems like a dream to have you here, and if it is I don't ever want to wake up. You may need to keep telling me it's all real for a while."

The sight of Eli, his excitement and sweet words made Lizzie feel as if her heart literally skipped a beat. "Thank you for the compliment, Eli. I feel lucky as well. I look forward to reminding you it's all very real. If I'm assuring you a year from now, it will mean you still feel as if it's a dream," Lizzie smiled.

"Why did we wait so long to get together? We've known each other since we were young. We're both in our twenties now and it seems all those years were just wasted."

"The years weren't wasted Eli, it just wasn't meant to be sooner. I believe these things happen in God's time. We have the rest of our lives to be together."

"And I hope it's at least two hundred years, my love. Mama and Hattie must have gotten up before daylight to start work in the kitchen. They'll have a feast prepared for dinner."

"I hope they don't work themselves to the point of exhaustion, Eli. I'm worried about Mama. She looks a bit frail and this wedding may be too much for her."

"Mama will be alright. I haven't seen her so excited and happy in a long time. She's enjoying every minute of this."

"Reverend Downey and Mrs. Barbara will be here in less than two hours. We'd better get busy ourselves, Eli. I am just so excited."

"Just think in two hours, you'll be Mrs. Lizzie Roads. I pray that God will give us many happy years together."

After the ceremony, Samuel and Sammy sat at the kitchen table as Hattie spooned steamy sweet potatoes into Mrs. Roads' fine china. It was the last dish to add to what Hattie thought was a fine wedding feast.

"Mam, Massa Roads and Miss Lizzie didn't jump da broom or nothin'. They just hold hands and say some words. Is they really married?" Sammy asked.

"Of course they is, Sammy. I told you they do it different than we do. Whichever way it's done, it's done and they is married. Go wash your hands before we eat and stay away from that black lamb. You startin' to smell like sheep."

Sammy, finding it difficult to sit still indoors asked, "Mam, when we gonna get our surprise from Massa Roads? Maybe he forgot."

"Hush up, Sammy. They gonna hear you talkin' bout stuff you don't need to be talkin' bout. Do like I say and wash up."

Sammy, head hanging and shoulders slouched, walked outside with the soap Hattie had given him to scrub his hands thinking about the surprise. *Mam say it might be somethin' bad, but Pap say if Massa Eli give us a surprise, it be somethin' good. Maybe the surprise be a new red wagon like in the order book at the store. No, can't be that cause the surprise be for me, Mam and Pap, and they don't need no wagon. Guess I got to wait like Pap say.*

"Samuel, wonder if Sammy is right and Massa Roads has forgot about the surprise," Hattie said as soon as she was sure Sammy was out of hearing distance.

"Now Hattie, you know when Massa Roads say a thing, he mean it. When he ready to tell us, he will. That looks like a tasty roast, Hattie, and the sweet taters, um um. I can't wait to sit down to the table. What could be takin' Sammy so long to wash up? Hope he ain't already forgot what you said and foolin' with that sheep. That boy loves that sheep as much as Massa Roads loves his new bride."

Sammy returned to the kitchen. Handing the soap to Hattie, Sammy heard Eli call, "Samuel, Hattie, Sammy, come in here a minute. I have something to talk to you all about."

Hattie nervously wiping her hands on her apron turned to Samuel and said, "Lord, here it come, Samuel. I's scared. Wonder if it be bad? Samuel, my knees weak. I might fall down. Hold my hand Samuel, and you too, Sammy. Lord a mercy."

As Samuel, Hattie and Sammy entered the dining room, Hattie full of trepidation, Eli said, "Please, sit down at the table. I want to explain something to you."

"No sir, Massa Roads, we can't sit down to your table. It ain't fittin."

"Yes, Samuel, I insist you three sit down. Mama, Lizzie, please sit down with them so they will sit."

"Reverend Downey and Mrs. Barbara, please sit on this side. I'd like for you to be witnesses to this occasion. This is something I have wanted to do for a long time. Lizzie and I have spoken about it and agree this is the day."

Hattie was so nervous that she put her hand on Samuel's shoulder, raised, almost tipping the chair and exclaimed excitedly, "Samuel, I told you it's gonna happen. Massa Roads gonna sell us off. I knows it was comin'."

"No, Hattie. Oh dear, of course I'm not going to sell you, not any one of you," Eli quickly replied moving close to Hattie. "I guess I shouldn't have said anything about a surprise. I didn't in a million years think you would conjure up such terrible thoughts. I'm truly sorry to have made you worry, Hattie. Now sit back down, calm yourself, and I will explain.

I'm not sure if you know what freedom papers are, but there's a law that a slave owner, if he so desires, can free his slave. The slave owner fills out the proper forms, registers them in the courthouse and gives a copy to the freed slave as proof of freedom. I've already filed each of your papers in the courthouse. I have copies for each of you and myself. Samuel, Hattie and Sammy, you are free and legally registered as free blacks in the courthouse."

Hattie turned to Samuel and exclaimed "I's gonna die. I's fixin' to faint. I don't know what I's suppose to do. I ain't never been free before. Say somethin' Samuel. Lord a mercy! Sammy, you a free boy to do what you want, go where you want and nobody owns you. Thank you, Massa Roads. Thank you, Mrs. Roads. Thank you, Miss Lizzie. Thank you, Jesus! Say somethin' Samuel!"

Eli couldn't help but laugh at Hattie's excitement and Samuel's inability to speak. It took some time to get Hattie settled down. Even though Hattie was unable to read the papers for herself, she clutched them close to her heart as she left the Roads' home.

Hours later she was still talking to Samuel about freedom and what it would mean for Sammy.

After Samuel, Hattie and Sammy went home and things began to settle down, Mrs. Roads commented, "Eli, you and Lizzie had a beautiful wedding. Reverend Jack Downey sure conducts a fine marriage ceremony. His wife, Mrs. Barbara, is such a sweet lady. The food was wonderful, but the most entertaining part of the day was when you gave Samuel, Hattie and Sammy their freedom papers. I couldn't believe how stunned Samuel was. He was unable to utter a single word."

"Yes, Samuel was unable to speak and it wasn't only because Hattie could not quit talking. It caught them completely unaware," Eli replied.

"Mama," Lizzie said, "I think it was a wonderful thing what you and Eli did today. It seems unjust for one person to have ownership of another."

"Thank you, dear," Mrs. Roads replied. "The fact of the matter is we inherited Samuel, Hattie and their daughter, Mable, from Grandfather."

Eli added, "Mable had a child. No one knew who the father was and soon after Sammy's birth, Mable disappeared. We've heard that she's in Detroit. We never attempted to pursue Mable, because Daddy didn't believe in slavery either. I only regret that we've waited so long to obtain the freedom papers."

"Did you know that Sammy wanted a second name and gave himself the name Sammy Lamb?" Eli asked recalling the story Samuel had told him at the store just prior to Lizzie's arrival on the stage. "He loves his little black lamb so much he named himself Lamb."

"Eli, Sammy seems to be such a smart child. Do you think it would be all right if I taught him to read and write? If I could give him school lessons, he could help out in the store."

"I was thinking along those lines myself, Lizzie. We will talk with his grandparents and see what they have to say on the matter. Speaking of Samuel and Hattie, they need to slow down a bit. With the right education Sammy certainly could take on any of the tasks required to keep the store in order. We'll talk to them straight away," Eli replied.

While Eli and Lizzie were making plans for Sammy's schooling the day after the wedding, Hattie and Samuel let the little boy sleep in just a bit. Mrs. Roads had sent them home with food, cake and instructions that Hattie take the day off. She had encouraged Hattie to sleep in hoping that she would recover from the wedding preparations and the emotional exhaustion that had overcome her at Eli's announcement of freedom.

Sammy woke up with his usual smile, quickly dressed into the clothes Hattie had left on the chair next to his bed and looked from the loft to see her pouring Samuel a hot cup of coffee. He climbed down the ladder that led up to his loft bed and said, "Mam, can me 'n Blackie go out back in Massa Roads little pasture where the grass is best? He sure likes it back there. It's just right outside the fence."

"Jus' for a few minutes, Sammy. You gotta go 'n work at the store in a little while to help yo Pap."

Sammy went out the back gate humming a gospel song he had heard at church. Sammy could remember word for word every song they sang. Little Bob was the preacher-elect, but any one of the congregation members could speak as the Spirit led. None of the slaves could read, but several had been taught the scripture by their owners. The slaves in and around the area were given permission to use an abandoned farm shack at the edge of town for a meeting place. Sammy loved to attend church because he loved to sing and play with the other children.

While Blackie grazed, Sammy talked to the lamb about how kind a person the new Mrs. Lizzie Roads seemed to be. It was then he caught a glimpse of Sims and Billy taking a short cut across the little pasture toward him and Blackie.

"Come here boy, let me take a look at that black sheep," Sims called out.

"Why you wanna look at my sheep, Missa Sims?"

"Here's your dime back, boy. Billy, put your rope on that sheep. You know what to do and get a move on it."

Sammy, fearing for Blackie said, "That ain't my special dime. Mine got a hole in it 'n you can't take my sheep. I'm gonna tell Massa Roads. He'll take care a you."

"Billy, run back to the house and get that no good dime that's in my money jar and bring it back. This stupid nigger won't take good money."

Billy placed a rope around Blackie's neck, tightened it and dragged the sheep away. Blackie's bleating brought tears to Sammy's eyes. "You can't steal my Blackie. Massa Roads will fetch the sheriff. Why you wanna steal my sheep anyway?"

"This ain't your sheep, boy. You know I just let you keep him and play with him for a while. I wouldn't sell you a good sheep like that for a dime. Nobody, not even the sheriff would believe a story like that."

Seeing Hattie approaching in the distance Sammy screamed, "Mam, Mam, come here. Hurry, Missa Sims done stole my Blackie! Tell him he can't do that, tell him Mam."

Hattie had been watching Sammy from the small kitchen window over the sink. Samuel had already left for the store. The sight of Sims on Roads' pasture on a Sunday afternoon struck her as odd. She had already started toward Sammy when she heard him calling for her wildly. "What all the ruckus 'bout?" Hattie said as she moved between Sammy and Sims.

"Billy done run off with Blackie, Mam."

"You can't do that, Missa Sims. What you want with Sammy's sheep? You can't jus' steal somebody's sheep." Hattie could see Sammy's worry and feel her own heart pounding.

"That's my sheep and you can't prove it ain't," Sims retorted.

"Everybody in this town know Blackie belong to Sammy. They know he give you a dime for that lamb. You can't take my child's sheep from 'im."

Billy returned at a run, "Daddy, here's that dime with a hole in it. Old Saul didn't want to kill that black sheep, said it was bad luck. I told him what you said. If he wants to stay in that shed this winter where he can keep warm, he better mind you. I swear he about had that sheep completely skinned when I left."

"Sammy, I's so sorry," Hattie said falling to her knees and pulling the boy close. Looking up she said, "Oh Lord, why this bad thing gotta happen to my poor child?" Then rising and turning to Sims, Hattie said boldly, "We tellin' Massa Roads tomorrow when he get in from his trip. Lord be with my poor Sammy."

Sammy pulled away from Hattie, overcome with a deep resolve.

"Daddy, that boy is lookin' crazy at us. He's peepin' through that hole in his dime."

"This is my special dime," Sammy said. "When I look in da hole at somebody, dey get a spell on 'em. I done seen you in da hole. If you put one bite a Blackie in yo mouth, yo tongue gonna swell up and choke you to death. And if you swallow any of Blackie, yo belly will swell, bust open and yo guts will fall on da ground. That be my spell on you." Sammy almost didn't recognize his own voice, steady, slow and deep. He could feel Hattie's eyes on him, but he could not stop the voice.

"Daddy, let's get outta here. He's crazy. Daddy, I don't feel too good," Billy said as he moved backward away from Sammy, almost tripping.

Sammy, looking straightforward at Sims now said, "You gonna have lots a bad things happen in yo family Missa Sims. Bad, bad things."

Sims and Billy quickly vacated the little pasture and headed for home, leaving Sammy crying for his little black lamb and Hattie wringing her hands.

"Mam, what I gonna do without my Blackie. Why they steal my poor little lamb? Mam, they kill my best friend. I hope that spell works. They need a lesson."

Hattie again pulled the child close, looked up and prayed quietly, "Help my child, Jesus."

As Sims and Billy made the walk back to the small house they occupied on the Roads' property, Billy asked nervously, "Daddy, do you believe in spells?" Not getting an answer, he continued, "I never did before today, but you can't be sure can you? Sammy sure looked like he knew what he was doing," he fretted as they walked home.

"Ain't no such thing as spells, Billy. That's hogwash." Sims stopped by Saul's shed and saw the dead sheep hanging from a porch rafter with hooks in its legs. Old Saul was nowhere around.

Billy passed Old Saul's place without stopping. Sims took the dressed sheep and carried it home. Billy did not want to see Blackie dead and skinned.

As Billy arrived home and opened the door to the kitchen, the sight of his mother on the floor made him scream. Calling out to Sims now nearing the house, he shouted, "Daddy, come here quick, something's wrong with Mama. She's on the floor. She's vomited. Daddy, I told you that nigger boy put a curse on us with that dime of his. Mama's dead!"

Billy jumped as his mother stirred and said, "No Billy, I just got real sick and must've fainted. Help me up. I feel a bit better now."

Billy, kneeling to help his mother to an upright position said, "Mama, Sammy put a curse on Daddy and me and that meat. He said that if we eat that sheep we'd die. I thought you was dead."

"What sheep are you talking about, Billy?" Mrs. Sims asked as Billy helped her into a chair.

"Blackie, Sammy's black lamb. We brought it home and had Old Saul kill and dress it out for us to eat."

"You mean you and your Daddy stole Sammy's Blackie and had him killed?" Turning to her husband, Mrs. Sims asked, "How could you do such a thing? You know Sammy bought that lamb from you fair and raised it from a baby. It was his pet."

"Shut up woman or I'll slap some sense in your head. You know I wouldn't sell a sheep like that for a dime. No one would blame me for takin' him back, plus I gave that boy his money back. Just clean up this mess you done made and cook us up some of that meat."

"I will not cook that sheep of Sammy's. Of all the things you've done, this is by far the worst. I can't believe with the number of sheep you have out in the pasture you would steal and kill a little boy's pet."

Sims, overcome with anger at his wife's words, hit her with the back of his hand. "I told you to shut up, woman. Just do like I say and keep your mouth closed. You'll cook that meat and thank me for puttin' food on the table."

"Daddy, I can't eat none of that meat. It has a spell on it. And, please don't hit Mama no more, she just sees things different than you and me," Billy spoke. Expecting his words would provoke his father's anger more, Billy moved away from Sims and closer to the back door.

Sims, unwilling to admit that he too had been shaken by Sammy's spell, replied, "Well, if nobody appreciates my hard work, I'll just give the meat to Old Saul. It's not that I'm afraid of some nigger spell. Everybody has always been against me even when I was a boy."

"Old Saul's not there," Mrs. Sims replied. "He picked up his few things and said he was leaving. He wouldn't tell me why. Now I know."

"Old Saul can't up and walk off just like that," Sims said angrily. "Billy, take that blamed sheep and drag it off in the woods somewhere. Get it out of my sight. It's caused enough trouble. I told you black sheep is bad luck, didn't I? Didn't I?"

The next morning Sammy was grieving over the loss of Blackie when he saw Eli walk out of his house. Sammy had been waiting outside the Roads' home, waiting for Eli to appear.

"Massa, Massa Roads, Missa Sims and Billy done stole my lamb and kill 'im and eat 'im. Massa, what I gonna do? He done kill my friend, Blackie, and eat 'im. He's a mean man, that Missa Sims."

Eli, surprised to see Sammy and hear the news about Blackie, took Sammy by the hand and led him home. Leading Sammy into the house, Eli asked, "What is this all about Hattie? Did Sims steal

Sammy's lamb?"

"Yes sir, Massa Roads. Yesterday while you was away, he and Billy come by and took Blackie. Say he gonna eat 'im. He give Sammy the dime back and say Blackie is his all along. Can he do that?"

"No, he cannot get away with stealing other people's property. I'll tend to this unfortunate situation immediately. Hattie, I obviously cannot get Blackie back if Sims has killed him, but I can rid this place of him. Something I should have done a long time ago."

"Here come Old Saul, Massa Roads. He comin' this way. Maybe he wanna talk. He wavin' his arms," Sammy said.

"Mister Roads, I'm glad you're back. I have awful news for you and Sammy. It's all my fault. I killed Sammy's black sheep, and I'm so sorry. I told them it's bad luck to kill a black sheep, but Sims said I couldn't stay in my shed this winter if I didn't. I didn't know at the time that it was Sammy's little black lamb. I really am sorry. Sammy, I'm curing the hide and it will take a couple weeks. I wish I had parted ways with Sims a long time ago."

"Missa Saul, I know you wouldn't a done it if you knowed it was Blackie. I don't hold no bad feelin' with you."

Eli was struck by Sammy's maturity. The child had seemed to come into this world understanding right and wrong.

"Thank you for seeing it that way, Sammy." Saul said. "I truly am sorry. I'll do my best with Blackie's skin. It'll be yours of course."

Eli was furious after hearing that Sims and Billy had stolen Blackie from Sammy. *Of course,* Eli thought, *Sims would never see it* that way. Everyone knew that Sammy had bought Blackie with his own money. I should get the sheriff and have him put in jail, but that won't bring Blackie back.

Eli was still fuming when he stepped up onto Sim's front porch and pounded on the door. "Sims, get out here. I want to talk to you now."

"What can I do you for, Mr. Roads?"

"You can get your lazy self, your family, your sheep and everything you own off my land. I have no use for a thief and a liar. With all you have, why did you steal and kill Sammy's lamb?"

"I never stole that boy's sheep. It was always mine."

"You are a liar, Sims. Sammy bought that lamb from you. You know it, I know it and so does everyone else in these parts."

"Best I reckon, accordin' to the law, a slave can't rightly own no property."

"Well, that may be true Sims, but Samuel, Hattie and Sammy are as free as you and I and have been that way for some time."

"Well now, that's something I didn't know and expect. Maybe no one else does either. Thanks for telling me. I'll make sure to let the rest of the good folks in these parts know."

"Get on off my land, Sims. You've got three days or I'll have you arrested for stealing. Now get out."

Sims left but not without spreading the news that Roads had freed his slaves and were paying them a wage proper for a white man. Most townspeople thought Eli was committing a dangerous crime. Some went so far as to refuse to do business with Roads Mercantile.

Not long after Sims left, people learned what he had done to

Blackie, but still didn't think it right that Sims was paid a pittance for his own sheep. Sims, of course, would blame all his bad luck on Eli Roads. It took all but a few dollars he had to his name to buy passage for his family to Atlanta, Georgia.

Once in Atlanta, Billy was caught stealing twice and sentenced to a year in the county jail. Sims, wanting to move on, left his wife in Atlanta because she refused to leave Billy. Sims went on to Jackson, Mississippi, and never took accountability for his actions.

"Mam, do you think they got lambs in heaven? I bet they do," Sammy said.

"They probably do, Sammy Lamb. You kinda look like a lamb a little yoself with that black woolly head and them big sweet eyes."

"Mam, Old Saul sure done a good job on Blackie's hide. I gonna keep it at the foot a my bed where I can pet 'im every day. I bet he in heaven. I miss Blackie still, Mam. I can't get 'im outta my mind."

"Sammy, I know how you miss Blackie, cause I still miss my little girl, your mama, every day."

CHAPTER FOUR

"Eli, come sit in the living room. I have something important I need to talk to you about," Lizzie said.

"Okay Lizzie, my love. Now I know what Hattie must have felt like when she was waiting for me to announce a surprise."

"Eli, you are going to be a father. I waited a couple of months to be sure. Eli, say something, you're just standing there with your mouth open. Why, you're not like Hattie at all. You look as stunned as Samuel did the day you gave them the freedom papers."

"I don't know what to say, Lizzie. Tell me again. No, don't. I do know what you said. You caught me completely by surprise. I'm going to have a baby."

"No, I didn't say that," Lizzie laughed. "I said you're going to be a father. I'm going to have the baby."

"Lizzie darling, are you sure? I'm the happiest man in the world. We're going to have a boy. Come along Lizzie, we've got to find and tell Mama together right now."

Eli stroked Lizzie's face from temple to chin, cupped her face with both hands and kissed her gently. He held her hand and led her out the front door to where Mrs. Roads was cutting roses.

"Mama, Lizzie and I have wonderful news," Eli said. "We are going to have a boy, a son, Mama. Lizzie is going to have a baby."

"Well, congratulations, Daddy, but I do suppose it could be a girl just as well as a boy. If you want a boy, I do hope it's a boy," said Mrs. Roads smiling at Eli's excitement.

Lizzie's pregnancy seemed to go by quickly. Mrs. Roads doted on her, and Sammy asked a million questions about the baby.

The townspeople seemed less excited about the prospect of a new baby, the joyous news overshadowed by Sims' talk about the Roads freeing slaves and providing an education for Sammy.

As Eli predicted, the baby was a big, healthy boy. The baby resembled Eli, and Lizzie named him Eli Roads. Not Eli Zebulin Roads, or E. Z. Roads, just simply Eli Roads.

"Looks like we might have a problem," Eli mentioned to Lizzie the day after the baby was born. "We both can't be called Eli."

"I have a simple solution my dear. We'll call you Eli and the baby Little Eli. I don't see a problem with that," Lizzie answered, unable to take her eyes off the beautiful boy. "You don't want to be called E.Z, and I don't like that either."

"We might call 'im Babe," Sammy said with a big grin on his face as if he had solved the world's biggest dilemma. "He be a babe alright."

"We'll give that some thought," Lizzie said as she smiled at Sammy. "We all call you Little Sammy from time to time. I think we'll call him Little Eli like we call you Little Sammy. That makes you two alike."

Sammy was pleased by Lizzie's comments and thought it fitting that both he and Eli had only first and last names and none of the extra names that Hattie thought were nonsense.

The next day Lizzie was sitting on the front porch with Mrs. Roads asking questions about what kind of baby Eli had been.

"You know, Lizzie," said Mrs. Roads, "the one thing that sticks out in my mind is that Eli cried louder than I ever thought possible of a newborn."

"That's odd because Little Eli barely makes a whimper," Lizzie replied.

As they were talking and taking turns rocking Little Eli, Sammy bounded through the gate with a letter in his hand. He was waving the letter wildly, "Mail, Mrs. Roads. I got you a letter. Might be important. The postal clerk give it to me, and say bring it to you straight away. I didn't dawdle at all."

Lizzie asked Sammy where it had come from, confident that his recent reading lessons would permit him to sound out the address from which the letter came.

"It be from Dee-troit. Where that be, Miss Lizzie?"

Lizzie thought Sammy's grammar would be her next priority. "That is Detroit, Michigan, Sammy. Do you remember when we discussed the states?"

"Yes, Miss Lizzie, I do," said Sammy as he handed the letter to Mrs. Roads.

"Michigan is a northern state," Lizzie said.

"Thank you for the letter, Sammy," Mrs. Roads said as she looked at the envelope. She asked Sammy to go to the store and have Eli come to the house when he had a moment to spare.

Sammy wasted no time and took off at a run.

"That boy always goes like he's going to a fire," Mrs. Roads said. "Lizzie, the letter is from Sammy's mother, and I want Eli to read it before Sammy knows about it."

Mrs. Roads told Lizzie more of Mabel's story. "Mabel had little Sammy out of wedlock and didn't want anything to do with the child. She ran away when Sammy was just a few days old, leaving Sammy with Samuel and Hattie. We heard after she was gone for some time that she was in Detroit. Samuel and Hattie are rearing Sammy as if he is their own child, and they've told him wonderful things about Mabel. I know that Hattie loves Mabel and wants Sammy to love her just as much. I fear, however, that Mabel's departure so early in the child's life may have left him with little connection to her. Hattie is really the only mother Sammy has ever known."

A short time later Eli came from the store and asked what had happened to result in Sammy carrying on about a letter from the great northern State of Michigan.

"It's from Mabel," Mrs. Roads said, handing Eli the unopened letter. He opened the envelope and read the letter aloud to Mrs. Roads and Lizzie.

Dear Mr. Eli Roads,

I really do not know how to begin or what to say, only that I made a terrible mistake nine years ago when I left my baby and the responsibility of his care with my parents and your family. I did not realize at the time that my mother, father and child were the most important people in my life. I have since grown up. I have desired to write this letter for a long time, but I could not get up enough courage to do so before now. I am so ashamed of my past actions and want to make up for them to each of you.

I have been fortunate to have access to an individual who has periodically kept me informed about my family, but now I have lost that connection. The last word I received was of your wedding and the freedom papers you extended to my family. While I am not so presumptuous to expect the same kindness, I am aware that your family did not pursue me when I left without a word. I am teaching school in Detroit and earning a good living. I can well afford to take care of my family now and would like them to come and live with me.

I would be forever grateful if you could extend me another kindness and read this letter to my son and parents. While I long to tell them that I love them, I would rather show them. If they will come for a visit, I will pay their train fare. I do appreciate, Mr. and Mrs. Roads, what you have done for my family and for me.

I beg forgiveness from each of you and would consider it a favorable sign if you would honor my letter with a reply.

Yours truly,

Mabel

"Well now, isn't this a surprise out of the blue?" commented Mrs. Roads wiping tears from her eyes. "I didn't think that we would ever hear from Mabel again. This is nothing short of a miracle."

"After we close the store this evening, we'll get Samuel, Hattie and Sammy over here and read this letter to them. They are free and whether or not to go to Detroit is their decision to make. I agree that this is a miracle. It's wonderful news. I just don't know if Hattie can take another surprise like this one."

That afternoon Eli could hardly keep from telling Samuel and Sammy about the letter. At closing time, Eli asked Samuel to bring Hattie and Sammy over to the house after supper. "I have another surprise for you all, but I'm not sure Hattie can deal with the suspense."

"She'll be fine, Massa Eli. We'll be along after supper," replied Samuel.

"What you reckon the surprise be?" Sammy asked Samuel after they left the store. "Might be somethin' good. Bet it is, Pap."

When they walked into the kitchen where Hattie was preparing their evening meal, Sammy said with a big smile, "We all got to go to the big house after supper, Mam. Massa Eli got a good surprise for us."

"What kind of surprise you talkin' 'bout, Sammy Lamb? You know I don't take to surprises. What he talkin' bout, Samuel? I have us a good supper cooked, and now I won't be able to eat a bite. Why you have to go and tell me now?"

"It's gonna be alright, Hattie," Samuel said. "You know it can't be bad comin' from Massa Eli."

They ate in silence, Hattie nervously picking at her beans and cornbread.

"We jus' as well get it over with," Hattie said as they walked out the back door after supper. "Now, Sammy, don't you go and say nothin'. Let yo Pap do the talkin'.

After supper the three walked down the path to the Roads' family home, still silent and in single file.

Mrs. Roads ushered them into the parlor and went and sat next to Lizzie on the couch.

"We hopes this ain't gonna be bad, Massa Eli," Hattie said as she wringed her apron in her hands.

"It's not bad, Hattie," Eli replied. "Make yourselves comfortable in the chairs there." Eli pointed and with a little coaxing they finally sat.

"We received a letter today by post, Hattie, from Mabel. She…"

Before Eli could continue, Hattie jumped from the edge of her chair and shouted, "Heaven have mercy, is my sweet Mabel all right? Is my poor baby all right? I knowed it was gonna be bad, Samuel."

"Hattie," Eli said, "it's nothing bad at all. Now give me a chance to tell you the good news. Mabel sent a letter, a letter that she wrote herself, with the desire that I read it to you."

Eli took the letter from the envelope and read it with no interruptions. "Now," he said, "do you want me to read it again?"

"No sir," Hattie said. "I can almos' say it by heart."

"What you wants us to do, Massa?" Samuel asked. "We don't know if goin' to Detroit be the right thing to do."

"I can't tell you what to do, Samuel. This is a decision for you and Hattie to make. You all are free to decide. I know it will be different for you to do this, but just think on it for a while. You certainly don't have to decide this instant and not even tonight. Talk about it tonight, sleep on it and talk it over again in the morning. I find that works best when I have an important decision to make." Eli turned to Hattie and asked, "Are you excited to have news from Mabel?"

"I don't know what I is, Massa. It be a letter from my baby girl and she want to see her mama and daddy. I think I's gonna cry."

"I beg yo pardon, Massa Eli, but I thinks I gotta get Hattie to the house. We gonna think on it like you say. Come on Hattie, Sammy."

Eli handed the letter to Hattie. As she clutched it to her small frame, Eli realized how frail she seemed in comparison to the strong, wiry determined woman he had become accustomed to over the years.

Hattie left the Roads' home, stooped over and wiping the tears from her eyes. "I don't knows what to do, Samuel," Hattie said that night as they lay side by side. "Does you? We can't jus' go and leave the Roads family, but I sure wanna see my baby. Jus' think, Samuel, she be a school teacher. Can you believe it?"

"She seem to be doing well for herself all right," Samuel said feeling proud of Mabel as he drifted off to sleep.

Sammy alone in the loft bed was thinking, *she ain't my mama. She done run off and left me when I was just a little baby. She might wanna see Mam and Pap, but she sure don't like me. I ain't goin'. I'll just stay here with my Roads family.*

Both households were contemplating the decision to be made.

"Eli, this is going to be a hard decision for them to make," Lizzie said as she sat brushing her hair at her dressing table. It was the last thing she did each night before going to bed. "What do you hope they do?"

"I hate to see them go, but I think they should if only for a visit.

They can always come back."

Eli, Lizzie, Mrs. Roads, Hattie, Samuel and Sammy all went to bed that night knowing the letter from Mabel was a turning point in each of their lives.

For three days no one in either household mentioned the letter. Hattie walked around in a daze, misplacing almost every utensil she used in the kitchen, unable to concentrate on anything. Samuel was silent, watching Hattie and waiting for her to make up her mind.

"Samuel," Hattie said breaking the silence about the letter on the fourth day after receiving it, "what you think we oughta do? If we don't go, I ain't ever goin' to see my baby again. If we go, I don't know what Massa Roads will do without us. I wanna see my little girl, Samuel. We gonna go 'n see her 'n then we gonna know what to do. Alright?"

The next couple days were turmoil with emotions changing from excitement to worry and then back again to excitement. Eli had Hattie and Samuel fitted with new clothes, a trunk and all the necessities he thought they would need for their travel to Detroit.

The evening before they were to leave, Eli and Lizzie went to the little house to say their farewells to Hattie, Samuel and Sammy and give them their stage tickets to Knoxville and train tickets on to Detroit.

"Samuel, I want you to take these papers to Mabel. She may not feel she deserves them, but I want her to have her freedom papers like you, Hattie and Sammy. I purchased and registered them for her at the same time as yours. I hope this will assure her that we harbor no ill will toward her for leaving. Mabel should know, like you and Hattie, she is welcome to come back to our home anytime she pleases. Here too is twenty-five dollars. You better let Hattie keep it. Buy what you need," Eli said.

Hattie and Samuel were astounded by Eli's and Lizzie's generosity. Hattie hugged Lizzie and then Eli back and forth crying as she went from one to the other with Samuel just saying, "Lord, Lord."

"Where is Sammy?" Lizzie asked.

"I be in my room," Sammy said as he climbed down the ladder of the loft. As soon as he stepped from the last rung he turned to say determinedly, "I ain't goin'. I made my decision, and I am staying with the family that stayed with me."

No one knew what to say, not even Hattie. They all stared at Sammy sobbing. "Mam, Pap, I loves you both, but I just can't go. Don't make me. I'll just run off and come back if you makes me go."

Hattie put her arms around Sammy. "Don't you wanna see yo mama, baby?"

Sammy looked up into Hattie's eyes. "Mam, you be my mama, and Miss Lizzie be my mama, and Mrs. Roads be my mama, too. I reckon I got three mamas. I be a lucky boy, don't you think?" tears rolling down his cheeks.

"Massa Eli, does you mind if Sammy stays?" Hattie asked. "No need makin' him do somethin' he don't wanna do."

"Sammy, are you sure you don't want to take a train ride? You can always come back if you don't want to stay in Detroit. You should go see your mother," Lizzie said. Having come to know Sammy well, Lizzie was not surprised by his conviction and determination.

"No, Miss Lizzie. I wanna stay right here."

"I guess it's settled then," Eli said. "Hattie, Sammy can stay. And Sammy, if you ever change your mind all you need do is let me know."

"Yes sir, I will," said Sammy as Samuel lifted the boy in his arms. It pained him to leave the child behind, but he knew Hattie was right.

The next morning the stage was ready to depart at seven o'clock sharp. Samuel boarded the coach wearing the first suit he had ever owned and Hattie donning a new red dress, white hat and white apron. "You ain't dress proper lest you got your apron on," she had said to Samuel.

As the coach pulled away, Hattie waved her handkerchief at the Roads family and Sammy until the coach turned the corner and his small frame was out of sight.

"We are going to miss those two," Mrs. Roads said to Little Eli, gently bouncing the bundled baby as they walked back to the store. "Things won't be the same without Hattie and Samuel."

Lizzie spent all her spare time teaching Sammy reading, writing and arithmetic. Often, she would have Sammy completing lessons in the mercantile so she could be of assistance to the customers when Eli made deliveries. She and Eli could not ignore that requests for deliveries along with the number of customers decreased gradually since Eli had banished Sims from his property. They knew that many of the townspeople disagreed with their decision to educate Sammy. Some blatantly said so.

Eli and Lizzie found out very soon how intelligent Sammy

was and in short time he mastered each subject and lesson presented. "Eli, he needs to go to an actual school," Lizzie said to both Eli and Sammy one day. She encouraged Sammy not to stop learning.

Eli tried to find a school but none would admit a black person. It wasn't acceptable by society's standards so Eli and Lizzie provided Sammy with every book and paper they could get their hands on. Sammy especially looked forward to the medical journals that came addressed to the mercantile each month.

Eli pulled old copies of *The Weekly Register* dated early 1800's out of the attic. His father had subscribed to the publication so that Eli would be well read in current political, historical, geographical, scientific and astronomical ideals, facts and findings. When Lizzie noticed that Sammy was most drawn to biology and medical essays and facts, Eli subscribed to the *Monthly Journal of Medicine*. Sammy devoured the American and English journals and essays found in its pages.

Each time Sammy read a publication, he found himself curiously drawn to the information about the publisher. The notation regarding the publication of *The Weekly Register* indicated it was printed by Franklin Press on Water Street near the Merchant's Coffee House in Baltimore. The notation made Sammy wonder if Mam and Pap had the opportunity to frequent a coffee house in Detroit.

"Your mother may be able to help you find a school," Lizzie said one day as they were completing an accounting lesson.

"No thanks, Miss Lizzie. Not now. Maybe someday," Sammy replied.

The Roads family and Sammy continued to receive letters from Detroit. Mabel had taught Samuel and Hattie to write their names, and the letters bore signatures from each of them. Hattie and Samuel had Mabel convey that they liked Detroit, but missed Sammy and the Roads family. Mabel thanked Eli for her freedom papers. The papers were framed and hung in her classroom.

Time healed the wounds between Samuel, Hattie and Mabel. The three became closer than they had ever before.

A year later Mrs. Roads died. Eli's and Lizzie's marriage grew strong, but the death of Mrs. Roads and the departure of Samuel and Hattie left a void in their lives. More and more customers shopped elsewhere and the town's younger families moved away looking for opportunities that would sustain them. By the time Little Eli was eight years old, the Roads family found themselves existing on a meager income.

"Eli, I received an answer to the letter I wrote to Uncle Edward. He writes there is so much opportunity in Nashville, and we should consider opening a store there. He says that businesses are booming in Nashville."

"Lizzie, we do need to talk this over again with Sammy and Little Eli. As for myself, I'd like to try it, but I want to know what you think and how you feel about such a move."

"I think we should give it a try," Lizzie replied. "We can't ignore that things are not going well here, and I don't see it getting better. Hattie and Samuel indicated in their last letter that they plan to stay with Mabel in Detroit. She has a good job and would like them to live with her permanently. Mabel wants to take care of her parents. I know that Sammy wants to stay with us wherever we go. While Sammy doesn't want to go to Detroit now, I'm hoping that he will reunite with Mabel one day. It's been such a long time since he's seen Hattie and Samuel."

Lizzie knew that neither she nor Eli could make Sammy go to Detroit, but she held out hope that he would one day see his mother and continue his education.

"Ralph Daly has wanted to buy this land for the last three years," Eli replied. "I'll meet with him tomorrow and if he's still interested, we'll sell, load up our Conestoga wagons, map out a route to Nashville and take off. Since you agree we should give it a try, I think we've come to our decision."

"Oh Eli, it's all happening so fast. Do you think this is the right thing to do?"

"We've talked about it for over a year. Everything feels right. If we are going, let's load up and go."

"Yipppeee!" a shriek preceded the little frame that jumped from around the corner. "Can we start now? Sammy and I weren't spying, Daddy. We just came into the house and heard you talking. Can I drive one of the teams?" Little Eli asked full of excitement.

"We'll all have to take a hand in driving and walking, son. A couple days tending to business, loading the wagons and then we'll be on our way." Eli found himself feeling as excited as Little Eli.

"We'll need provisions for at least three months," Eli said to Lizzie when they were gathering up their supplies. "We should be able to make the trip in two months if all goes as planned, but it's best to plan for a longer time and the unexpected. No doubt the roads will be a challenge in places, and there will certainly be some high hills to climb between here and Nashville. We will have to let the horses graze and rest on the way. I expect we can travel six days and rest on the seventh. On Sundays we will rest and observe the Lord's Day."

Eli had to buy four more horses for the second wagon.

"Eight big horses seems excessive for the four of us, Eli," Lizzie said as he led the new horses into the corral.

"The truth is Lizzie, I wish I could find a couple extra," he replied. "Four to a team is barely enough. We'll have a heavy load and these horses will be constantly pulling."

As the Roads prepared for their journey, their remaining few friends came by to say their goodbyes and wish them well. On the last day of August in 1842, Eli and the boys finished loading the wagons.

PART II
The Journey

CHAPTER FIVE

Just as the sky was showing pink in the east, the two wagons pulled out and headed west. Eli and Lizzie were in the lead wagon. Sammy, now seventeen, and Eli, eight, followed in the second wagon, jubilant that the long awaited trip had begun.

"Ready or not, love, we're on our way. This place has been my life until today, and now we're leaving everything behind. It's like I'm leaving a part of me behind. Are you more excited or anxious?"

Lizzie answered, "I haven't lived here all my life like you, Eli, but in the nine years I've lived here I've loved every minute. I do believe we'll grow to love Nashville as well. I just know it."

Four hours later it was close to eleven o'clock. They stopped beside the road in a well-watered, grassy field and unhitched the teams. Lizzie prepared lunch, and they picnicked as the horses grazed.

"We've come about twelve or thirteen miles in four hours," Eli said as he ate his cold cut sandwich. "We should let the horses rest for a couple hours, travel four more hours and then camp for the night. If we can keep this pace the trip will be a cinch. The reality is that once the terrain gets steeper we'll surely make less headway. Twenty miles a day will be exceptional. I'd settle for that."

The hills became steeper in the afternoon, and as Eli predicted they traveled fewer miles during the afternoon hours. About four o'clock the horses were beginning to tire. "We better call it a day," Eli said to Lizzie as they entered a little meadow covered with lush grass interrupted only by a bubbling spring.

Not long after they dismounted the wagons, the clouds grew dark and the wind began to blow. "Sammy and Little Eli, let's hurry and stake out the horses. It looks like a storm's coming. We'll take shelter in the wagons," Eli said.

The rain came down in sheets and didn't let up until midmorning the next day. "We have to take what comes, love," Eli said to Lizzie as the rain dissipated. "There's nothing we can do about Mother Nature."

When the rain stopped, the men, including Little Eli, began to search for enough dry wood to build a fire.

"We need to cook a good meal," Lizzie said. "You men haven't eaten anything hearty. We'll just have to get a late start today." She unpacked a bucket that she had carefully packed with two-dozen eggs.

"I'll scramble half a dozen and save the rest for another day. Maybe we'll find a farm up ahead where we can buy more eggs along the way. Little Eli, you peel some potatoes and Eli, you slice some bacon. We will have a feast."

After eating Eli and Sammy hitched the teams. Little Eli helped Lizzie wash the dishes and pack up the leftover food.

"Mama, are you as excited as I am about going on this trip? I'll bet this is the way people on the wagon train west felt," Little Eli said to Lizzie.

"I do feel adventurous. It's very exciting."

"Well," Eli said, "getting started at noon is better than losing the entire day. If the road isn't washed out we'll be lucky. The rain really came down all night."

Every stream and creek in the area was overflowing but the roads proved to be in good shape. That evening Sammy was talking to Eli about the horses. "Mr. Eli, we better take it easy with these horses. They've been grazing the last few months, not doing much else, and these wagons are mighty heavy. We can't afford to lose even one."

"You are right. We should stop and rest them more often."

"Daddy," Little Eli whispered excitedly, "look over by those trees. There are two deer. Think I can shoot one? I've never shot a deer before. Can I, please?"

"Quietly get the rifle and see if you can get that young buck, the one with the spikes."

While Little Eli could hardly contain his excitement he had no trouble loading the rifle. He took care to move quietly and the deer had not moved as he prepared to take a shot.

"Take your time," Sammy whispered squatting next to him, "and gently squeeze the trigger. Don't pull or you're likely to miss."

Little Eli was no novice with a rifle. He had been shooting for almost two years, but he had not felt this kind of excitement before. Heart pounding, Little Eli thought about all the instruction his father and Sammy had given him in the past. He listened to Sammy, took time to aim well, squeezed the trigger and the deer fell in its tracks.

Little Eli turned and with a big grin asked, "How's that?" He wanted to jump up and down but thought it too child-like so he restrained himself.

The deer was dressed, the wagon packed and they were ready to travel again. They took their places on the wagons and for the next four hours the wagons moved as fast as the muddy roads would allow. The sun shone bright and by evening the roads were beginning to dry. Eli chose a place to camp beside a stream. The horses were staked, and the boys built a fire for Lizzie to cook.

After searching the area for dry firewood, Eli cut the venison steaks for Lizzie. It was a familiar chore, butchering, and one that had been part of his duties at Roads Mercantile. Lizzie lightly floured the steaks and added them to the cast iron skillet Eli had placed above the fire.

"Deer steaks all around," Lizzie said as she filled each plate. "Eat up, men. Thanks to Little Eli we have enough venison to last a week if the weather cools. Fellas, I do believe we have us a sharp-shooter in the group," she said as she patted Little Eli on the back.

Few words were spoken during supper until Eli said just before taking his last bite, "Lizzie darling, I have never enjoyed a better meal."

A heavy frost, almost a light blanket of snow, covered the ground the following morning. No one was very hungry after having had a huge supper. Lizzie decided to keep it light with coffee and flapjacks.

"We'll get an early start this morning," Eli stated, "and rest the horses more often throughout the day." All, including the horses, were ready to head out that morning. The air was cool and fresh and the sun had just cleared the treetops. "Move 'em out," Eli ordered giving a raise and shake to the reigns to start the horses and wagons moving.

"Look how the leaves are starting to change color," Lizzie said. "I just love this time of year. When I was a little girl my daddy told me fairies came out at night and painted the leaves to make people happy. It was so easy to believe."

"It does make a soul happy to see such vibrant colors," Eli agreed, "and the changing of colors has just started."

Every time they climbed a hill they stopped to let the horses blow before they started again. At noon the horses were unhitched and hobbled to water and graze.

"We've probably made twenty miles today," Eli said as the end of daylight neared. "Tomorrow is Saturday and the next day we'll have a day of rest. How are you holding up, love? Getting tired?"

"A little but it's just a new experience for me. I can't imagine doing this for a year like the pioneers did moving west."

The land was beginning to flatten out and the wagons moved easily over the terrain. Saturday they made good time and covered more ground than they had any of the previous days.

"Eli, let's stop a little early since we've made such good progress," said Lizzie. "I have to wash a few things and if I could get some help, it would go faster. Maybe the boys can cook supper, and you and I can do the laundry."

"Be glad to oblige, my love. We'll find a good place."

As dark descended the washing was finished and almost dry. The boys had prepared supper and they had eaten. "No need getting up early in the morning, Lizzie. I told the boys that tomorrow is our day to rest so sleep in if you can."

The next morning Lizzie woke alone in the wagon to the smell of fish frying. "Hey out there, do you all have enough fish to spare? I sure would like some."

Sammy called back, "Plenty to spare, Miss Lizzie. Come help yourself."

As she stepped out of the wagon Lizzie saw Eli and Little Eli coming down a steep hill. She filled her plate with fish and Sammy poured her a hot cup of coffee. "What are those two men of mine up to, Sammy?"

"They wanted to climb that hill and take a look around to see what's ahead."

"What did you boys see, the Pacific Ocean?" Lizzie chuckled as they entered the camp.

"No, Mama, but there may be some houses up ahead. We saw what looked to be smoke from a chimney rising up in the sky."

"Now wouldn't it be nice to be able to talk to someone who lived way out here?"

"What are you going to do with all those fish, Sammy?" Lizzie asked. "That's enough for an army."

"Well, there should be enough here for three meals. We'll eat what we want now, and I'll smoke and dry what's left. If we keep them cool they'll last a long time."

After everyone had eaten, Eli got out his Bible, read some scripture and gave a devotional. After giving thanks for their safe travels, they all went about their own interests. It was truly a day of rest and leisure. Eli thought that even the horses had a relaxing day.

The next morning they decided on another early start. The temperature had dropped during the night and a cold north wind was blowing. The sky was blue without a cloud to be seen. Lizzie pulled her shawl up over her head and tight to her body. Looking up to the sky, she thought about how it was the color of the ocean off the coast of South Carolina. She had vacationed there during childhood with her father.

"I hope there are people up ahead, Eli. We need to stock up on vegetables, and a little woman gossip would be nice."

"I think you'll get your wish, love. I noticed cows over in that meadow and I can hear dogs barking ahead."

When they topped the next hill they could see a large barn and a farmhouse with a few small out buildings. A man was walking toward the perimeter gate.

"I think he wants us to stop," Lizzie exclaimed excitedly.

"Mornin' folks, name's Art Hector. Pleased to have you come on in for a spell. Wife's name is Essie 'n my brood, well, can't member mosta their names."

As they drove their wagons up to the house, Lizzie saw a petite woman with a little baby in her arms and surrounded by children. The oldest appeared to be a boy about twelve. Lizzie stepped down out of the wagon and walked to where Essie stood. "My name is Lizzie. It's good to meet you. Hope you don't mind company barging in this way."

Essie did a little curtsy and invited her into the house. "Children, you go finish your chores, and then if you promise to be good you can come and visit with Miss Lizzie."

Outside, the men talked and Eli explained their plans to Art. "Yours is the first farm that we've seen since we started traveling."

"Not many people travel this a way, Mr. Roads. We're a bit off the beaten path. A few freight wagons about all that comes by here. Hate to tell ya but you ain't gonna make it much further like you are."

"What makes you say that, Art? Is something wrong?"

"I'll say it is. It's your set up. Ain't gonna climb the next mountain."

"What mountain are you talking about? I don't see any mountain."

"Up the road a ways, not the tallest I ever saw but it sure is steep. Four horses won't pull your wagon up that hill, Mr. Roads, just won't do it. You'll kill them horses if you try it. Them ain't pullin' horses. Them's stagecoach horses made for lots of runnin', not for pullin' heavy loads. You oughta have mules or oxen, they the best for freight."

I did buy the four horses hitched to my other wagon over there from the coach line, but he said nothing about not being able to pull freight."

"Reckon he wanted to sell them horses or maybe he didn't know."

"What do you suggest I do, Art? We have to get to Nashville. Is there a way around the mountain? We have to go on."

"To go south, you'd have to backtrack the way you come and go down through Georgia and then north. I just don't know. The mountain gets taller that away."

"There has to be a solution to this problem. Do you have any mules or oxen that I can buy or borrow?"

"No, not enough to do ya any good, but there might be a way if ya wanna try it. You can hitch all your horses to one wagon and maybe they can take it over. Unhitch and come back for the other one."

"We have to give it a try. It just may work."

Eli explained to Lizzie what they had to do to cross the next mountain. "Art said that you and Little Eli are welcome to stay here while Sammy and I take over the first wagon. Sammy could stay with the first wagon while I bring back the horses and take the second wagon over. We might just make it work that way."

Lizzie turned to Essie and asked, "Are you sure that it wouldn't be an imposition to have me and Little Eli here longer?"

The young woman looked pleased and answered, "It will give us more time to visit, Lizzie. I would love to have you stay and the children to be able to play with Little Eli longer."

"Odis," Art said to his oldest son, "you hitch up Big Clyde and go along in case these folks need extra help pullin' the wagons." Odis was no stranger to hard work, and Big Clyde was the hugest horse that either Eli or Sammy had ever seen.

"I'd go myself but I gotta get my hay in while I can."

Eli and Sammy hitched all eight horses to the first wagon and departed from the Hector farm as Lizzie, Little Eli and the Hector children waved farewell.

The pull up the mountain was steeper than any Eli had encountered, but moving at a slow pace, the eight horses had little trouble making the climb. Descending the mountain was more difficult. It was hard for the brakes to hold the wagon. Almost three hours later, the first wagon rested safely at the bottom of the mountain.

"Sammy, I'll take the horses back while it's still daylight, but I won't try and cross back here tonight. I expect I should see you tomorrow about noon."

Eli and Odis returned to the Hector farm just as it was getting dark and supper was ready. "Had no trouble going up but it was hard to brake going down such a steep mountain. We need to make sure the brake on the other wagon is in good shape before we leave," Eli said to Art.

The Roads and Hector families became close friends in the short time they were together.

"If you ever get to Nashville, Art, look us up," Eli said. "Thanks for all your help in getting us across that mountain. And, most of all, thanks for your generosity and kindness."

"Don't mention it. Once you're t'other side, you in North Carolina," Art hollered as they were driving away.

"The Hectors are some of the nicest people I've ever met," Lizzie said as she turned around from waving. "They even restocked our food supply."

"Yes they are. Thanks to Art, we'll know what to do if we face this problem again," Eli said gratefully.

They had no difficulty taking the second wagon over the mountain. Sammy was waiting with food prepared when they

"We are officially in North Carolina I suppose," Little Eli said.

"That's right, son. We have a couple hundred miles more and we'll be in Nashville. We're making really good time considering the rain, the steepness of the mountain and all the other unexpected obstacles," Eli added. "Let's allow the horses a good rest and get an early start in the morning."

"I didn't know there's such a difference in freight and stagecoach horses," Sammy said, "but Mr. Hector sure seemed to know."

"Yes, and now we know," Little Eli said in a matter of fact way.

The next two days proved good for travelling. The weather was cool and the sun shone bright which lent warmth to the air. Three days after crossing the mountain as they looked for a place to make camp for the night, Lizzie spied what looked like to be a burnt wagon a little off the trail.

"Let's camp over here by the creek, love." Eli said. "It will make it easier to water and graze the horses."

After supper it was still early so Eli and Lizzie decided to walk over to where she had seen the wagon. "It's been burned alright," Eli said as he peered into the charred hull.

"Look over here, Eli, it's an old trunk," Lizzie said as she opened the lid. "Oh my, it's full of baby clothes. I wonder why a family would have left it here."

"Lizzie, put the lid down," Eli felt a growing uneasiness. "Look there! There are three graves and one is a baby's. Let's get out of this place. There's no telling what happened here."

Eli pulled Lizzie away from the rubble and cautioned, "We

should wash our clothes and take a hot bath. All these remains are bad signs and we may have exposed ourselves to whatever caused these people to be buried here. Better to be safe."

Lizzie thought about the death of the small family on the walk back to camp. *Who buried them? Had some survived to continue on their journey heartbroken by the loss of loved ones?*

Once they returned to their campsite Lizzie told Little Eli and Sammy what they had found and cautioned the boys, "Do not go near the wreckage. Three people are buried there."

Eli and Lizzie set about the task of heating water, bathing as best they could and washing their clothes in boiling water. "It's probably nothing to worry about, my love. Let's get a good night's sleep."

The next morning after a hearty breakfast they headed out as usual. "I believe we traveled the most miles in a day yet," Eli commented as their night camp was put away. "If the weather stays good, we'll be there before you know it."

The next day proved just as good for traveling but before making camp for the evening Lizzie began feeling sickly. "I think we better stop, Eli, just as soon as we can find a suitable place."

"Lizzie, your face is mighty red. Are you running a fever?" he asked as he lightly touched her cheeks and forehead. "You are burning up. There is an opening just ahead, love, there by that creek. We'll pull in there so you can rest."

A few minutes later when they stopped, Lizzie was shaking uncontrollably from chills. Eli had Sammy and Little Eli make camp and heat water. He prepared some hot tea for Lizzie. *What should I do?* Eli thought to himself. *What kind of medicine do we have?*

Maybe Sammy will know what to do.

Eli called, "Sammy, come here for a minute. I need to ask you something. Hurry. It's important. Little Eli, you stay where you are. Your mama is very sick."

Hearing the urgency in Eli's voice, Sammy moved at a run.

Eli shared his suspicions with Sammy about the contaminated trunk of clothes, the three graves and Lizzie's chills and fever. "I don't know if any of what's happening now is related to the demise of that family, Sammy. What should I do? I know you've read a lot of medical books. Do you have any suggestions as to a course of action, any medicines we might have to give her?"

"I don't know anything for sure, Mr. Eli. We can see if she can drink hot tea, and we can bathe her face with cold water from the creek. Maybe quinine will help. I just don't know if we have anything that will ease her chills and fever or really help her at this point if she was exposed to some kind of contamination or disease."

Eli had a small bottle of quinine they had stocked at Roads Mercantile. It was an important medicine for plantation owners in the treatment of malaria, common on the rice plantations in South Carolina.

Sammy steadily delivered cool water and Eli bathed Lizzie's face. An hour later Lizzie had not responded to the medicine. More than feelings of helplessness overcame Eli. He too began feeling chilled and feverish.

"Sammy, there is nothing more you can do to help me tonight with Lizzie except pray. Stay close to Little Eli in case he needs you. And Sammy, take care of him if things take a turn for the worse. I will see you in the morning." Eli didn't let Sammy know that he was experiencing the same symptoms that had overcome Lizzie.

Sammy hesitated to leave Eli alone to take care of Lizzie. Eli's statement about things possibly taking a turn for the worse concerned him, and he was unable to sleep. His thoughts were on something he read in his medical journals about Lizzie's symptoms of high fever and chills. There were several illnesses that could cause the symptoms, typhoid, cholera and about fifty others. *If I were to make a guess,* Sammy thought, *I would say its cholera, and if I'm right, there's no hope for either. All I can do is make them comfortable and pray.*

Eli, barely conscious at two o'clock in the morning, never knew Lizzie passed away. Sammy woke Little Eli and together they did their best to keep Eli comfortable only to watch him succumb to the sickness about midmorning.

"I'm so sorry, Little Eli, for you losing your mother and father this way. You know we have to bury them as soon as possible. They may have died of cholera or some other contagious disease. We are also going to have to burn the wagon they slept in and their clothes. I'm afraid there is still no guarantee that we won't get sick ourselves," Sammy said full of grief.

Little Eli felt dazed but responded, "Up there, Sammy, on that little knoll. We'll bury them there. It's a beautiful spot. Just inside this valley that looks so peaceful. Mama would have liked this place."

"I agree they'd like it here, Little Eli. I just know they would," Sammy said to reassure.

"No need to call me Little Eli anymore, Sammy. Since I'm the only Eli left, call me that." Eli felt a sense of responsibility for completing what his parents planned.

"Okay, Eli, you are the head of the family now."

Eli and Sammy planned to bury Eli's mother and father on the knoll just inside the entrance of a peaceful looking valley. Cognizant of contamination, Sammy insisted they tie bandanas across their faces and wear work gloves that they would later burn.

Both Eli's and Sammy's movements were mechanical. Bewildered, they took apart the wagon that Eli and Lizzie traveled in just hours before. Using some of the boards, they built two coffins, wrapped the bodies in blankets and placed them carefully inside. They dug one grave large enough for both coffins, hardly a word exchanged between the two, each suffering an unspeakable grief.

Sammy watched the tears streaming down Eli's face and was unable to find words to comfort him. *Eli's such a strong boy,* Sammy thought, *dealing with tragedy, digging this grave, at just eight years old. I guess he is already a man.*

"Sammy, this is Sunday. Will you get Daddy's bible and read some scripture?" Eli asked. "It would be proper."

Sammy read the Twenty-Third Psalms and then they covered the coffins.

"We'll burn the rest of the wagon and the clothes and pray for the best." They kept the fire going till way up into the night until everything was ash. Exhausted, they went to sleep.

"Where are you going, Sammy?" Eli asked the next morning

as he climbed out of the wagon rubbing the sleep out of his eyes. Sammy was saddling one of the horses.

Sammy had woke early not able to sleep, "I got me a job to do. I'm going back to burn that trunk and wagon. It may be the cause of your parents' deaths. We'll never know for sure, but if it has been contaminated with some kind of disease, we don't want anyone else exposed. I'll be back tomorrow evening. You just wait around here and rest."

Sammy rode the youngest horse and left camp at a canter. *Took us two days traveling together to get here after Lizzie and Eli were exposed to the wagon*, he thought to himself. *I should be there this afternoon riding this horse.*

Eli dressed, poured a cup of coffee and ate a couple pieces of fry bread that Sammy had cooked. *Things will be different now*, he thought to himself. *It's just Sammy and me. What in the world should we do? Mama and Daddy always read the Bible first thing in the morning and discussed what they were going to do that day.* Eli randomly opened the Bible and there before his eyes was the Book of Samuel. *I didn't know that Samuel was a Bible name*. He began to read and came across the name Eli. He felt that his father had a hand in opening this book to him.

After reading for some time, he remarked aloud, "Samuel and Eli were good friends in the Bible, and here we are together again." He closed the Bible thanking God for showing him this passage and praying that God would continue to show them the way.

He checked the horses making sure they were staked out where they could get to water and grass. Eli walked to and up the knoll where they had buried his parents only yesterday. He fell to his knees at his parents' grave and spoke aloud, "I don't know what to do now, Mama. I didn't realize things could change so fast. I'm going to try and remember the things you and Daddy taught me. I'm just glad I have Sammy here to help me."

Eli walked back to camp and sat down on a fallen tree near the horses. He was overcome by the thought that he would never again see his mother and father. He allowed himself to cry. Looking up to heaven, Eli said, "I promise that I will always try and live like you taught me. I love you Mama and Daddy." The knowledge that his parents would want him to be strong brought him a small measure of comfort as he made the commitment aloud.

Eli went back to the wagon, picked out a big red apple they had gotten from the Hectors and ate it down to the core. He started to throw it away and stopped. *Wonder what will happen if I plant these seeds.* He got the shovel, went back up the hill to the burial plot, dug several small holes and planted the seeds. *Now we'll just see what happens.*

Eli decided to explore the area around the campsite. *I haven't been walking much since we started this trip. Think I'll follow this creek a ways and see what this valley looks like.* The further he walked, the wider the valley became. The grass was so tall that he had to walk next to the water. *What a fine farm this would make. When Sammy gets back we'll have to check this place out a little more.*

The leaves seemed even more yellow and gold than they had yesterday, with a little red scattered throughout. "Looks like a cave," Eli said aloud. *A cave could come in handy one day,* he thought as he approached the entrance. The cave's opening was about six feet tall and ten feet wide. He walked inside and it opened to a large room. *I'll bring a light and explore this with Sammy when he returns.*

As Eli walked back to camp, he realized he had been thinking about this place as home. *But what about Nashville, the store and the plans his parents had?* "I can't go off and just leave them here all by themselves in the middle of nowhere, can I?" he asked himself feeling tears well up in his eyes and looking up toward the hill.

Around mid-day Eli was hungry and decided to fish. "Man," he said aloud, "every time I throw in, I catch one." He thought he would do like Sammy and catch enough to smoke and dry. *These dozen ought to be enough to try out Sammy's smoking method. If it works, I can surely catch plenty more.* After eating all he wanted, he built a small lean-to about six feet long and four feet tall. He built a small fire in the back. The smoke had only one escape and that was where he hung the fish. *Looks just like Sammy's and look at that smoke.* He slowly smoked the fish all afternoon until he went to sleep.

"Wake up in there," someone yelled. "You planning on sleeping all day?"

Eli jumped up, pulled his pants on and looked out the wagon. It was Sammy. "Thought you said you'd be back this evening."

"Didn't want to leave this little kid I know by himself too long. Thought he might get scared and I didn't want that."

"Aw, Sammy, you know better than that. I'm not scared."

"I know, I'm just joking with you. I got the job done early and decided to ride all night. Let's fix something to eat. I'll catch a couple hours sleep and then you and I have some things to talk about."

"There are plenty of fish in the lean-to. You tend your horse and I'll make biscuits and coffee unless you want something else."

"That sounds just fine. I could eat a bear, but I'll settle for biscuits and fish."

Sammy unsaddled and staked his horse. He walked over to the campfire and poured himself and Eli cups of coffee while waiting for the biscuits to finish. "You'll make some woman a good cook, Eli. These biscuits are as good as any I've ever eaten. Pass me a couple more."

After eating four biscuits and several pieces of smoked fish, Sammy told Eli, "I'm going to get in the wagon and take a little snooze. If I'm not up by noon, wake me."

Eli re-staked the horses in a new area where the grass was tall and lush. *This is getting to be a real job moving eight horses around. I need a better system.*

"What you got to eat? I'm starved," Sammy asked as he came out of the wagon some time later.

"How about the last of the venison stew over a cathead?" Eli grinned thinking about the word his father had used for biscuits as he removed the iron pot from its hook over the fire. "One of us better go kill another deer. This one is gone."

"That shouldn't be a problem around here. I've never seen so many deer," Sammy replied.

As they finished the biscuits Sammy asked Eli, "Have you been thinking about what you want to do? We need to make a plan."

"I've been thinking of little else, Sammy, but first I'd like to know what you want to do."

"Eli, I wanted to live with your parents because they loved me and I loved them. I feel like you're my little brother. We're both still young. I'm sure people consider us kids, but I think we can make it at anything we set our minds to. If you want to go on to Nashville and build a store, we can surely do that, and if you want to stay here and build something, I'm for that as well. Money is important, but it's not everything. My preference would be to stay here and see what we can build. What about you?"

"I was hoping you would say that, Sammy, because that's what I want, to stay right here." They looked each other in the eye and shook hands, both excited and happy with their decision.

"Sammy," Eli said after they had made their pact, "the money that my parents had from selling the place and store is in the strong box I put in our wagon when we burned theirs. I don't know how much money is in that box but it should be considerable. Maybe we should find a safe place for it. I looked around yesterday and there's a cave a little ways down the valley. Maybe we can make use of it and put our supplies there until we build a place. First thing we need to do is something with our horses. I believe we can build a pole corral big enough for two or three and turn the rest loose in this valley. Every couple days we can switch them. I don't think they'll leave if we build a fence across the entrance."

Sammy smiled at Eli, "Are you really only eight?"

"Let's start now, Sammy. We can start cutting poles for the corral. It'll be a lot of work but a lot of fun too."

Since the decision was made to stay where they were and put

down roots, Sammy and Eli started making plans to build a house, barn and store in the middle of nowhere on a road rarely traveled. "People will come one day," Sammy assured Eli. "I just know it, and we'll have supplies for them when they get here."

From daylight to dark they worked. In three days, the corral was built. Three horses were corralled and the others were turned loose in the valley. Grass was plentiful in the valley and alternating the horses would insure each had sufficient time to graze. Sammy and Eli built a fence and gate across the small opening to the valley.

During supper that evening, Sammy said, "We need to know where we are, Eli, and where we can buy the supplies we need. Did your parents have a map showing the route to Nashville?"

"I don't remember seeing one but if they had a map it would probably be in the strong box with the money. Let's get it out and open it. Maybe you can handle it better than I, it's kind of heavy. The key is taped to the bottom."

"Okay, if there's a map in the strong box it should be marked with roads and towns." Sammy removed the strong box from under the bed where Eli had stowed it away and unlocked the pad lock.

"There must be three or four thousand dollars here, Eli, and gold." After looking through the box Sammy found the map. "It's just a hand-drawn map. Now let's see if we can figure out where we are."

"The trail we are on is lined in red from where we started and all the way to where we planned to go on to Nashville," Sammy said running his finger along the map. "That river we crossed on the ferry was the Tennessee. The next night we camped by the burnt wagon, that I think was here. Two days later we stopped here." He pointed to a spot on the map where he thought they were. "It looks like Chattanooga is the nearest large town, smaller ones to the north and west. This is not a bad place to be. There are no people here yet, but I believe we will grow."

"The cave is close enough to keep an eye on, let's move most of the things we don't need right now into the cave. Let's hitch the wagon up, drive as close as we can and pack the rest of the way."

In a few hours everything that wasn't needed was either secured in the cave or the wagon. "Eli, we're going to have to build a house to live in for now. Then we'll build a store on the front of it later."

Eli replied, "I'll cut this chestnut oak tree. It's right in the way."

"I'd rather you not. When that tree grows big, it will be the showpiece to the entrance of this valley. We'll sit under its branches and talk about old times and drink cold lemonade. I can see it now."

"It's only about ten inches thick, Sammy. It'll have to do a lot of growing between now and then."

"You see that old tree over there laying in two pieces?" Sammy asked. "It looks like lightning struck it. See how it looks burned in the middle? I'll bet that's the mother of this little offspring. I say give this tree a chance and our grandchildren will play under it one day."

Little did they know that Sammy's words would be more prophetic than either could imagine.

PART III
The Community

CHAPTER SIX

The weather turned colder over the next month. Eli and Sammy worked cutting, notching logs and fitting them together for their little house. It was the last of November when they split and nailed shingles on the roof. A week before Christmas they moved into the small log home.

"It's our first home, Sammy. It's small but a lot bigger than the wagon. I'll go hunting, and we'll have a venison roast to celebrate. We can prepare the last of the root vegetables Mr. Hector gave us to go along with the roast. I can't wait to plant our own garden," Eli said as Sammy carried in the last of the kitchen supplies from the wagon.

"That sounds good. If you don't mind staying by yourself a few days, I'll take a couple packhorses and find my way to Chattanooga. I'll pick up some things we need. Before I go, you get your rifle and go get that deer. Being in our new home is cause for celebration."

Eli wasn't out of sight of the house when he spotted hoof prints from three deer. He eased along the tracks and found the deer under a huge oak tree pawing snow, looking for acorns. He chose the smallest and with one shot made the kill. The deer would provide enough meat for a few weeks.

Sammy built a fire in the fireplace and had the iron pot hanging over the coals. "Water's hot," he said when Eli opened the door carrying an expertly dressed shoulder roast.

"The rest is hanging in the smokehouse. I'll tend to it tomorrow. It's getting colder outside. It'll probably freeze tonight."

After eating their celebratory meal, they agreed it was exceptional and wasted no time planning their next undertakings. "If there's a lumber mill along the way to Chattanooga," Sammy said, "we might look into buying mill-cut lumber for the store. It'll be faster than building with logs. I'll see what's available that we can afford."

As Sammy prepared the pack horses and mounted his ride the next morning, Eli said, "See if you can find a plow and any other farming tools, and some fruit trees, garden seeds and ammunition."

"Anything else?" he called back almost out of hearing.

"Man," mumbled Eli, "I guess I really do miss being in the mercantile business. I would give anything just to browse around a well-stocked store." Eli recalled the stacks and smells of Roads Mercantile. The smells of the small food counter that offered cold cut meats, cheese, rice and flour, the stacks of fabric and leather and the sacks of feed kept in the back room all mingled together had added to the experience of being in the store. He remembered delivering groceries in a small red wagon that his parents purchased when the one Sammy used could no longer be repaired. *The new store,* Eli thought, *will possess the same good smells and be home to new memories as precious as the ones I'll never forget.*

What should I do today? Eli thought as he ambled back to their new little house. *Maybe I should wash the clothes in the laundry bag. It's nearly full. No, I'll wait till tomorrow. Maybe catch a few more fish and smoke them. No, that's no fun either.* As he was sitting in front of the fire trying to think of something more interesting to do than chores, there was a knock on the door.

The knock was so unexpected. Eli didn't know if he should answer it or make out like no one was home. Stunned, he thought, *they've seen the smoke in the chimney. They know someone is around.* After the third knock, he cracked the door just enough to see Mr. Hector and his son, Odis.

Eli, relieved, opened the door.

"Come on in, Mr. Hector, Odis. It's cold out today. There's a pot of hot coffee. Let me pour you both a cup. What brings you this way?"

Art and his son accepted the coffee. Art went on to tell Eli, "My horse fell and badly hurt his leg right outside your fence. Thought you folks went to Nashville."

Eli explained to them about his parents getting sick with a high fever and dying within a few hours and his and Sammy's decision to stay here and build a store.

"I truly am sorry, son, about your folks, but ya can't open a store way out here. There's nobody to buy your stuff," Art replied.

"We've decided to give it a try anyway, Mr. Hector. Like my Daddy use to say, you never know until you try. Sammy is on his way to Chattanooga now to pick up a few supplies. We're about out of everything."

"How about selling me one of them horses you have? Mine's unable to travel anymore, at least for a while."

"We have five out there, Mr. Hector. Pick the one you want. Sammy has three with him. Can't sell till I talk with my partner, but you can surely use one. You're welcome to leave yours here until he gets better."

"We're on our way to see my brother. He lives about forty miles west of here. He's ailing mighty bad," Art offered in way of an explanation for their passing through.

They led the injured horse out to the corral and Art Hector caught and saddled another. "Don't know how long I'll be, but when we come back by, I'll return your horse. Mine might be better by then. We should be back through in maybe a week or more."

"Mr. Hector, would you by chance have an extra milk cow you'd like to sell?" Eli asked.

"Just might, son. Got a young Jersey that'll freshen this spring. She'd make a gooden. Might work up a deal if ya want. You be careful out here by yourself, son. Anything can happen."

"Hope your brother gets better, Mr. Hector. Bye Odis."

"Thank ya kindly, son. Thank ya kindly."

After the Hectors went their way, Eli got excited about the possibility of a milk cow. *Won't Sammy be surprised? Art might have extra pigs and chickens. Well, let's start with the cow, then maybe the others. Now I know what I want to do. Start building a couple of stalls for animals. Art is right. I really have to be careful here by myself.*

"Don't be careless, Eli," he muttered to himself, "especially with an ax."

Eli worked four days alone cutting cedar posts and poles that grew abundantly on the hillsides. He hurriedly cooked and ate each day, focusing on the work. Each night he slept like a baby. After five days Eli thought, *I probably have enough posts and poles to get started, but I better wait till Sammy gets back. That ought to be soon.*

Eli realized he had little to wear and that he'd need to wash clothes. Reluctantly he heated water in the wash pot, put the clothes in, swished them back and forth with lye soap, then let them set and soak. After they cooled enough to handle, he rubbed them on the scrub board that had been his Mama's, then packed the bundle of shirts and pants to the creek and rinsed them out. "Nothing to it," he grumbled to himself as he wrung them out and hung them on the fence to dry. "Just took all day, that's all."

That night when he went to bed, Eli's mind raced with thoughts of all the things that he and Sammy could do to build a successful farm and store. This place where Eli and Lizzie were laid to rest was a place where people would come and get what they needed for their homes and farms. "What people?" he remembered asking as he fell asleep. "Where are the people?"

When Sammy returned, Eli was dragging dead, seasoned trees from the woods. Sammy came in leading his packhorses loaded heavy with supplies.

"Still hanging around I see," Sammy said with a big smile. "I could sure use a cup of your fine coffee."

"There's a pot half full inside. I hope you have more coffee in your packs. We're almost out."

"Got ten pounds of coffee packed on Old Bud plus a lot more. We have two wagon loads of supplies right behind me and two more coming next week."

"You must've cleaned out every store in town, Sammy. Why so many supplies?"

"Made some good deals," he said as he and Eli walked into the house. "No one seems to have cash money now days. When they found out I was buying with cash people were ready to deal. I also talked to a man that has a sawmill about twenty miles from here. He said he could cut all the lumber we needed. He has two grown sons that know how to build and they'll help us for a dollar a day each."

"Mr. Hector and his son, Odis, came by a few days back on their way to visit Mr. Hector's sick brother. One of their horses took a pretty good injury to the leg, and I loaned him one of ours. He wants to buy one of our horses, but I wanted to talk it over with you first."

"We sure don't need all eight of them. If you agree, let's sell one."

"He has a young Jersey milk cow that's going to have a calf this spring and we may be able to work out a trade. We need a milk cow, Sammy."

"Okay by me if that's what you want."

They were unloading and shelving food and supplies when the two wagons arrived.

"Let's unload this one out by the corral. We'll have to build a shed to house these things. The other wagon with feed and grain for planting we'll unload in the cave. It'll stay dry in there," Sammy said.

Three hours later everything was in its place and the two

drivers climbed into one of the wagons and drove off.

"They're leaving one of the wagons, Sammy."

"Yeah Eli, that one belongs to us. We need a wagon like that because our Conestoga wagon is too big for everyday use. Maybe we can sell or trade it to someone."

All afternoon the two of them worked on cutting the tree trunks Eli had dragged up to the house for firewood.

"I see that you accomplished a lot while I was gone. What are all the cedar poles for?" Sammy asked.

"We'll need a couple of stalls if we get a milk cow. Maybe we could raise a few chickens and pigs as well."

"We'll have all the livestock we need in time, Eli, but first you and I need to concentrate on the store."

"You're right, but I'm so excited. I want it all now."

"Well then, we'll start tomorrow laying out the foundation. I'm really tired from the ride from Chattanooga. Let's call it a day."

The following morning Sammy was up before daylight. By lamplight he started sketching a rough layout of the buildings and placement of each. "Eli was right," he said to himself. "This is exciting."

The following afternoon Sammy and Eli were working on the foundation for the store when Art Hector and Odis rode up on their way home from visiting Art's brother. "Tuberculosis is what the doctor said. Might live if he moves out west to Arizona," Art said. "Reckon they'll be movin'."

"Will they need a big wagon, Mr. Hector?" Eli asked. "We have that one we moved out here in."

"That's just the kinda wagon he needs. What you askin' for it?"

"Make me a fair price, Mr. Hector."

"He ain't got no cash and I don't either. Maybe we can work out a trade."

"We do need all the help we can get now that we've started this building. That is if you have the time," Sammy said.

"Got plenty of time. Won't have much goin' on with the farm till March, still a couple a months yet. Is it a deal?"

"It's a deal, Mr. Hector," Eli and Sammy agreed.

"Odis, you think you can ride home by yourself and tell your Ma so she won't be worried?"

"Yes sir, Daddy," Odis replied.

"Get Abe and Big Clyde and bring them back with ya. Abe and you can drive this wagon to your Uncle's house after you get back. Better not leave till morning. Sammy, what do ya want me and Odis to do today? We still have a bit of daylight left."

"Instead of everyone working on this one building, we can divvy up the work and start the pole barn. We'll have two more men next week when they deliver the lumber I purchased," Sammy said. "Why don't you and Odis go and cut some poles? Eli, if you don't mind, you can cook supper. I expect we'll have four hungry men about dark."

"My oldest daughter, Lisa, is a cracker jack cook. If you boys want, she can come back with Odis and cook for us while we're here. It'll give us an extra hand."

"That would be great," Eli said. "I hate to cook."

"Everything seems to be working out," Sammy said at supper that evening. "If the weather holds, with this many workers, we should get a lot accomplished in the next two months."

Over the next several weeks, good weather persisted, lumber deliveries were made and the builders concentrated on building. In two months the store was finished with the exception of the installation of glass for the windows. The pole barn was ready for livestock.

Big Clyde bred three mares Eli decided to keep for brood mares. Art Hector agreed to bring back the milk cow along with a start of chickens, pigs and a pair of hound puppies that he said was a must on a farm.

Eli and Sammy kept the three mares and two geldings. The other three horses they gave to Art along with a little hard-to-come-by cash money and the big wagon for his brother. A large portion of land was fenced off for pasture for livestock and another for planting corn and other crops. By mid-summer a substantial amount of work had been accomplished, but there were still no customers for the store.

"Signs! Signs are what we need, Sammy," Eli blurted out one morning. "We need to let people know where we are. We need to place signs at cross roads, at the ferry and on all the roads where people travel around us. The signs should have a name for the place, the distance to get here and arrows pointing in this direction. Then the people will come."

"We haven't even thought about a name, Eli. What can we call the place?" Sammy asked.

"Lamb's Creek is the only name we can call it. It's your creek. You were the first to dip water out of it when Mama was running a high fever. That's what we'll call it, Lamb's Creek Community Store. Boy, why didn't I think of signs before now?"

"You know if we want a community, we'll have to lay out building and farm sites to draw people. We need to get information about the Homestead Act your daddy told us about so we can avoid any land and ownership discrepancies that may arise," Sammy noted.

Sammy and Eli decided it best to travel to Chattanooga together.

The next morning, the weather did not look promising but Sammy and Eli decided to start the ride to Chattanooga as planned. They each pulled two extra horses with packsaddles for the supplies they would carry back to Lamb's Creek on the return trip. On the afternoon of the third day, they began to see a few houses and farms.

"Eli, that's Lookout Mountain," Sammy said pointing ahead. "Chattanooga is built at the base of the mountain." As they neared the mountain, Sammy led Eli through a ranch gate and into a large stable.

"Lo, Sammy," a boy just starting to grow whiskers greeted them.

"Good to see you again, Jim," Sammy replied. "This is my partner, Eli. If it's available, we'll take the quarters I had before."

Sammy and Eli dismounted and turned the horses over to Jim. Eli followed Sammy into a tack room with two cots stacked in the corner of the room. Before Eli could ask, Sammy answered his question, "The reality is, Eli, black folks can't get accommodations in towns like this. Our money's good enough for buying supplies but black folks just don't seem to be good enough to rent a room for a night. In fact, you'll have to be the one to file the claim tomorrow on the property because I'm not able to own property."

Eli had removed his hat and now swung it against his leg, "That's just not right."

"I agree, but that's the way it is. I know the rules and for now that's good enough." Sammy thought, *one day I hope to change the rules.*

Eli and Sammy shared the sandwiches they packed for their trip and a little conversation with Jim before retiring to their cots. Their first stop the next morning was a sign shop a few doors down from the stables. "We want two dozen signs a foot high and thirty-six inches long that read 'Lamb's Creek,'" Eli told the painter. "We plan to use them as road signs, and we'll add the arrows and distances on them based on where we stake them." They settled on a price and were assured they'd be ready the following day.

"Next stop," Eli said with uncontained excitement, "is the Homestead Office." Eli told the story of their move from South Carolina to Tennessee to a rather agreeable, stout office manager. The manager asked his age and explained that he was not old enough to lay claim on land. "I tell you what, young Eli, your determination seems to be far beyond your years, so I'll just neglect to record your age on this particular transaction. If you don't make mention of it I expect neither will I. How does that suit you?"

"It suits me just fine, sir," Eli's disappointment disappeared. The manager worked deftly to fill out the forms hoping to get the boy and the negro on their way before anyone else might enter the small office and question their business. The manager gave Eli brief instructions and the business was complete.

With business concluded, Eli and Sammy walked through the streets of Chattanooga. Eli asked, "Sammy, do you think that Lamb's Creek will ever be this big? I've never seen a place like this. Look at the buildings. Some of them are three levels tall." Eli was completely awed by the buildings and the number of people.

After purchasing supplies, picking up their signs, a can of red paint and a couple of paint brushes to put the finishing touches on the signs, Eli and Sammy loaded their pack horses. As they rode out of town, they placed the first signs with approximate mileage not too far out of Chattanooga.

As a result of the signs, several wagons with families did make their way through Lamb's Creek. Mostly they expressed disappointment. The families were looking for an established town with a school and a church. No matter how hard Eli and Sammy tried to convince the few people brave enough to follow the signs to stay, the community was not well enough established to entice them to stay.

Four months after placing the signs, the Jenkins family rode through and decided to make Lamb's Creek their home. There were three members of the Jenkins family, Mr. and Mrs. Jenkins and Sonny, their twenty-three year old son. Sonny planned to return to the College of William and Mary in Virginia as soon as he saw his parents settled.

"There's a place two miles north of your store we'd like to file on," Mr. Jenkins informed them. "We'll need a good amount of building supplies, fencing and food until we're able to provide for ourselves. I could also use some help building if you know of anyone."

"We can supply your materials and maybe even offer a little help. I'm sure we can work out something. There's a lot of good land south, down this valley, but north is just as good. When do you plan to get started and what do you plan to do first?" Eli asked.

"I'll show you what we plan to build and you can bring the materials as soon as you're able. The rest we can talk about when you bring the lumber. We're going up there now to set up a temporary camp." Mr. Jenkins laid out a rough sketch of a house and barn on the counter and discussed the details. A list of materials was figured and approved by Jenkins.

They agreed on an initial delivery of materials. "Be looking for you as soon as you can make it," said Mr. Jenkins as he smiled, nodded and departed to claim his new homestead.

"This first order is a large one," Eli exclaimed excitedly. "I knew people would come."

The materials arrived within a week and both Eli and Sammy rode out with the delivery wagons. "This is a beautiful place, Mr. Jenkins. If you want, I can stay four or five days and give you a hand to get started. I can come again in another few days. In the meantime, we'll be looking for more help," said Sammy.

Eli went back to take care of the store and their farm. There, sitting on the steps to the store was a young man a few years older than Eli. He was whittling on a stick.

"Figgered somebody would be along directly. Lookin' for work. Ain't too particular about what it is. My name's Bill Lions, and I work hard."

"It's nice to meet you, Bill," Eli extended his hand. "My name is Eli Roads. You're in luck. We need someone willing to work hard on our farm. The Jenkins family, who live a couple miles north of here, need some help building their farm. Do you know anyone else looking for work?"

"Not at the moment. I can bed down in the barn if it's all right with ya. I'll unsaddle my horse and start workin'. What do ya want me to do first?"

"Take care of your horse and come in the cabin in back of the store. I'll fix us something to eat. I haven't had anything but a cup of coffee and a biscuit this morning. I don't think I can do anything else until I eat."

Bill led the horse to the barn and then walked over to the house. Eli asked him to come in and have a seat at the small table he and Sammy used for meals.

"Seen ya signs comin' this a way. How many folks live 'round here?"

"Just Sammy, my business partner, me and like I said, the Jenkins family. They're building a place two miles north of here. That's where Sammy is now, helping them out."

"Well, I reckon towns start small. Give it time," Bill said.

"Glad to have you here, Bill. How about a chunk of this venison, some cold biscuits and hot coffee?" Eli was surprised to learn that Bill was only sixteen. His dark brown eyes and the start of a walrus mustache gave him a much older appearance.

"My mama lives in Nashville, works at a restaurant. She says I got itchin' feet like my pa. Can't seem to stay in one place long. Reckon she's right. Already been lots a places, but I need to rest a while. This looks like a good place for now," Bill said.

Both young men worked hard from early till late the following day. When Sammy came in Eli introduced them and suggested Sammy take Bill to help the Jenkins with their building.

"He's working me to death," Eli moaned. They all laughed.

Two days later, two additional wagonloads of material and supplies arrived. Sammy did take Bill to the Jenkins' place to work a few days.

"Two more weeks or so and we'll be able to move in," Mr. Jenkins commented one day. "Then we'll stop until spring. We'll get our winter's wood cut and work on a couple out buildings till then. I'd like to go ahead and settle my account with you and Eli, Mr. Sammy."

"Just what we agreed on for the materials and supplies. You can pay Bill direct for his labor. I don't want to be paid, I was just being neighborly."

"You are a good neighbor, Mr. Sammy, but I feel that I need to pay you something."

"One day I may need your help. I'll let you know."

That fall the corn and hay crops were immense. The barn was filled with corn and hay and a half a dozen stacks were scattered along the creek. Bill never seemed to tire and Eli never got enough rest. Their bodies were growing in size and strength, their muscles hard as rock.

Friendships usually take time in the making but it was different with Bill and Eli. Right from the beginning there was an immediate trust, respect and closeness. Eli learned that Bill was always at the ready to be called on day or night. He met each job with a fierce determination and tackled problems head on. *The one thing he never does,* Eli mused, *is get tired.*

"You know it'll be three years next month that we came to Lamb's Creek," Eli said one evening. "It doesn't seem that long. Look at how much has been accomplished."

"We've certainly been blessed, but we need more people to share our valley and build this community. They come but they don't stay."

"I know, Sammy, but if they can't settle down, we don't need them. We need the kind that sticks."

Sammy smiled thinking that Eli had picked up some of Bill's sayings.

The winter was cold and long but Bill never stopped working. He laid the foundation for a two-room bunkhouse, gathering stone and building the walls two layers thick. "Be a good storm shelter," he said. "Never knowed when ya might need one."

"That man never stops working," Eli grumbled one night. "Guess I better help with that stone house he's building. Wish he would stop for just one day."

But Bill didn't stop and at the end of winter the stone was laid, doors built, the stone floor finished and ceiling joists and rafters up. "All we need is to roof it and it'll be finished. See what you can do, Eli, if'n ya don't sit on ya duff all the time? Let's go and split some shingles." In three more weeks, the bunkhouse was complete. "All it needs now is somebody to live in it and plant some flowers."

"It sure does look like a house, Bill. Maybe it needs a picket fence." As soon as he uttered the words he thought, *oh no, I shouldn't have said that.*

"You said the right thang, Eli. Let's build it. Then ya can marry up and live here and raise a passel of kids."

"Seems to me that you were the one intent on making it all pretty. With all that work you did, I think you should move into it," Eli said, irritated by the fact that his comment left him wide open for Bill's teasing.

"Oh no, not me. When ya build a fence around a house that means ya lookin' for a wife. Not me ole boy, not yet," Bill laughed.

Just as time marches on, so do some men. Bill Lions was beginning to feel a familiar hankering to move on. Spring and summer passed and Bill felt more and more restless. "Reckon I'll be movin' on fellers," Bill stated at breakfast one morning. "Need to go and check on Mama. Been here more than a year. Best place I ever been. Hate to leave ya boys but somethin's callin' me."

After breakfast he saddled up, said his goodbyes and rode west. "Be back to see ya later. Keep my job open." Bill hollered as he rode away.

"That was all of a sudden," Sammy commented while he and Eli were doing the dishes. "He gave us no warning at all."

"That's Bill. I could tell the last few days that something was on his mind. I would catch him just looking off into the distance, dreaming like. We're sure going to miss him around here. He said that he'll be back, and I just bet he will," Eli said.

Most of the hay had been cut and stacked. After the barn was full and the corn had been pulled and placed in the corncrib, several more families passed through but did not stay. They bought supplies and moved on.

One Saturday morning as Eli was sweeping off the front porch to the store, a covered wagon being pulled by two paint horses pulled up in front. A slender man with flaming red hair got down and tied the horses to the hitch rail. "Need a few supplies if the store is open, friend. The horses need rest and some oats or corn if it's available."

"We can fix you and your horses up, mister. If you want to come on in the store, I'll take care of your horses for you."

As Eli was unhitching the horses from the wagon, a girl about eleven years old opened the flap on the wagon and stepped down. They looked at each other for a moment, and then the girl turned away and walked up the steps to the store with Eli turning to look after her. *Never have I ever seen such red hair before in my life,* he thought, *not that bright of a red.* He watered and fed the horses and pitched some fresh hay into the stalls still thinking about the girl.

Back in the store, Eli found himself unable to keep his eyes off the girl with the flaming red hair. He felt mesmerized and the feeling both excited and irritated him.

Sammy chuckled to himself as he watched Eli try to subtly steal glimpses at the girl. "Eli," Sammy said calling him over to the counter, "this is Reverend 'Red' Willis. He would like a place for he and his daughter to rest up for a couple of days. Do you think we can quickly fix up the new stone bunkhouse with a couple makeshift beds for them? They can eat with us."

"Reverend Red, this is Eli. We're partners in this venture."

"Nice to make your acquaintance," Reverend Red said extending his hand to Eli. "Nothing fancy," said the Reverend, "just a place to get out of that wagon for a little while."

"I'll get Bill's bed ready," said Eli. "Everything's been washed and I just need to make up the bed. I guess I'll have to make a pallet on the floor in the other. I'll fix it up now." Eli walked away abruptly, embarrassed by the way he felt.

"Don't take it personal, ma'am," Sammy said to the girl. "He's just never seen anyone with such beautiful red hair before. He's fascinated, that's all."

"Missy, Mr. Sammy. My name is Missy, and I'm used to it. It doesn't bother me any."

"Well, Missy, I understand being stared at. People stare at me sometimes because I'm black. I know the feeling and the best thing to do, like you say, is just don't let it bother you."

When Eli finished with the bedding he returned to the store and started stocking and straightening items on the shelves.

Missy walked straight over to Eli, hand extended and introduced herself, "Hello, Eli. I'm Missy Willis. I appreciate you fixing up the stone house. I don't think I could sleep in that wagon one more night. It gets old after a while and I'm looking forward to sleeping in a bed again."

Eli shook Missy's hand, aware that his skin was damp and his throat was dry.

"I'm Eli. Guess you know that and you're welcome," was all he could muster and turned back to the shelves, flustered.

They all talked for a while and Reverend Red asked if there was a church and how many families lived in the area.

"No church yet and just one other family besides Eli and me," Sammy replied.

"Do you think we can have services here in the morning?

Tomorrow is the Lord's Day, and I would sure enjoy observing it with you fine folks."

"I'll ride over and see if the Jenkins will come," Eli said. "Is about ten in the morning all right?"

"That will be fine, Eli."

Finding his voice again, Eli turned to Missy and asked, "Would you like to ride, Missy? It's just two miles away."

"Yes, I'd love to. Do you have an extra horse?"

"You sit tight. I'll be back in a jiffy with a little horse I trained myself," he said.

In a short time, Missy and Eli were riding side-by-side talking as if they had known each other all their lives. Eli told Missy the story of how he and Sammy came to be at Lamb's Creek and about his experiences building the store and farm.

Missy was not quite so open but did say that she and her father were looking for a church or a place to build one.

"We need a church real bad," Eli said almost to himself. "Just ahead is where the Jenkins family lives."

After Eli and Missy extended an invite, Mr. Jenkins replied excitedly, "You bet we'll come. We always went to church where we lived before." Mr. and Mrs. Jenkins were talking excitedly about going to worship the Lord in the morning as Eli and Missy prepared to depart.

"The Jenkins family will be here in the morning, Daddy," Missy told them excitedly when they returned to the store. "I just know it will be a good service."

After a mid-day meal, Reverend Red retired to the little stone house to prepare his sermon and Missy to her bed to get some long-awaited rest.

Eli and Sammy talked about asking Reverend Red to stay a while and maybe start a church at Lamb's Creek. They decided that they would approach him after the service the next day. "Sammy, why don't we cook a venison roast and all the trimmings for tomorrow and invite the Jenkins to eat with us and maybe the Reverend will preach again tomorrow evening."

"Good idea, Eli. We'll go all out."

That night at supper, Sammy explained their plans about inviting the Jenkins to eat with them and maybe having an evening service.

"I'd be delighted to preach a morning and evening service, Sammy. Nothing that I'd rather do," said the Reverend.

After their visitors left, they put the roast on to simmer so it would be tender for lunch after the Sunday service.

"We'll get up early and prepare the rest of the meal in the morning."

The next morning Reverend Red said, "No breakfast for me," as he entered the little kitchen. "I'm going to save up for whatever it is that smells so good. Missy will be over in a few minutes."

All three of the Jenkins family came a little early. Eli placed a bench and three handmade chairs on the porch of the store at Missy's request.

"It's such a beautiful and warm day. I thought it would be nice to have the service outdoors," Missy exclaimed. "Just look at the leaves changing color. I believe this is my favorite time of the year."

The Jenkins sat on the bench, Eli and Sammy on two chairs behind them and Missy on a chair in front.

"Missy will lead us in singing this morning," the Reverend said. "She has planned two congregational songs and a special, her own rendition of *Amazing Grace*."

Everyone joined in the singing, and it sounded like they had practiced harmonizing before. When Missy began to sing *Amazing Grace*, all were astounded at her beautiful, controlled voice. Eli sat spellbound. Mrs. Jenkins wiped tears from her eyes with her handkerchief.

After the song, Reverend Red asked if someone would volunteer to lead in prayer before the sermon. After a moment, Missy prayed, "Lord, thank you for sending Daddy and me here to Lamb's Creek. Thank you for giving Daddy this opportunity to preach. Amen," followed by another "Amen" from Mrs. Jenkins.

"Bring them up in the way that they should go, the scripture says and that is what I want for Missy," Reverend Red stated. He went on to preach on the miracles of Christ in the Bible, noting that miracles are still being performed today, that He answers the prayers of His children when they call upon Him and that salvation is offered to all that believe.

Reverend Red never raised his voice, as was the custom of many preachers. Instead, he softly preached, completely holding the attention of everyone in the small congregation.

Eli could not remember ever hearing anyone expound on the Bible like this. His parents had their family devotions but this was different. He knew that he had a lot to think about. After the sermon, there was a song and the preacher concluded with, "Now that we have partaken of our spiritual food, I understand that we are all invited to partake of some mighty good physical food.

Amen."

The men moved the seating to the back of the house where they all gathered at a picnic table and generous helpings of roast, vegetables and cornbread. Mrs. Jenkins had prepared apple pie and the dessert was the final touch to what everyone agreed was a great meal. Most all the food prepared had been raised in Lamb's Creek on their small farms.

While they were eating, Sammy asked Reverend Willis if he would consider staying in Lamb's Creek and serve as their pastor. "Eli and I have talked about this, and we believe the Jenkins will agree, we need a church. If you and Missy consent, I'm sure we can work something out."

"I do thank you for the offer, Brother Sammy, but this is something I'll have to pray about before I can give you an answer. It's the Lord's choosing not mine. I will say this much, we'll stay here until God gives me an answer."

"We'll have our services early this afternoon so that the Jenkins will have time to get home and do their chores before dark. Now, I should go and prepare for that time. If you'll excuse me, I have a lot to pray about."

The evening service was just as heartfelt as the morning's had been.

That night before they went to bed Eli asked Sammy, "Do you think the preacher will stay and be our pastor? I sure hope he will."

"Maybe, depends on God. We will wait and see."

The next morning Sammy cooked breakfast for the four of them while Eli worked on the morning chores.

Missy came over when she saw Eli return to the house.

"Morning, Missy," Sammy greeted her. "Tell your father the food is ready."

"Won't do any good, Mr. Sammy, he's fasting. He won't eat until he gets an answer to his prayers. He fasted five days one time before we left Ohio. He didn't know if he should stay there or go somewhere else. He just drank a little water and prayed. You can see the results yourself. We're here. It may be today or a week."

"What in the world is fasting? Not eating?" Eli asked.

"Yes, the Bible teaches about praying and fasting if you want an answer to prayer. A lot of people pray but not many fast. They give up too easy. It's in the Bible. You can read it for yourself. If you like I'll help you find it."

"No, not now, but maybe later, I'm too hungry to fast," Eli answered.

Reverend Willis fed and watered his horses and helped around the barn but never partook of anything to eat. Three days later he sat in Eli and Sammy's small kitchen and said he reached a decision. He would stay on one condition.

"Anything within reason," Sammy said. "What is the condition?"

"That we start a church building. I'm happy to work here on the farm or the store in my spare time, but the Lord's work comes first. I know that the church can't pay me, but if Missy and I can have room and board, we'll work for our keep."

"What do you think, Eli? It sounds like a good thing to me," Sammy said.

"Me too," repeated Eli. "I'll go tell the Jenkins family. I know what they'll say and they are probably waiting for an answer. Would you like to ride, Missy?"

"No, not this time, Eli. If we are staying, I need to help unload the wagon and get my room organized."

Sammy worked with the Reverend to sketch plans for the church and a small addition of a kitchen and bedroom to the little stone house. Most materials were donated by the sawmill owner and goods dealers who provided supplies to the store. A dozen men came with the supply wagons and helped start the two projects. The wagons traveled back and forth bringing supplies and new workers. Reverend Red preached each Sunday and some of the volunteer workers without families stayed to listen. In two months both buildings were completed and furnished on a Saturday.

"There will be a surprise for you and Missy in church tomorrow, Reverend. No peeking till then," said Eli.

The next morning was Sunday and a crowd of people stood outside the church waiting for the preacher and Missy. People had come from the sawmill community and even as far away as Chattanooga for the first service at Lamb's Creek Church.

"Let the preacher and Missy go in first," Sammy said to the crowd.

He opened the door for them and when they entered, Missy let out a squeal and ran to the front of the church. Sitting off to the side of the pulpit was a brand new, shiny piano. Missy immediately sat and started playing hymns and singing in her full beautiful voice. The people followed suit as they filed in and stood at the pews.

Sammy stood in front of the pulpit, welcomed the crowd and said, "All of what you see was given to the church by God, through our generous friends, suppliers and the workers that gave many hours of their time. Even the new piano was donated," Sammy announced, "and we thank you all so very much."

Sammy introduced Reverend Red. "This is what God can do, brothers and sisters, if we seek his divine will in our lives. Let us thank him," the Reverend began.

Pastor Red Willis preached the best service Eli thought he had ever heard. Several people in the congregation rededicated their lives to the Lord.

After the service, Sammy was concerned about feeding so many people. They had little food prepared. "No need to worry," one of the visiting women declared. "Most everyone brought a picnic lunch with them. There'll be enough and some to spare."

After eating, several families begin to reveal they had brought more than just food. They pulled out their own musical instruments, fiddles, a banjo and even a triangle. Missy and two more women took turns at the piano. There were two additional hours of mountain gospel music following lunch.

"This is a good sign, Sammy," Reverend Red exclaimed as the music was coming to an end and people starting leaving for home. "Some of these people will be camping out the next two nights before they get to their homes. They went to a lot of trouble and expense to see that we had a successful start in our church and I know the Lord will bless them for it."

"I never would have guessed that we would have such a turnout," Eli said, "never in my born days."

The only ones for evening service were Sammy, Eli and the Jenkins family, along with Missy and the Reverend.

When all were assembled, the preacher motioned for them to sit down. "We'll not have singing and preaching this evening. We had a bountiful amount of praise and worship today. What I want to do is to tell you a little about myself. It's more than a testimonial, a confession, if you will. I should have done this before I agreed to be your pastor. If you don't want me to stay after I reveal these things about myself, I'll understand."

"First, I've not always been a man of God. Until a year and a half ago, I was nothing but a drunk and a brawler. I made whiskey. I drank whiskey. And, I sold whiskey. My wife and myself were two of a kind, always fighting and drinking. My mother took Missy in and raised her in a Christian home as she tried to raise me. She sent her to school, gave her piano and music lessons and raised her in church, the same way she had me. I wanted nothing to do with church, although I'd attend with my mother on special occasions and did hear the word preached."

"I was a rowdy and rebellious young man in jail as much as out. On one occasion I was arrested for fighting, being drunk, making and selling liquor and several other things. They literally threw me in the jail cell. I was so drunk I didn't care. They did give me a trial after a while, although I was surprised. 'Six months,' the judge said scolding as he read the charges and looked at me over the top of his glasses. 'And I don't want to see you in my court again. Understand?'"

"I said, 'I do understand, your Honor, and you won't see me again.' I had plenty of time on my hands to think about a lot of things. My mama and my little girl were foremost on my mind. I made myself promises that I knew I would not keep. One night they arrested the old man they called the town drunk. The next morning he woke, looked at me through bloodshot eyes and vomit all down his front, stinking and disgusting, said, 'You in here again?' he slurred when he spoke. 'Keep it up and you'll be just like me.'"

"Well, let me tell you, that gave me something else to think about. At that moment I felt another presence in that room. That presence had a voice and it said, 'There is a better way, you know.' I looked around and saw no one except the drunk that had passed out again."

"I knew there was a better way. I also knew I had a beautiful nine year old daughter that needed a daddy. I knew I needed my mother, the one person that truly loved me and would help me change. I knew my wife would be no help. I knew that it was Sunday and I was overcome with a desire to be in church with Mama and Missy."

"I frantically picked up the metal plate that they had brought my breakfast in, started banging it on the bars and yelled until Earl, the jail keeper that day, came to see what the trouble was. The drunk never made a sound. 'I want to go to church, Earl, with my Mama.' 'I can't let you out, Red, you know better than that,' Earl replied. 'Yes, you can. You let me out, Earl, and loan me some clean clothes. I want to go to church and be saved. God just spoke to me and said that there is a better way. You know the Lord, Earl, and that better way is Jesus. Now let me out and let me borrow some of your clothes. I promise I'll come back as soon as church is over. Hurry, Earl, or I'll be late.' Well, Earl did as I asked and even drove me in his wagon to the church. 'Red, you better be back as soon as church is over or I'll lose my job. I may anyway,' Earl said as I got out of the wagon."

"Mama and Missy were surprised when I walked in and sat beside them."

"The preacher preached a salvation sermon that Sunday and I still remember it almost word for word. It surely had to be God dealing with and speaking to me, and I accepted the Lord as my Savior that morning at five minutes to twelve. I quickly explained my circumstances and told them I had to go back to jail. But now that I knew the Lord, I knew everything would be all right. I'd soon be out and back with my family."

"Needless to say, Earl was relieved when I showed back up at the jail after church. 'Have a little faith, Earl,' I said. 'I'm like you now. I've accepted Christ as my Lord and Savior.'"

"I witnessed to the drunks, to Earl who already knew the Lord and to everyone they put in jail. I just felt I had to tell everyone about Jesus and what he'd done for me. They let me out two months early, maybe because I was bugging everybody or they could see the change in my life."

"My wife said that it wouldn't last and that I'd soon be like I always was. When she realized I had really changed, she left. 'I ain't gonna be a wife to a so and so redheaded preacher. I'm leaving and you can keep the redheaded girl, too. I don't want either of you.'"

"Mama passed away a year later, and Missy and I felt the Lord wanted us to leave Ohio. That's how we've come to be here. You decide if you want us to stay or go. We'll abide by your decision."

Tears were rolling down Missy's face when the preacher finished his confession. She walked over to where he was standing and kissed his cheek and said, "I love you, Daddy, for who you are and for being so honest." They walked out of the church together.

Each member of the congregation was moved by Reverend Red's story. They had a quiet and brief discussion, unanimously voting for Reverend Red to stay.

CHAPTER SEVEN

Eli's two hounds set in to barking. It was a rainy, bitter cold night in March and the first winter after the new church was built. No new visitors had stopped in Lamb's Creek that winter.

"Someone is out there, Sammy," Eli spoke just as they heard a light tapping at the door.

Sammy opened the door and there, completely soaked, stood a middle-aged woman and a young boy.

"Come in, ma'am," Sammy held the door against the wind and rain. "Come on over by the fireplace."

Eli put more logs on the fire and said, "These people need to get some dry clothes on." He went into the next room and picked up two blankets and brought them to the woman and boy.

"Ma'am, you can go in that room, take off your wet clothes and put this blanket around you. We need to dry your clothes. Son, you can stay in here and do the same thing," said Sammy.

Eli provided them each with a dry change of clothes. He took the wet clothes and hung them on a clothesline stretched across the room in front of the fireplace.

"My name's Sammy Lamb and this is Eli Roads."

"I am Martha Lewis, and this is my son, Orville. Our buggy lost a wheel down the road a ways and we saw the light in your window. We stopped to see if we could find someone to help us."

"Eli and I will go and see about your rig. You and Orville sit in front of the fire and try to warm up. We'll have our pastor and his daughter come over and make some hot tea."

Sammy explained the situation to Pastor Red and asked if they would sit with the travelers and fix some tea while they fetched their buggy.

Sammy and Eli found the rig about a quarter mile away. Not only had the wheel come off, the axle was broken.

"We can't do anything now about this buggy, Eli. I'll get these two suitcases and you unhitch the horse and put her in the barn. In the morning we'll see what we can do about that broken axle."

When they got back to the house, Reverend Red and Missy were sitting with Mrs. Lewis and Orville drinking tea.

"Bad news and good news," Sammy said. "The bad news is your buggy has a broken axle. The good news is, I think we can fix it just not tonight. We brought your suitcases and horse back with us. In the morning we'll see about tending to your rig. We'll fix a place for you tonight. Eli and I will sleep in Bill's room in the barn. Ma'am, you and Orville can sleep here," motioning to his and Eli's rooms.

Mrs. Lewis said that she and Orville could sleep right where they were in front of the fire but lost the argument with Sammy.

The next morning Sammy and Eli finished their morning chores before returning to the house. Reverend Red intercepted them, said that Missy had prepared breakfast and invited them to join them at the parsonage. Mrs. Lewis and Orville were already there.

"Good morning, folks," Sammy greeted them when he walked into the parsonage. "Sleep good?"

"Best night's sleep in days," Mrs. Lewis replied. "The ground is to walk on not sleep on. Thank you, Sammy and Eli, for giving up your beds."

Mrs. Lewis explained about the decision to come to Tennessee where her deceased husband was born. "We should have waited till later on in the year, though. We spent most of the winter in Knoxville and decided to come farther south. People in Knoxville say this is the prettiest part of Tennessee, and I believe they're right. We've been seeing the signs for Lamb's Creek a long time now. How large a town is it?"

"Ma'am," Reverend Red said kind of embarrassed, "what you see here is it, except for one more family two miles north. The town has been kind of slow getting started, but it'll grow."

Mrs. Lewis looked surprised and asked, "You have a store and a church and only three families? Forgive me for being so blunt, but that almost seems absurd. How would someone like Orville and I go about living here? Are there any extra houses available?"

Sammy replied, "No, Mrs. Lewis, there are no houses but lots of land. Of course houses can be built if you have the finances."

"How much money will it take to build a four-room house similar to this one? I would like to have a barn, smaller than yours, for a couple of horses, chickens and other things. Most of all, I'd like a place for a garden."

"Ma'am, for about a thousand dollars, you can get what you

want. You can homestead ten acres in Lamb's Creek valley if you want to settle here, and we'll help to build your house."

"I'll pay you two hundred dollars, Mr. Sammy, if you get my house built. That's just to see that it is done right."

"You have a deal, Mrs. Lewis," Sammy shook her hand and added, "welcome to Lamb's Creek."

Eli and Sammy were elated to have another family join their community.

Reverend Red invited the newcomers, Eli and Sammy for lunch. "What you been feeding that boy, Mrs. Lewis?" Reverend Red asked as they watched Orville, Missy and Eli walk toward the barn after lunch.

"Reverend, it's always hard for people to believe he's only ten years old. From time to time I forget myself. It worries me that all he thinks about is wrestling. He will wrestle just anyone, big or small, makes no difference. He was the undefeated wrestling champion at the school he attended back home and that included the high school boys as well. He even challenged and beat his instructors. They said he could be national champion one day, but I don't want him to go that way."

"Orville picked the buggy up so Eli and I could chock it while we worked on the axle this morning," Sammy added. "It seemed like nothing to him. That boy doesn't know his own strength."

"He'll get around to asking each of you, Reverend Willis and Sammy, to wrestle with him. Don't do it, please."

"My fighting and wrestling days are over, Mrs. Lewis. Maybe in my younger days I would have considered it, but not anymore," laughed Reverend Red.

Mrs. Lewis picked a little nook off the main valley, about twelve acres of land and a quarter of a mile from the store, to build her home. Sammy contacted his suppliers and the materials arrived a few days later along with some of the workers who had helped on the church. Only a few weeks into the build, Mrs. Lewis expressed surprise that the construction of her home was progressing so fast.

"It doesn't take long with this many good workers that know what they're doing," Sammy said.

In less than two months time Martha and Orville moved into their new house. Orville, as predicted by Martha, had challenged every worker at some time during the build to wrestle. Most took his challenge and all that did lost. At times, Orville would take on his opponents using only one arm.

Wrestling wasn't Orville's only talent. He could sing. Orville and Missy were soon doing specials in church each Sunday.

"Daddy, what do you think about Orville?" Missy asked one evening as they were sitting and reading next to a slow-burning fire. "Do you think that he'll ever grow up?"

"What do you mean by grow up? He's already a grown man in size."

"I don't mean that way. I mean to mentally mature not just grow in size. He is so handsome and can sing so well, but all he thinks and talks about is wrestling. He's so immature. He makes me so mad at times I just want to scream."

"Missy, you have to remember that he's only ten years old. He's still a child regardless of his stature. His mind will catch up, just give him time."

"I guess you're right, but he still makes me mad. I had a crush on Eli when we first moved here but not anymore. We are best friends, though. Daddy, I wish there was a girl my age living here. I sure would like to have a girl to talk to."

"You know what you should do then? Pray for one. Maybe the Lord will send someone here."

"I'll do that, Daddy. Will you pray for me to have a girl friend as well?"

"Yes, we'll start tonight in our prayer time together."

Missy and Reverend Red were earnest in their prayers. Reverend Red saw changes in Missy sometimes daily and felt as if time was flying by. Missy resolved to wait patiently on Orville to mature and God to answer her prayers. She felt as if time stood still in Lamb's Creek. It was almost a year before her prayers were answered.

"Eli, why don't you go and hunt a couple deer? We've been out of venison for two weeks now, and I know the other families could use some fresh meat. If you take a pack horse, it'll be easy to bring them back," said Sammy.

The next morning Eli was eager to start the hunt. With his rifle, favorite riding horse he'd trained himself and a pack horse, Eli rode off to the east to another little valley about two miles' distance. It was the last of February. The morning air was cold but the sun was coming up clear and bright. *Just breathe in that fresh air,* he thought. *Doesn't it feel good?*

As Eli approached the place he had in mind to hunt, he spotted a wagon, a campsite and a young girl cooking over an open fire. Three horses were picketed a little ways off. *They must have been here a while*, he thought to himself. *All the grass has been eaten close to camp.*

As he entered the camp, the girl called out for him to stay where he was, "There's sickness in the camp. Don't know what it is."

Eli's thoughts returned to his parents. Their deaths were from some kind of sickness, *but they had died in just a few hours after becoming sick.* "How long you been here?" he called back.

"Eight days today," the girl said. "It's my daddy and he's bad sick."

Eli knew he would be taking a chance but said to himself, "I have to help if I can," so he rode into camp with the girl protesting for him to stay away.

"Look," Eli said, "you need help. If you have been here that long and your father is still sick, you need to have someone help him. I live about two miles west of here in Lamb's Creek. There's a man there that may know what to do. Let's hitch up this wagon and get you and your father to our settlement. Now don't argue. Just do it."

Eli looked in the wagon at the man. *Lord, he thought, this man isn't going to make it if you don't help.*

Eli drove the team up to his and Sammy's house. Sammy, seeing the wagon approaching, knew something was wrong when he realized Eli was driving a strange wagon with his horses tied behind. He went outside to meet them as they pulled to a stop.

"Got a sick man and a wore-out girl in the back. He's been sick and camped out over a week. I found them when I was hunting two miles east of here. Sammy, you need to take a look at him."

Sammy lifted the canvas on the back of the wagon and stepped in. The girl was sitting, holding her father's hand. "Tell me, miss, about your father. What happened to make him sick?"

"We thought he just had a cold but he kept getting sicker. Now, I don't know."

Eli felt his forehead. "A little fever, but not much. Does he cough a lot when he is awake?"

"Yes."

"He's semi-conscious. How long has he been like this?"

"Two days since he spoke a word."

"Eli, get Reverend Red over here. We'll put this man in Bill's bed in the barn. You kill one of the young roosters and make chicken soup as quick as you can. Better yet, let Missy make the soup after you kill the rooster. Mam always said chicken soup cures any ailment."

Eli ran to get the preacher and explained what was going on then killed and cleaned the rooster.

"I can take it from here, Eli," Missy said.

When Eli got to the barn, the man had been undressed and put into bed. The preacher had built a fire in the little cast iron heater and the room was warming up.

Sammy came in with two bottles of medicine from the store.

"I think he has a severe case of pneumonia. We have to get some of this medicine and some nourishment in him. He's severely dehydrated."

"Ma'am, here's some tea to give to your father. Eli, help her to give him just a few drops at a time. We don't want him to strangle. Once Missy has the soup ready, we'll give him some of that for nourishment. Now we have to get this medicine in him as soon as possible," Sammy explained.

As Eli gently lifted the man's head so his daughter could administer the drops of tea, she said, "I'm Sara Darby and this is Bruce Darby, my father. Everyone calls him Major Darby. He's a retired Major."

"It's nice to meet you, Eli. I don't know what I would have done had you not come along and been willing to help," Sara said.

Sara turned to Sammy and asked, "Can you help my father?"

"We'll try, Sara. Maybe it wouldn't hurt if you were to ask Reverend Red here to plead your father's case to someone that can really help."

All that day, slowly but surely, they successfully got the medication and chicken broth into Major Darby's system.

"Sara, you should go with Missy and get some nourishment and rest so we don't have two patients on our hands," Sammy said. "Someone will stay here with your father."

About ten o'clock that night, the Major was coherent enough to ask about Sara and their whereabouts. Sammy explained what happened and that Sara was nearby, all right and resting.

"Major Darby, you have to drink as much as you can and continue to take this medicine. You are a very sick man. I believe you have a bad case of pneumonia and people die from this. Get your body where it can fight for you. Drink, drink, drink the water and tea. You are dehydrated. Do you understand?"

The Major acknowledged with a nod, drank a whole cup of warm broth and took the medicine before falling back to sleep.

The next morning, Sara entered her father's room and asked Martha, the current attendant, about how he made the night. Before Martha could speak, Major Darby opened his eyes and smiled faintly, "I am going to be fine, Sara. I don't know how you found these people, dear, but I am glad you did."

Sara was relieved. She thanked Martha and insisted that she go home to get some rest. "Mrs. Lewis, I'll sit with him now." By the end of the day the Major said, "If I take one more swallow of that broth, I will float plumb away."

Each day the Major regained more strength and in a few days, he was able to walk around outside. He was instantly drawn to the small community and the people.

"Nice place you have here, Sammy," the Major said on one of his brief daily walks. "Nice people, too."

Sara moved into the Willis' house and shared Missy's room. They became close friends, revealing secrets and expressing ideas and hopes for the future. "I wish you and your daddy would stay right here in Lamb's Creek, Sara," Missy said one night as they climbed into their beds. "Why don't you ask him?"

Sara had never really wanted to leave her previous home but being in Lamb's Creek made her rethink that sentiment.

"Daddy, what are your plans now that you are feeling better?" Sara asked one morning as they sat on the Willis' little porch in the warm sun.

"I've been thinking about what our next steps should be these last few days, Sara. When your mother became ill and I resigned my commission in the Army to take care of her, I had no idea all this would come to pass. When your mother passed, I was completely at a loss for what to do. My Army commission, the one thing I knew how to do, was gone, and even worse your mama was gone. I had you, a little girl for whom I was ill equipped to take care of. All I could think was that I did not want to stay where we were. I did the most foolish thing I could have done. I took you out of your school, away from your friends and exposed you to dangerous situations this past year. I still don't know what we should do, Sara, but I'm going to do something I should have done before now. I'm going to ask you, not tell you." Major Darby took Sara's two hands in his and asked, "What would you like to do?"

"Daddy, I knew your heart was broken when Mama died. You were under a lot of stress and doing the best you could. I would really like to stay here for a while, at least until you are strong enough to travel again. This just might be where we belong," Sara replied.

With Major Darby's decision to stay in Lamb's Creek, the population grew to eleven. Another home was built just past the church and the community was beginning to take shape. After the Darby house was complete, Sammy suggested they start another home for whoever would arrive next.

Eli replied, "Won't do any harm that I can see. Let's build it."

The house was about finished when a family pulled up to the store asking for directions. "How far to get to where the weather is warm?"

"How warm do you want the weather, mister?" Eli asked.

"You want warm or do you want hot?"

"Warm will do fine. My wife says she's tired of being cold. She grumbled so much we left Vermont to find a warm place."

"Well, I've never been to Vermont, but I suspect it's a lot warmer here in Lamb's Creek than it is there. We have a new house here in town that's almost finished, and it's for sale."

"No, not a house, a farm is what we want with good rich land."

"Well, mister, we have the best farm land you can find anywhere, and like I said it's got to be warmer than Vermont. The land is free to homestead. You can't get it cheaper than that. My name is Eli Roads. My partner and I'll be glad to help you find farmland and get settled."

The man turned to his wife and said, "Mama, this is where we stop. No more travelin' to hunt a warm place," and then back to Eli, "our name is Hinsen and we're glad to meet you, Eli."

"Come in the store, Mr. Hinsen, and bring your lovely wife. I'd like you both to meet my partner, Sammy Lamb."

Mr. Hinsen helped his wife down from the front bench of the wagon. Eli noticed that she was expecting a child. Mr. Hinsen disappeared around the back of the wagon only to reappear with a two-year-old boy.

Eli introduced Sammy to Mr. and Mrs. Hinsen. "Sammy, Mrs. Hinsen wants a place that's warm. She's tired of being cold. The Hinsen's come from Vermont and want to farm. I've already told Mr. Hinsen about homesteading and that we can help him find a place."

Sammy replied, "The land that joins ours to the south is as good as any around. Let's show them that land. It's got good grass and lots of water."

"We have a big family, Mr. Sammy. My wife, she has nine brother and sister. Me, I have eleven brother and sister. Mama here, she wants a large family like our people had in Norway. I say I help what I can. We need lots of good land for a large family."

The land adjacent to Eli's and Sammy's proved to be just what the Hinsens had in mind. Sammy helped them with the homesteading process and building a three-room house with a large kitchen. "Mama will cook a lot when we get our family. Need a lot of cooking room," Mr. Hinsen told Sammy.

Every Sunday the community members gathered at the church to hear Reverend Red preach one of his heart-warming sermons. This Sunday was no different, except that as the preacher started his sermon, a visitor walked in and sat on the back row. After the last Amen everyone turned to exit and Eli saw the visitor clearly for the first time. "Bill, you ole rascal," Eli shouted from his pew.

Eli and Sammy converged on Bill, pumping his arm and patting him on the back. The others watched the excited exchange and moved to join Sammy and Eli in welcoming the man they called Bill. "Everyone," Eli exclaimed, "this is Bill Lions. He helped us start this settlement. He practically built the parsonage himself. Major, the room and bed where you stayed when you were sick was Bill's room when he was here before."

They introduced Bill to all the newcomers and everyone was excited to finally meet the man they had heard so much about. "Is my job and room still open?" he asked Sammy as they walked the short distance from the church to their home.

"You bet it is. We were wondering when you would show up.

How is your mother doing? Tell us what you've been up to."

"Mama's fine and I just been ramblin' around like usual. Looks a lot different than when I left here. She's growed quite a bit. A church, more houses and people. I knowed it would happen given a little time."

Eli and Sammy spent the afternoon telling Bill about their experiences with the people of their settlement.

"Eli, that Major's girl, Sara, I'd say is most likely gonna be the lucky girl to win your heart. I seen how she acted around ya. Right pretty too. Boy, ya done growed since I seen ya last. Near about a man I'd say."

Eli's face reddened at the mention of Sara. "Aw Bill," Eli said, "don't go and start teasing me." They all laughed but Eli couldn't deny the feelings he had for Sara lately. He wondered how he would go about talking about how he felt to a girl like Sara. *Maybe Bill can give me some pointers,* and Eli decided he would ask Bill the next time they were alone.

"Just tell him how you feel," Missy said to Sara after church as they prepared lunch for themselves and their fathers. "Just go to him and say 'I love you Eli, what are you going to do about it?'"

"First of all, I don't sound like that at all, and I can't do it, Missy. He needs to say it first. I don't see you saying that to Orville," Sara replied.

"Orville is just a boy. Eli is a grown man. There is a difference," Missy said.

Bill asked Eli to walk over to the barn and help him tend his horse. Eli decided it was the right time to ask Bill for advice about talking to Sara.

Bill seemed to think on it for a moment before responding. "Never told a girl I loved her other than Mama. That's different. I guess you'd just walk up to her like ya do to your horse and say, 'Sara darlin', I love ya, and this fall I want to marry ya if that's all right.' Maybe that would do the trick. You never know about women. Their thinkin' is different then ours."

"I can't do that Bill," Eli replied. "That would be kind of crude."

"Well, she'd know how ya felt about her. That's what ya want. You can practice on me if'n ya want to."

"I'll think about it, Bill. Maybe you are right," Eli replied, not feeling any more decided about what to do.

"One thang I'm sure of Eli, these thangs have a way of workin' themselves out. Right now me and you need to concentrate on the plowin' and the plantin'. Now that's somethin' we both knowed a lot about.

Sammy was spending his days helping Mr. Hinsen build his house and barn. While Eli and Bill took care of the farm, Sara and Missy worked in the store so the men could get in the spring planting. They also prepared dinner and supper for all the men so they could focus on their work.

The Major, not quite over his illness, had not regained all his strength. He spent a lot of time on the porch of the store resting and napping in an old rocking chair. He listened to the girls talk about Eli, Orville and the future. He was aware that his daughter had a crush on Eli and thought, *Eli just might be the right one for her. They are both young, but Eli's circumstances forced him to grow up early on in his life. Comes a time when a boy becomes a man and puts away childish things. Eli is a responsible young man. Most importantly,* the Major believed, *he is in love with Sara and it won't be long until he tells her how he feels,* he thought to himself as he watched Eli and Bill come in from the field for dinner.

"Major," Eli said as he came up the steps, "Bill and I have decided to build a bedroom off the side of the store for you to rest in and keep an eye on the girls while they tend the store. It could be used by anyone who might need it from time to time. We'll start the building just as soon as we get the planting in."

"I'm not much at building," the Major replied, "but I would like to help if you don't mind."

Reverend Red helped Martha Lewis and Orville plant their garden and build the extra shed and outbuildings needed on their homestead. Orville took care of the heavy chores and the Reverend the lighter work.

"You two make a good team," Martha commented as the three of them were building the chicken coop. "I didn't know a preacher was capable of accomplishing so much work."

"I've not always been a preacher," Reverend Red answered.

The Tennessee summer was hotter than usual that year. Work continued through the heat. Families settled in, visited and got to know their neighbors. The townspeople discussed building a school but with only two school-age children, Orville and Missy, they decided a school building could wait until there were more.

Mrs. Lewis volunteered to help Sara teach Missy and Orville two or three days a week until a full-time schoolteacher was needed. School started for the first time that fall in Lamb's Creek.

Cool weather was much appreciated when it finally arrived

and with it another family.

"Name's Jackson," the stranger said to Reverend Red as the new family pulled their wagon to a stop at the church one Sunday morning. "We are homesteading in a little valley a couple miles east. We thought we might join you folks in church this morning."

"Welcome Mr. Jackson. I'm the pastor of Lamb's Creek Church, Reverend Red Willis. We're pleased to have you and your family in our church and our community."

After the service Reverend Red introduced each family in turn to the Jacksons. The Jackson family included Mr. and Mrs. Jackson, their son Hiram, Jr., twelve years old, three younger daughters, Ora, Mercy and Lila, and Mr. Jackson's mother and father. The Jackson family had moved into the valley where Eli found Sara and the Major over a year ago.

"We're camping out now," he said, "until we can build. We'll be needing supplies from your store, Mr. Sammy."

"That's what we're here for, Mr. Jackson." Sammy replied. "We'd be glad to help you out. We also have three or four extra hands if you need help building."

"That would be wonderful, but we don't have the means to hire extra help."

"Free labor, Mr. Jackson. We all help each other in our community. Let's go see what you need and find out how we can best help."

With the addition of the Jacksons there were over twenty people in Lamb's Creek community, and the community decided to conduct school five hours a day, five days a week on a trial basis. The Jacksons moved into the new house that Eli, Sammy and Bill had built in their spare time for no one in particular.

"I know it's small," Sammy stated, "but with everyone pitching in, we'll have your house built real soon."

"It's a castle compared to a covered wagon and a tent, what we've been living in the past few months," replied Mrs. Jackson.

The Jackson's house was finished in January and the barn one month later. To celebrate, the Jacksons hosted a community party in the new barn. Everyone in the community came to the party except the Jenkins family. Since no one had seen them since church last Sunday, Eli and Bill decided to ride out to their farm to make sure all was okay.

As Eli and Bill arrived at the Jenkins' house, four strange men came out onto the porch.

"We're looking for the Jenkins family," Eli stated.

"Well now, sonny, them folks done moved. Sold us the place and moved on. We bought it from 'em lock, stock and barrel. Can we help you with anything else?"

"No sir, I guess not. We're having a community party over at the Jackson's new place, two miles east of Lamb's Creek. Maybe you'd like to join us," Eli said.

"Might just do that, sonny. We'll be over in a while. Got a little more work to do. You know how it is when you have a farm."

"Let's get on back to the party, Eli," Bill said, and when he was sure they were out of hearing distance, whispered, "somethin's wrong. Come along, quick."

"What do you make of that, Bill?" Eli asked.

"Don't know, but don't like what I see. The Jenkins didn't just up and sell their place. You know that."

The two rode back to the party and relayed the conversation with the strangers to the others.

"I think somethin' is bad wrong," Bill said. "We need to look around that place. I knowed they were lyin'. If'n they come to the party, me and Eli will take a look around."

About thirty minutes later, the newcomers arrived at the party. "Our family name is Paine," the oldest of the men said when they showed up a little later. "Just call me Daddy Paine. You folks have any grub? Me and my boys are kinda hungry."

Sammy replied, "We'll eat in a while, but first tell us about the Jenkins family. They didn't say anything to us about selling out."

"First off, I don't tell my business to no niggers," he snapped back at Sammy.

Several of the women gasped at Paine's rudeness.

"And second," Paine continued, "t'aint nobody's business that we bought them folks out. Come on boys, I get the feelin' we ain't welcome here. Let's get on back home."

Everyone stayed quiet until the strangers left. Martha Lewis was the first to speak. "We need to get the law out here and look into this. I think Bill's right. Mr. and Mrs. Jenkins thought too much of their place, this community and of us to up and sell without a word to anyone."

"There's no law out here," Sammy said. "The closest lawman is likely in Nashville or Chattanooga. We'll check around and see if we can find anything, some kind of evidence that there was foul play. If we do find foul play, we'll contact the authorities."

The exchange with the Paines and worry about the Jenkins put a damper on the party. After dinner and a short visit everyone retired to their respective homes, feeling they had lost something very important.

The Paine clan seldom left the Jenkins farm unattended. When one or two would go into Lamb's Creek for supplies, they were obnoxious and loud. Daddy Paine especially worked hard to intimidate the townspeople.

Sammy cautioned each household to be watchful. They all agreed should they be approached at their homes by the Paines, they would send for help and shoot if necessary.

"The Paines have taken away a measure of our peace," Mrs. Jackson said at the store one day, "and made us afraid for our children."

A couple times Bill and Eli caught the entire clan gone from the Jenkins' homestead, did some investigating around the farm, but found nothing they could call evidence.

With the passage of time, routines returned to normal, but uneasiness settled over the community with the abrupt departure of the Jenkins and the Paine clan close by.

Eli began calling on Sara the following spring. He brought her little gifts from the store or flowers that he picked.

"Can't get that boy out in the field now days. Reckon we gonna lose this crop if'n he don't hurry up and do somethin'," Bill said to Sammy.

The next day Bill said, "Eli, ya been foolin' around too long. We gotta cut some pickets and build a fence around that little house nobody lives in. We gonna plant some flowers and ya gonna marry the Major's daughter soon. Now let's get busy on that fence."

Everyone knew what Eli's intentions were when he and Bill started the picket fence around the empty house.

"I guess we have to get married now, Sara," Eli said the day they finished the fence. "Bill's not going to be put off any longer." He sat with Sara after dinner on the front porch of the Willis' home.

"I guess so. No telling what he would do if we don't," Sara said still patiently waiting for Eli to say the words she needed to hear.

"Sara, by the way, what I want to say is, well, Sara, I love you." Then, unexpectedly Eli knelt down in front of her, grabbed her hands in his and asked, "Sara, will you marry me?"

"Yes Eli, I will marry you. I love you too."

Reverend Red married Sara and Eli three days later and the entire community celebrated. At the wedding reception Sammy called the bride and groom aside for a private conversation.

"That was as nice a wedding as I have ever seen. It reminded me of your mother's and father's back when I was a young boy, Eli. You two remind me so much of Eli and Lizzie. I know they would be proud to see how you turned out. I surely am proud," Sammy said.

Sammy continued, "This may not be the best timing to tell you about my plans, but I intend to leave Lamb's Creek in about a week. I've been thinking of Mam, Pap and even my birth mother, Mable. I'm going to Detroit to see how they're doing. I've also decided to do something your parents always wanted for me and that's to pursue my education. This community is growing and almost everyone here is a solid citizen, capable of taking care of whatever comes up. That is, all except for the Paines, and Eli, they bear watching. I'll tell the others about my plans this week, but I wanted you and Sara to be the first to know. I'll make sure you know how to reach me and do my best to keep you informed of my progress. I love you both and pray God's blessings are with you. The store is yours to do with as you please."

Eli and his new bride were taken by surprise at Sammy's announcement. They didn't know what to say or do.

Later that evening when they were alone, Eli asked Sara, "What are we going to do without Sammy? I don't know if we can make it without him. He's always been here for me. We have to persuade him to change his mind."

"No," Sara said in a loving voice, "he wants to see his family. Don't you see that he's wanted to do this a long time? He just waited until you had someone else in your life. He's a very good man, Eli. You've been his family during his separation from Samuel, Hattie and Mable, but you have to let him go make his own life. We have each other and with God's help and the people of Lamb's Creek, those here now and the ones to come, we can make it. Sammy knows that."

"You're a jewel, Sara. I remember my daddy always calling Mama his 'love.' Do you mind if I call you 'my love'? That is what you are."

"I would like that very much. I do love you so."

A year after Sammy's departure, Eli and Sara had a son. They named him Roger Darby Roads.

Two new families moved into the surrounding area, each with children. The community was growing.

"I've been thinking about something, Sara, and want to know what you think about it," Eli said. "I don't want the store for just us. I would like for it to belong to everyone who is part of Lamb's Creek. We could let everyone bring their excess goods, things grown or made, and trade for what they need. We'll be here, or someone will, to see that the trades are fair. We'll continue to purchase things that can't be raised or made. We'll call it Lamb's Creek Community Store."

"That'll be a little different. I like your idea. Since there's not a lot of money, this will help everyone. Let's have a community meeting after church Sunday and see what everyone thinks."

Everyone at the meeting thought it a very good deal for the residents of the community and very generous of Eli and Sara.

The community store became the hub of activity in Lamb's Creek. As Eli and Sara watched Roger grow, they often commented on the passage of time.

The morning of Roger's eighth birthday, he said, "Mom, the Major is out by the gate talking to Daddy."

"Roger, that is not the Major to you," Sara said. "That is your Granddaddy. You need to remember to call him Granddad."

"But Mom, everybody calls him Major. He always wears army clothes."

"Roger, just do what I tell you to do. Now, sit up and be still so I get your hair trimmed nice and straight."

Eli entered the house. "Sara, I just talked to your father. He wants to call a meeting this evening of all households. Says it's important to the community. Six o'clock at the community store."

"Eli, I don't like the way people are talking. All the talk of war scares me, and Dad calling a meeting cannot be good."

"I guess unrest is everywhere now. We do need to keep abreast of what's happening. I've never seen the Major look so worried."

"Eli, you're the one the community looks up to so please keep the meeting under control tonight," Sara pleaded. "Most everyone will be rational but if the Paines come it could spell trouble. Please be careful."

For the remainder of the day, Sara and Eli did their best to make Roger's birthday special. They hiked and picnicked. Eli and Roger fished in their favorite spot on Lamb's Creek. Sara knew the carefree spirit of the day only skimmed the surface of their lives like sunlight on the creek. It was what was lying underneath the shimmering surface that scared her.

In the evening, Eli and Sara walked silently, hand in hand to the store for the community meeting. The unrest that characterizes war had settled on Eli. He thought about the realities of what was driving a nation to be at war. Some men would be driven by greed and a lust for power. Some would see the death and destruction of war as an atrocity while others would take advantage of the defenseless for personal gain.

"Luther Paine, you and your three sons find empty chairs and sit down. You cannot make people that are already sitting move. If you would get here early enough, you could pick your place."

"Who made you boss around here, Eli Roads? You can't tell us where to sit. We go and come as we please and you can't make us do different. We came here to say our say and we'll do just that," Luther Paine said loudly.

"The Major has the floor now, Luther." Eli's look made Luther think twice about continuing to make trouble. "You will wait your turn like everyone else. You four men in the back are appointed to keep the peace. If anyone makes anymore disturbance, throw them out," Eli interjected, "Okay Major, tell us why you called this meeting."

"Folks, two days ago I spoke with General John Atwood of the Union Army. He informed me that the war is escalating at a rapid rate. The General said Tennessee and every state north, south, east and maybe all the way to the Mississippi River will be in the war soon. I called this meeting so that we as a community could come up with a plan to be ready to protect our homes and property if the need arises. Maybe we…."

Luther Paine interrupted, "I say if you're talking to the Union Army, you need to be shot for a traitor. I think…"

"Luther Paine this is the last time that I am going to tell you to shut up. If he so much as breathes hard, physically remove him," Eli said to the men assigned to keep order. "We are not here tonight to pick sides but to try and protect our community. Now Major, continue, and once you say what's on your mind, we'll proceed with an orderly discussion."

"What I was about to say," the Major continued, "is that we may be able to form a militia in each of the surrounding towns to keep a watch for each other."

"Is there anyone else that would care to make a suggestion? Now is the time to do so," Eli continued as moderator.

"Yes," Luther Paine immediately stood, "I would like to talk if your majesty would permit me."

"Speak your peace Luther as long as you keep a civil tongue," Eli replied.

"Well, I guess my tongue is about as civil as the next man's, and what I think is as important as what you or the so called Major thinks. I say martial law be declared, and me and my boys will enforce it. No strangers should be allowed in our town because they may be spies. Every family could put up a little money each month to pay for safekeeping. What do you think?" Luther asked with a smirk on his face.

"That is the most ridiculous thing I've ever heard," Eli felt the need to stand up to Paine. "We are not trying to protect the army from the townspeople, we are trying to protect the people, their homes and properties from scavengers like you."

"If that's the way you feel, you and your town can go to blazes. This town'll come begging us to help one day and then it'll really cost you. Let's go boys. I can tell we're not wanted here."

Once the Paine family departed Eli addressed the assembly, "Does anyone else have a suggestion or care to make a statement? Anyone? If not, each of us should think about what we've heard. This is Friday so let's meet again on Monday evening and see if we can come up with something that will benefit our community. Meeting adjourned."

"Eli, do you think that we need a militia? Do you really believe the armies are that close?" Sara asked as they walked home after the meeting.

"My love, a militia the size our community could put together will do little good defending against an army. But, it might help against the scavengers and looters that seem to go along with war."

"Eli, look at that moon, it must be a full moon. Just see how big and bright it is, almost like day. And to think not too far away a war is going on with people dying and looking at the same moon. Little Roger is just eight and I wish I could shield him from such horrible times."

The residents of Lamb's Creek were consumed with thoughts of war following the community meeting. That Sunday at church, Reverend Red Willis reminded the congregation of the meeting scheduled the following evening and encouraged them to pray for wisdom to do the right thing.

Monday evening, the Major visited Sara, Eli and Roger about an hour before the meeting.

"Daddy, do you have any ideas about what the community should do other than what was discussed the other night?" Sara asked. Not waiting for a reply, she continued, "I sure hope we don't have to deal with the Paines again."

"Doubt they'll show up tonight, Sara. Eli put them in their place and they didn't like it at all."

"Daddy, would you tell Roger that it's alright to call you Granddad instead of Major?"

"Roger, there are a lot of people that call me Major, but there is only one boy that can call me Granddad."

"Yes sir, I'll call you Granddad from now on. Granddad, do you think when I grow up that I might wear your Major uniform sometimes?"

"When you get big enough it's yours."

There was unrest in the hearts and minds of the people of Lamb's Creek. They were concerned with more than just forming a militia and protecting their settlement. The war was being fought close to home and the Nation was split. Families were fighting against one another because of differences of opinion, loyalties and personal convictions.

The Major and Eli talked privately about asking for volunteers to join the regular armed forces. They decided not to discuss it publicly until they heard what the people had to say at the next meeting.

As the Roads family left their house that evening they joined other families walking to the meeting and wagons driving in from homes farther away. The mood was somber and hardly a word was spoken. It was more like a funeral procession than a community meeting. Most knew that whatever would be decided would likely change their lives forever. Every family was present except for the Paines and that helped to lessen the tension.

The meeting was called to order and there was complete silence. Reverend Red was asked to start the meeting with a prayer. Reverend Red asked that God's blessings be upon the meeting and the decisions to be made that would affect each person in the room. He asked that God's Divine Will be done.

Eli started the meeting letting everyone know that it would be recorded. He called for comments, "The floor is open for discussion and recommendations. Who will be first?" No one moved or made a sound. It was as if a stifling fear had overcome each person crowded in Lamb's Creek Community Store. A place that had previously been so full of lively discussions, Reverend Red's testimony, Orville's wrestling challenges and Sara's attempts at matchmaking, was now dark and silent.

There was a long pause and people began to fidget. The Major stood up and said, "I move that we form a militia."

Another pause and someone stood and said, "I second the motion." It was Revered Red. Everyone seemed to relax a little.

"Will there be any discussion before we take a vote on this motion?" Again, silence. "All in favor of organizing a militia stand and be counted. Everyone stood. "The motion is passed unanimously. Thank you. Is there anymore business to be taken care of at this time?" Eli asked.

The Major stood again. Sara looked at her father and then at her husband. She had seen them talking in private by the front gate early that same morning. Her fears were coming true, and Sara wanted to wake up from what she felt was a bad dream. *I can't wake up because the war is real. Is everyone around me insane? How can they all so politely make decisions about going to war? O God*, she thought, *please don't let this happen.*

"I am not going to make a motion, but I do want to take the pulse of our settlement in relation to organizing a unit of volunteers to join the Union Army. Tomorrow there will be two lists posted in the store, one for the militia and one for the Union Army. I ask that you each think on this and pray about it with your families tonight. May God direct you in your decisions," the Major said.

Sara felt a strong wave of uneasiness and weakness come over her. She could not focus on her surroundings. She felt faint and wondered how many wives and mothers felt as she did. Still, she had a few days to convince Eli that he must not go. She and the community needed him here.

The next morning Sara and Eli arrived to a line of men and boys from ages fourteen to sixty-five waiting in line at the store to sign up for the Union Army or the community militia.

My God, Sara thought, *are they all mad? Do the men so want to neglect their families and go off and get themselves killed? What is wrong with these people?* She had so wanted to confront Eli that morning but didn't know what to say or how to say it. Maybe in a day or two things would calm down, but no, she thought, Reverend Red was there, sixteen year old Orville was there, fourteen year old John Spikes and even sixty-five year old Albert was there. Every man in the community except the Paine clan seemed to be there. She stood numb, faint and then Eli's voice brought her back to the present, something about a key and unlocking the door. Then she felt his hand, gentle at her waist.

"The store key Sara, hand me the key, love." Eli unlocked the door and guided Sara in. She walked back to the storeroom where sacks of flour and grain had become fewer and fewer since the war began. She sat on a wooden keg of nails. If she didn't get some release, she might explode so she allowed herself to cry, silently. She prayed, "Lord, I do not understand. Please help me. I need your strength." As she prayed, she knew that she was not alone. She felt strengthened by her prayer and the feeling that God would make her stronger.

Sara opened her eyes to the Major riding up on his high-stepping, buckskin gelding. Her father had cared for the horse since it was a three-month old colt. Its mother had been shot out from under him during a minor confrontation in Ohio.

The Major dismounted his horse and assured the men that the

store would open momentarily and the business of signing up would begin. As he entered the store, Eli was preparing tables and chairs for enlistments.

"Major, we have a problem. Everyone outside wants to join the troops and none want to be a part of the militia. We're going to have to consider some rules and regulations for the volunteers. There needs to be an age limit for enlisting in the Army, and we have to consider the needs of the men's families," Eli said.

"Eli, we'll interview each one individually in your office. Those younger than eighteen or older than forty-five will be excused from the regular army sign-up, but they may be right for the militia." The Major called Reverend Red in first and said, "We'll begin with you, Reverend. Come with us to Eli's office."

"Reverend, you make us respect you more for your willingness to join the regulars and we understand you feel a need to support your country. Don't you think you are needed here in our community?"

"I guess I'm torn between our church in Lamb's Creek and my duty to my Country. You tell me what I should do. I feel I should be in both places."

"We know that's impossible Reverend. You could fill a very needed place in the Army if you insist on enlisting. That would leave Lamb's Creek without a spiritual leader. The people here are going to need your spiritual guidance and comfort more than ever in the months to come. The decision is strictly up to you. If you decide to stay here, you would be my first choice to head up a community militia. Everyone trusts and confides in you. I'm sure that all would support that decision."

"When you put it that way, I guess staying here in Lamb's Creek may be where I belong. Thank you for your advice." When Reverend Red opened the door to leave, Orville stepped in and closed the door.

"You have to listen to me, Major and Eli," Orville said anxiously. "You know that I'm the strongest man in this county. I've out wrestled just about everyone with my left hand behind my back. I was born to fight. It's a natural thing for me."

"Orville, we all know how you love to wrestle and there's no doubt that you're the best in the county, but Orville you don't meet the rules for enlisting. First of all you're only sixteen. Second, your mother would be left alone and I don't think any of us want that. She's not able to do all the work on the farm alone. It's just not possible for you to enlist. I'm sorry," Eli said.

Ten men signed up and only six were accepted. Four had large families and were encouraged to stay home and care for them. They were asked to join the community militia. Everyone was agreeable except for Orville.

Now that the enlistments for the Union Army and community militia with Reverend Red Willis as senior officer had been worked out, Eli still had to discuss his own plans with Sara and Roger.

It was right where the community store now stood that he lost his mother and father from cholera twenty years ago. He had been only eight years old. He and Sammy Lamb, a former slave, were the first two to settle this little community. He, his father, mother and Sammy who had been seventeen left South Carolina on their way to Nashville to open a store. No one knew how they contracted the disease, but after only hours of a high fever, they succumbed. Eli and Sammy buried them on a small knoll overlooking the valley and creek they later named Lamb's Creek after Sammy Lamb. Now Sammy was gone and he had to make the hardest decision of his life, stay and watch over his family and the community he had started or give his all if necessary for his Country. He was torn and did not know what to do. He prayed, *help me Lord to know.*

Sara left Missy in charge of the store. At noon, men were still attending enlistment meetings. She decided to take Roger home and prepare lunch for Eli and her father. Sara made peace with the fact that she had no control over the war or the men's decisions. *I have to turn it over to God,* she thought. In fact, she was surprised that she could feel such a deep peace during such a difficult time. On the walk home, she thought about how Missy must be feeling having watched Orville be the second in line to meet with the Major and Eli. She wondered if Orville would ever recognize the depth of feelings Missy carried for him.

Sara watched Eli coming through the front gate walking toward the house. She could see heaviness in every movement of his body and his face twisted in agony. "Eli, what's wrong? Are you all right?" Eli only groaned. Sara said, "Here, sit while I get you some water. What happened?"

"Nothing happened. Everything should be all right but I feel so tight in my chest and I don't know which way to turn. I have wrestled and fought in my mind and heart in trying to make this decision, the hardest decision in my life. Help me please Sara, would you?"

"I know just how you feel. This morning when I saw all those men and boys standing outside the store I knew that it meant war and that some would never come back home. I thought I was going to die but prayed for God to give me strength, and He did."

"I have prayed that prayer too, but to no avail." Eli replied. "I feel that if I go it would be wrong and if I stay here it would be wrong. So what do I do, Sara?"

"Daddy will be here in a few minutes, let's wait and ask him. While we wait for him, come sit down in the kitchen and eat. Lunch is on the table."

There were similar conversations in six other homes in Lamb's Creek Community. The six men who joined the Union Army were single and lived at home, but their families were sorrowful and didn't want them to go. The men were excited and felt lucky to be going to war.

"Here's Daddy now. Let's see what he thinks," Sara said as the Major walked into the kitchen and sat next to Eli. "Daddy, do you think Eli ought to stay here or go to war with you?"

"I can't make that decision for Eli. That's for you and him to decide. I can tell you with certainty that he is needed in both places. His Country needs good officers and he would be that. On the other hand, he's the one that everyone in and outside this community comes to when there is trouble. I will not persuade Eli in either direction, but I, and my six recruits, will be leaving for North Carolina in two days. This war has been going on for over a year and could go on for another year or longer. There've been a lot of men killed on both sides and more will die before it is over." The Major hugged Sara knowing there was little he could do to console his daughter.

That evening when Eli helped Roger get ready for bed, his mind was still clouded with uncertainty. Leaving his family and community to go fight in a war was certainly no call to glory in Eli's mind. The need to protect his family, community and to hold the Nation together did feel like a call to duty. *I need to be a man of integrity, someone that does the right things at the right times,* Eli thought. Roger's excited voice pulled Eli from his thoughts.

"Daddy, can I look at Sammy's treasures again?"

"Roger, you have seen them a hundred times."

"I know Daddy, but I like for you to tell me about them."

"Well, get the box from under the bed and bring it here. We surely have plenty of time."

Roger ran to get the box. "Here's the box. Can I get them out? I like to feel the little black lamb's skin. It's so soft. Feel it, Daddy. Tell me why it's so special."

"Well, Roger, I wasn't born yet and Sammy was just nine years old. He was a slave then and lived with his grandparents, Hattie and Samuel, who were also slaves. You see that dime with a hole in it? Hand it to me because it goes along with the sheepskin. Sammy found this dime out in the road, his first dime. He put a hole in it so he could tell it from other dimes. Sammy called it his lucky dime."

PART IV
The War

CHAPTER EIGHT

Once Eli came to an answer to the question about whether to enlist in the Union Army or stay in Lamb's Creek with the militia, he wasted no time in talking to Sara. She seemed to already know his decision.

"I'll write you, Sara. I'll miss you and Roger more than I can say. Guess I'm already homesick and haven't even left home. Make sure you keep the doors and windows locked and be aware of all that goes on around here. Lord, there is so much to do, and I don't know where to start."

"You go see Daddy," Sara said. "Tell him your decision and I'll start your packing."

Eli left the house on the run. *I have to talk to the Major, and I have to see Reverend Red about the militia,* he thought.

Eli came upon the Reverend sweeping the front steps of the church. "Reverend, I've decided to join the Major's Regulars. Do you think you'll have any trouble with the newly formed militia? I'll do what I can to help you get organized between now and in the morning."

"No need, Eli. I think everything is up to par. I figured that would be your choice. Wish I was going with you all."

"Reverend, it's sure a load off my mind knowing that you'll be here with the families of our community. There's one thing I really want to stress. The Paines are going to try something when we leave. I don't know what they'll do exactly but you are the authority here as commanding officer of the militia. Keep your men close, your eyes open and do what you have to do to keep our community safe."

"Don't worry about us. You have enough on your mind. God's blessings be on you and your family."

Eli made his way to the store to find the Major talking to Missy.

"Good morning, Eli," the Major greeted. "I thought you'd be here sooner or later. Are you making arrangements to leave in the morning?"

Eli nodded to assure the Major.

The Major continued, "You'll be Captain in this group. I hope you'll accept the commission."

"It seems that everyone but me knew what I would decide. Why didn't someone advise me? Major, where are we going when we leave here? I'd like to tell Sara if I may."

"Eli, I'll have supper with you, Sara and Roger. We'll map out a route and make plans tonight. Until then, spend as much time as you can with your family. It could be a while before you see them again. We all thought this war would be fought and won by now but that's not been the case."

Eli and others in Lamb's Creek spent the day with their families making preparations for those who would stay as well as the journey that lay ahead. Eli thought, *so the die is cast. Decisions made by the people of Lamb's Creek over the course of just a few days have passed the point of no return and will change their lives forever.*

That evening the Major and Eli mapped out their travels to Knoxville and then after supper the Major took Roger home with him for the night.

"Thanks for getting your father to take Roger to his house tonight. It's so quiet and peaceful here it doesn't seem possible there is a war going on just miles away."

"Let's not talk about the war. There's been too much of that. Look at all the moonflowers, so big and white in the light of the full moon. They almost glow. It's a shame they only bloom at night. I find it curious that they fall off the vine as soon as the sun shines on them." The sense of heaviness that Sara felt made it hard for her to focus on the beauty that surrounded them. She felt tears escape her eyes and said, "I love you. It will be so hard not to have you here with Roger and me. We'll pray that you stay out of harm's way. Just watch out for danger and keep an eye out for Daddy if you can. Just hold me tight. This night is what I will remember until you come back home to me."

"And you, my love, I will see you, this moon and the moonflowers every time I close my eyes no matter what is happening around me. It's this that'll get me through the tough times ahead. I love you with all my heart and there's something I would like you to do."

"What is it, Eli?"

"When I ride out with your father tomorrow, please stay in the house. If you come out or I hear you cry, I won't be able to leave.

Would you do that for me?"

"Yes, I'll do that. I don't think I can bear to see you ride away. And please, my dear, come home to me as soon as this war will let you go and you are able."

The night seemed like minutes. The sun came up at its usual time. The birds sang and the townspeople rose, prepared for whatever the day held. Everything appeared the same as other mornings, but at daylight, eight soldiers rode away from Lamb's Creek. Two of the riders had very heavy hearts and wondered if they were doing the right thing. Their sense of call to duty kept them moving forward, away from Lamb's Creek. The other six soldiers felt a sense of adrenaline and excitement, thrilled at the prospect of standing with a hundred other men facing the enemy and engaging in combat. *We'll show them rebels how to fight,* they thought, unknowing that some of them would never see their homes and loved ones again.

Major Bruce Darby, Captain Eli Roads and six Union volunteers rode at a canter en route to Knoxville. The only external identifier that the men were off to war was the blue Union uniform worn by the Major. The others could not be identified as such, dressed in ordinary civilian clothes. The terrain was typical to Tennessee with steeply rising hills and falling hollers between. Game was abundant and they planned to hunt along the way to Knoxville, about sixty-five miles away. They carried little with them, not wanting to take sustenance needed by their families and friends.

"Nothing quite like riding through beautiful country like this on a fine horse to make a man glad to be alive," the Major said.

"We'll stop early afternoon and eat then go a few more miles. Should be there in about four days."

"It sure is fine country, Major, but so is Lamb's Creek. I still have doubts when I think about what we are doing. Do you?" asked Eli.

"Sometimes I wonder about the sense of it all. I think you're a little homesick already. By the time we get to Knoxville you'll be better. Let's stop over there by that creek. We can take a break and there's plenty of grass for the horses. No need to be in a hurry. This war has been going on for over a year."

"Major, I got me a fishing line. Mind if I catch some?" Bill asked.

"Help yourself. A good mess of fish will do us all some good."

About thirty minutes later Bill had more than enough fish for the small group. The horses grazed heartily in the small meadow. The recruits were in good humor talking and even bragging about what they would do once they encountered the enemy. After a short break, they moved on.

Around two thirty the Major called for another stop. "Picket the horses, boys, and build a fire. We'll cook us a meal and rest up a couple hours before night camp. Which one of you men want to cook? You can take turns if you like."

"I caught 'em. I'll cook 'em. Someone can make the biscuits and coffee."

"Bill, you know how to fry fish?" Hiram asked.

"Boy, I been a cookin' fish longer than you been a walkin'. Just stand by and watch. I tell ya what, instead of just standin' there, you can help by gettin' me some mud from the creek."

"You don't use mud to cook fish, Bill. Whoever heard a such?"

"Just shut your lips boy and get me that mud. I'll teach ya how to cook the best fish ya ever ate." Bill packed the fish in mud and put them in the coals. When the mud dried and started to crack, he pulled the dried mud off, the scales came off along with the mud and left only the white flakey meat of the fish. "Now boy, ya see how it's done?"

After a couple hours of rest, the soldiers rode for another hour and stopped for the night. The horses were picketed, a fire was made for coffee and a few leftover biscuits from earlier were shared. The men were tired and didn't have much to say. Bedrolls were laid out and soon everyone was sleeping.

The second day proved to be a lot like the first except in the afternoon they arrived at the Tennessee River. The ferry was on the other side and as they were waiting to cross, a military coach with a twelve-man guard detail stopped to await the ferry alongside them. Major Darby and Eli walked over to the coach as General Martin stepped out. The Major and the General immediately recognized one another having been friends in past years. They greeted each other fondly.

"I haven't seen you in years, Bruce. Where are you headed?"

"General, I'm headed to Knoxville with a small group of volunteers from Lamb's Creek, Tennessee. Need to contact General Atwood and find out what he wants us to do."

"I'm going to a camp just east of here and would be glad to have you and your volunteers ride along."

"This is my son-in-law, Captain Eli Roads, General."

"Eli, this is General Martin, an old and dear friend of mine. We grew up together back in Ohio."

"I am honored to meet you, sir."

"Major, you and Captain Eli ride with me. Your men can fall in behind mine. I can fill you in on what's happening in the War Department."

General Martin relayed details about the war and added, "Politicians, ought to shoot them all. They're the people that have this country in such a mess. Wouldn't even be a war if it weren't for the politicians. Even Lincoln says freeing the slaves is unconstitutional. It is States' rights. Each state governs itself in this matter. It's also true that something has to be done about it but in a lawful way."

The Major replied, "I certainly don't believe in slavery. If the truth be told, neither do God-fearing men, even in the South. The people in Washington wanted the war for their own benefit. It just didn't turn out the way they thought. Thousands, no hundreds of thousands, killed on both sides, thousands more mutilated and maimed."

Eli rode silently, listening.

"I haven't witnessed devastation at this level in my life and the devastation grows every day," the General continued. "People shouldn't be shooting one another. We should be holding the politicians accountable."

Three more days on the road brought them to a camp of twenty thousand Union troops gathered east of Knoxville. Eli and the Lamb's Creek volunteers were issued blue uniforms and allowed to keep their own firearms.

"Cap'n Eli, I need to talk to you, sir."

"What is it Bill?"

"Look who come riding into camp a little while ago," Bill said as he pulled Orville from around the side of a tent.

"Orville! What in tarnation are you doing here?" Eli surprised and angry shouted, "You know well and good you were to stay in Lamb's Creek and take care of your mother. How did you get here?"

"I followed you here, nearly lost you a couple times. I left Mama a note. There are enough people back home to look after her, and Captain Eli, sir, the fact that you never knew I was following you means I'll make a fine soldier."

"Orville, you're only sixteen years old. This stupid thing you've done shows how incompetent you really are. You didn't follow the orders I gave you back at Lamb's Creek, so why am I to think you can follow orders here?"

"Captain, if you send me back I'll just go and join up with another troop. I bet I've already seen at least a hundred boys in this camp alone that are my age or even younger. Sir, you got to let me stay. This is my destiny."

"Bill, take this hard-headed boy out of my sight before I do something I'll regret. I need to think."

Eli had war on his mind and now he had Orville, *this hard headed, disobedient boy to watch out for. Lord, what am I going to do? I can't fulfill my duties and babysit an undisciplined boy. Why me? I better write Sara and let her know we arrived all right and that Orville is here with us.*

Orville Lewis followed Bill to a tent nearby and waited as instructed. He wondered what Eli would do and thought, *surely he'll decide that my fighting skills and hard work will benefit the Army.*

Orville couldn't remember a time he didn't want to fight. Not because he was angry or mad but because using and feeling his strength, wrestling someone to the ground, was just about the best feeling he had ever had. He knew it worried his mother, his schoolteacher and even his friends. He couldn't help that his mind was always drifting to thoughts on techniques to tangle, countermoves to being pinned and escapes.

Before moving to Lamb's Creek, while his father was still alive, Orville had seen a wrestling match at a county fair. His father had pointed out the catch-as-catch style and told him that wrestling dated back to the beginning of time. It had even been recorded as drawings in caves. He told Orville that in New York City there were organized wrestling tournaments. The thought of this excited Orville and he could see himself as a man wrestling.

At age sixteen Orville stood six feet tall and his withy body was that of a man's. His mama cautioned him that he needed to exercise his brain as much as he did his brawn. When the daydreams would take over and the excitement of the possibilities of what he could do in the ring were more real than the lessons being chalked on the board at school, he would hear his mama say, *"The power of the mind, Orville, is as important as the power of your arms. Don't you just work your arms and legs, work your mind."* Her words would always help him refocus. He didn't want to disappoint his mother. *She had enough of that in her life.*

Work never bothered Orville. Memories of his father had started to fade, but what he remembered was working alongside his father. Those times had always been happy. So it was that happiness with work and wanting to please his mother that kept Orville focused.

Orville routinely wrestled his friends at school. His friends never hesitated, trying, knowing that they didn't stand a chance and that Orville would not hurt them. At sixteen Orville had wrestled every able bodied man in the community and those he encountered passing through. *Everyone except for Eli*, Orville thought. Eli teased Orville that as long as they didn't wrestle Orville would remain undefeated.

Eli penned a letter to Sara and Orville waited for his decision. Eli felt a heaviness and he thought about how Sara would feel the same when she relayed the news to Martha.

Six weeks later the letter was delivered to the Lamb's Creek Community Store. "Sara, hey Sara, you got a letter!" Missy exclaimed as the post arrived.

"Oh Missy, it's from Eli. My first letter."

"Sara, would you like me to open it? Look at your hands shaking."

"No, I want to open it. I'm going to the back. I want to be alone for a few minutes."

Sara sat, closed her eyes, lifted the letter to her heart and willed her hands to stop shaking. Once she felt settled she used a letter opener to gently cut the envelope.

Dear Sara Darling,

The first thing I must write is that I love and miss you and

Roger. I would give anything to see and hold you just now. Please know that all is well and travels to our camp were safe and uneventful.

Along the way your father met an old friend, General Martin. We rode in with the General and his men to a camp near Knoxville. I am about as settled in as one can get amidst what must be at least two thousand soldiers.

Orville rode into camp after we arrived. I suspect that by the time you receive my letter, you will have communicated with Martha and know that Orville ran off to fight in the war. I would have sent him back but he is stubborn and would have signed up somewhere else. At least this way I can keep my eyes on him. Please tell Martha that he is with me.

We will be leaving here in two days time, but the command has not shared with us where we will be going. With meetings and preparations, my time is short and I promise to write more soon.

Being away from you has confirmed what I have always known - that you, Sara, are my home. Regardless of where this assignment takes me, my heart is with you and Roger.

Your loving husband,

Eli

Sara read the letter twice before returning to Missy. Missy waited for Sara to speak.

"We were right in figuring that Orville followed Eli, Daddy and the others to camp. We need to pass the word to Martha and the others. Eli wants Martha to know that he will do his best to watch over Orville. They are all well. Oh Missy, I do miss them so."

"I'll go talk to Martha now. She'll be happy to know for sure where Orville is and that he is with Eli. Can you take care of things until I return?"

"Yes. I'll be fine. I want to read the letter until I know the words by heart." *Oh Eli and Daddy, where are you both now?*

Each morning on waking, Martha's eyes went directly to the five-line note Orville had left prior to running off to join the war. Today was no different although she did have the comfort now of knowing that Orville was with the men from Lamb's Creek. Missy had run the entire way from the store yesterday to bring her the news about Orville.

Martha pulled on her housecoat, stepped into her heavy socks, and walked over to the kitchen to make coffee. First she lifted the note sitting on the shelf above the small wooden counter and brought it to her nose hoping to get some scent of Orville. She looked at the words and wondered if she had made a mistake coming to these Tennessee mountains that had meant so much to her late husband. *Did Orville need something more? Had I taken him to my home outside Boston would his fate be different? How can one ever know what the right thing is to do for another?*

The note from Orville read simply,

Mama,

I love you with all my heart. I must fight for this great State of Tennessee and the abolition of slavery. Fighting is what I do best. I do it for you, father's memory and in search of the truth.

Your son,

Orville

Martha was thankful for Missy's visit yesterday. Sara had come later to share the letter she received from Eli. At least now she had comfort in knowing that Orville was with Eli. In her heart she knew the inexperience of youth led to Orville's idea of finding truth in war. She would be able to make it through this day a bit easier knowing that Eli's watchful eyes were on him.

Weeks of worrying had taken Martha's appetite away. She had not thought about the change in her appearance until yesterday when Sara had expressed concern about her frailty. Today, Martha felt hungry when she woke. *Wasting away will do no good for Orville, the community or myself*, she thought.

Martha decided to cut some of the smoke meat from the smokehouse and fry an egg for breakfast. She dressed and coated herself against the cold. It was still dark outside. She lit the small lantern hung by the door for her early morning and late night trips to the barn or smokehouse. As she entered the smokehouse the small portion of pork was a reminder that she would have to butcher the last hog this winter with the help of some of the other ladies. Reverend Red would likely assist. The meat would be shared with the others. Each family was rationing what they had.

As she took her knife to cut a portion off the ham, she noticed the meat had been torn. She had been in the smokehouse only once since Orville had left, but the meat then had been smooth and intact. Martha was concerned not that someone had taken some of the meat but because anyone she knew that needed meat would know they only had to ask. Only a small piece of the meat had been taken indicating that someone was hungry and likely in hiding. *Were they here watching her now?* She quickly cut the meat and headed back to the house.

As she entered the house, she checked that the shotgun was loaded, propped it near where she worked to fix her breakfast and moved it to the table next to her as she sat to eat. Merrill had made sure she knew how to protect herself. She had always felt safe in the company of her husband and her son but now she had neither.

After she finished breakfast, Martha returned to the smokehouse and propped the small lantern in the window. It was still dark and she quietly left the small stone building and walked into the field, taking a long hidden route around to the barn. By the time she walked into the barn her eyes had adjusted to the darkness.

The moon, hidden behind clouds and fog, gave almost no light. She took cover in the first small stall. It had a ceiling unlike some of the other stalls that were open to the second floor joists. Martha had always been soft spoken, but now she needed to find that same strong voice that had given her the courage to venture to an unknown place and make a claim for land.

With one foot in the stall and one on the bare dirt floor of the first floor barn space, head tilted upward, gun raised to shoulder and her sight set on the ladder to the second floor, she shouted, "I know you are in here, and I just as soon shoot you without seeing you. I better see boots coming down that ladder right now or I'm going to fill this barn and you with buckshot."

The response was quick in coming. "I'm coming. Don't shoot." The voice was nervous. "I meant no harm. Only looking for a warm place to sleep."

"I'm not looking for conversation. I'm looking for boots,"

Martha voiced from deep within.

"Yes ma'am. I'm on my way. Please don't shoot."

They weren't exactly boots she saw but maybe had been at one time. The remnants of shoes appeared on the ladder, then legs, torso, hands raised and a face that looked to be about Orville's age.

"What are you doing in my barn, boy?"

"Ma'am, like I said, I meant no harm. I was just looking for a place to stay the night."

"Well, it seems to me that you're looking for more than just a place to stay the night because you've been eating from my smokehouse."

"I reckon I have, ma'am. Only took a small amount and I know that don't make it okay. I apologize. I just needed some rest."

It was then as the long thin body reached the rung of the ladder closest to the barn floor that Martha saw how bent and thin he was. The boy began to quiver and she knew he wouldn't be able to stand much longer. With the gun propped along the front barn wall, Martha moved toward the failing figure. She was struck by the combination of youth and fatigue. As she moved next to him he reached out to her. She supported him and told him to move toward the house.

Head hanging, feet sliding, they managed to make it to the house. *Dead weight* was what he felt like Martha thought. She immediately put him in Orville's bed, removed what little was left to his army-issued boots and only then did she recognize the tattered Confederate uniform. He was either in a deep sleep of exhaustion or unconscious now, but she washed his face, hands and feet. His feet had blisters that had become infected and she treated them with a salve that she, Missy and Sara had made for the store.

Martha hoped no one was looking for the boy and that he had truly been hidden in the barn. He slept intermittently throughout that day, talking in his sleep. While the boy continued to sleep, Martha took the mule and wagon to the store. It was the first Wednesday of the month, the day she was expected at the community store for supplies. These days, she often left with nothing but Sara and Missy would expect her nonetheless. She knew it would be important to maintain normalcy and hoped the boy would continue to sleep through her departure.

The boy was still asleep when Martha returned. She decided to make biscuits and fry some of the ham to busy herself. After cooking, she sat down to read from her Bible. She thought about how she had been so removed from slavery and this way of life that made no sense to her. *How did I come to live in a state so divided over the issue of slavery?* She thought how proud Merrill would have been to learn that Lincoln had been elected President and how equally disappointed to know that less than a year after the election, Tennessee, the state her husband longed for so much during his time in Boston, would secede from the Union.

The boy was coughing now and the sounds were different than those he had made during his sleep. Martha saw that he struggled to open and focus his eyes. *He likely will be confused at his whereabouts. How much does he remember about coming to be in Orville's bed?* She picked up a tin cup of water on her way to the boy. He stared at her, blinking, knowing and not knowing.

"Here, drink some water. Don't be alarmed. You're okay. I'm

not sure how much you remember, but I found you hiding in my barn."

"Thank you for the water. How long have I been here?"

"I'm not sure how long you were hiding in my barn, but you've been asleep here for a day and a night, and it is going on the second day."

"Well, I'm much obliged for your hospitality, but I best be on my way."

"Now wait just a minute. You aren't going anywhere until you have something to eat. Think about it, not only have you been sleeping for so long, you've been without food for that long too. You keep trying to get up from that bed and you're likely to pass out. Let me prop you up, and I'll bring you something to eat."

Martha opened up a cold biscuit and put it in a pan on the stove to heat. She melted some butter in the pan and put a couple pieces of ham on the plate. She poured a glass of milk and carried the plate with the meat and hot biscuit to the boy. "Well, I guess you could explain how you came to be hiding in my barn by starting with your name."

"My name is William Daugherty, ma'am. My friends call me Billy."

"Well, Billy, I'm Martha Lewis. I see by your uniform that you're a Confederate soldier. Do you suppose someone is looking for you?"

"No ma'am."

"Call me Martha please, Billy."

"Yes ma'am, I mean Miss Martha. I reckon they all think I drowned like most of my troop did retreating, crossing the

Tennessee River."

"Billy, where are you going?"

"I don't rightly know, ma'am."

"Well, I don't guess you have to know exactly right now. Just eat something, and I will heat up some bathwater."

"I'm thankful for your kindness, ma'am. I know I must smell something awful."

"Even the most awful smelling boy would likely be the most delightful to your family about now. I have a son. His name is Orville. He's fighting for the Union."

"Ma'am, I'm sorry. I reckon it's a miracle that you didn't shoot me for an enemy."

"You aren't my enemy, Billy. You are another woman's precious son. I would hope your mother would do the same for Orville if he took refuge in her barn."

"Well, ma'am, my mama died when my sister was born. I was only four, but what I remember about her makes me believe she would have taken your son in without any hesitation. She was a kind woman, Miss Martha."

CHAPTER NINE

"Hello little girlie. Looks like your mind is a hundred miles away. Now don't it boys?"

"Sure does, Cousin Sims. Have you ever seen such a pretty gal? I think this here is Eli Roads' woman."

"Eli Roads you say, from over South Carolina way? Use to know an Eli Roads back there years ago. Gave me an intolerable lot of trouble. Had his self a store back there. He was about the same age as me," Sims said to Sara. "Tell me woman, ya know the man I'm talkin' about?"

"I don't know what you are talking about. Who are you?" Sara replied defensively. She had no idea who the man might be but had an uneasy feeling about him.

"Sims is the name, and the way I see it can't be more 'n one Eli Roads less'n he had a son. That's it boys, this would be Eli's daughter-in-law. Where's the old man?"

"Now don't go scarin' this little gal, Cousin Sims. Ain't neighborly. No, just ain't neighborly," Luther Paine said and spit tobacco juice on the floor. "Heard Roads is gone a fightin' with the Yankees and that would be the wrong side. Always knowed he was no good. All these fightin' men leavin' this community unprotected. Sure is a pity."

"Daddy, some man's a comin'. I think it's that preacher, Red. Maybe we oughta skedaddle."

Sara was relieved to see Reverend Red. He looked at Sara with concern as he approached and asked, "Sara, these men giving you trouble?"

"No, not really Reverend Willis, but I'm glad you're here."

Reverend Red recognized the Paines and wondered who the man with them could be. "What do you men want? If you came for supplies, they are inside the store."

"Don't really see it as any of your business, preacher."

"Well, I'm making it my business, Mr. Paine. I have responsibility for both the spiritual and physical well being of the people of Lamb's Creek. I take both my clerical duties and lawful militia appointment to heart. So again I ask, what is your business?"

"Just passin' through preacher, just passin' through. Come on men."

Once some distance was between the group of men and Sara, she asked, "Reverend Willis, how did you know they were here?"

"Missy saw them coming and came to let us know."

"Reverend, that man Sims with the Paines said he knew Eli's parents back in South Carolina. He wanted to know where they were now. He seems to be some relation to the Paines. He made me very uncomfortable."

A couple of the other community militia rode up just as Paine and Sims were out of sight. "Alright men, I think we must assume that the Paines and this new man in town, Sims, are scouting out the town. We need to pass the word. If anyone sees them around, they should give the alarm. They are sure up to no good. We should all keep a sharp eye," warned Reverend Red.

Scouting the town was only a part of what Paine and Sims had on their minds. They had already ransacked a small settlement and a couple of homes some twenty miles east of Lamb's Creek, looting anything of value, destroying what they didn't want, raping and even killing those that resisted while wearing the uniform of the Union Army. They truly were a mean lot.

"Got me a grudge to settle with Eli Roads, cousins. He all but run my poor family and me off my own place just cause he wanted my little bit a land. Told all kinds a lies on me and I mean to get justice."

"Ain't no Eli Roads your age, Sims, and the young one is in the Union Army now," replied Luther.

"Don't never mind, I still want satisfaction and I do aim to get it, and soon. First thing in the mornin' we goin' to dress in our uniforms and hit that plantation west a little ways. Oughta be lots a fine things in that house. We'll make a killin' for sure." Sims laughed and Paine's son, Junior, felt uneasy.

Bright and early the next morning the five men woke to clear blue skies and a bright sun shining across the land. The Paines and Sims dressed in clean Union uniforms and rode west raiding houses and killing unsuspecting people. Their crime spree would shake several small communities in southeastern Tennessee.

Sims was the first to see the old plantation home. The men rode boldly through the open gate and down the live oak, tree-lined road that led to the two-story columned porch running the length of the front of the home. "Hello, anybody home?" Sims called out loudly.

An old man, Sims thought he must at least be eighty years old, stepped out from around the end of the porch, "What can I help you with, Sergeant? We're glad to have our soldiers come around for a visit. My name is Blount, Thomas Blount."

"We be takin' a census, Mr. Blount, of all the houses in this area. Be glad if you would bring all your valuables and set them on the porch."

The old man looked up and saw four guns pointed directly at him.

"Call all your people outside now, Thomas, or we'll burn your whole place down."

"There's no one on the place but my wife and two colored women that used to be slaves. I don't…"

"What you mean use ta?" Sims interrupted.

"Well, I gave them their freedom years back. We haven't had any spending money since before the war started, lost everything but the house and ten acres of land. There's nothing inside worth much."

"Paine, you and two of ya boys go get whoever is in the house out here. Then look around and see if he's tellin' the truth. Look up stairs and down."

"Cousin Sims, look at that there high yella girl. She almost white. I sure would like to have her all ta myself," Junior excitedly exclaimed.

"Shut up, boy. That gal belongs ta me. I'm oldest 'n I get first pick."

"But cousin, I spoke up first," Junior Paine said hopefully.

"Junior, don't argue with me. I'm in charge of what goes on here today."

"Thomas, what is going on here?" an elderly lady asked as she stumbled onto the front porch. "Three men are tearing up the house. For God's sake, what is happening?"

"Sims, everythang in the house wouldn't bring ten dollars. Big ole house and they don't have as much as we do," Luther Paine said as he reappeared with his boys on the porch.

The idea that there was little to loot made Sims angry. An anger that made his head instantly pound and his eyes burn. "Go on, get down off this porch," he demanded.

Thomas took his wife by the hand and walked down the steps as Maudey and Sari Lynn followed. Without blinking an eye Sims shot Thomas, Mrs. Blount and the old negro woman just as they reached the foot of the stairs.

The shooting, watching the bodies fall gave Sims some relief from the hammering in his head. "Tie up that wench, Paine. You two boys burn this place down. I figgered them to have a lotta valuables. Bring that girl and let's get before somebody sees the fire."

Someone did see the fire and smoke a long way off. He altered his course and road toward the smoke. As he rode up to the house the three bodies on the ground just a few feet away from the burned, smoldering house got his attention. The house had already fallen in on itself. The fire had burned itself out and the fireplaces on either side of the house were the only parts still standing. *Three people dead. No, two. One was still alive, but barely.*

The man knelt down next to the elderly black lady, and gently rubbing her forehead asked, "Ole Auntie, what happened?"

The woman blinked her eyes several times not believing the image. Maudey opened her eyes wide and with rattled breath said, "Mens dress like sojers in blue. Dey sure not sojers though. I pulled Massa Thomas and Missus away from de fire."

"You did good, Auntie. Names. Did you hear any names?"

"Sims 'n Paine. Dey got my girl, Sari Lynn. Find 'er, please. Dey kill us all," she said as her eyes closed for the last time.

Three people died and for what? The man thought as he prepared to bury the three bodies. *I don't have much farther to go to be home. I sure hope things are better there than here.*

The man, six foot three and two hundred and thirty pounds, wore a crisp white shirt, neat black pants and tailored coat. He rode a large, gaited, black gelding into Lamb's Creek late that evening just as most were finishing their day's work. Stopping in front of the store, he dismounted, tied his horse and surveyed the changes as he walked up the step. Sara and Missy had just walked out the door and came face to face with the stranger.

Startled, Sara said, "I'm sorry, mister. We just closed the store, but if you… Don't I know you?"

"It's been ten years, Miss Sara. The last time I saw you was at your and Eli's wedding."

"Is it really you after all these years?" Missy asked.

"Afraid so ladies. I've been riding over four weeks now. Is Eli around?"

"No, he's not. Eli and Daddy joined the Union Army some

time ago. Oh, Samuel, it's so good to see you again," Sara said as she reached up to hug him.

"It's good to see the both of you as well. I'm quite weary from traveling though. Is there a rooming house I can stay tonight? Let's talk and visit tomorrow."

"Lamb's Creek has certainly grown since you were last here Samuel, but there's no boarding house yet. There's the small, extra bedroom inside the back of the store. You are welcome to sleep there. You will also find a couple empty stalls behind the store where you can stable your horse. We'll see you in the morning. I can't wait to tell everyone you're here. I'll have to write Eli and Daddy tonight and tell them the good news. Come on Missy. Let's go tell your Daddy the good news. I am so happy."

Samuel was glad to be home. He had been on the road from Detroit nearly five weeks. *Lucky,* he thought, *that I didn't directly encounter military forces, blue or gray.* Hearing the battles fought in the distance had kept him cautious and made his journey longer than it otherwise would have been. He untied his tired horse and led him behind the store noticing that Eli had added quite a bit to the original store. *Guess things have been going quite well around Lamb's Creek.* He led the horse into one of the empty stables, gave him a generous amount of oats and a good rub down. "I'll give you a drink after you eat, Blackie, but now I have to check out that bedroom. See you in a few minutes, boy."

Sims and the Paine clan returned home, to the former home of the Jenkins family, after what proved to be a disappointing day. Sims told Junior, "Lock the nigger girl in the smokehouse. I'll tend to her in a little while."

Sari Lynn was left bleeding and scared. She had never been mistreated before nor had she been around such cruel men. Imagining the brutality in store for her, she decided to concentrate on a plan for escape.

Junior slipped away from the others so he could be alone with Sari Lynn.

Hoping she could appeal to Junior's sympathy, Sari Lynn told him how afraid she was and asked if he would help her get away.

"I sure am sorry they beat you like that," Junior said. "They had no call to. They coulda give you to me. I would treat ya better. Guess I could just kinda forget to lock the door. I know Cousin Sims is gonna take hide off my back, but I'll do it." Junior untied her, put her in the smokehouse and propped a small block against the door.

Before Junior made it back to the house, Sari Lynn ran to the woods. *Which way? There's a settlement.* She had seen it before when travelling with the Blounts, *but which way? It was by a creek. We just come by a creek a little ways before getting to the smokehouse. Is it the same creek? Maybe it is,* she thought and ran until she was sure her lungs would burst.

Someone was coming up behind her. Sari Lynn could hear heavy footsteps faster than her own. She looked back. It was Sims. *Oh, Lord, no. Please help me.*

Sims caught Sari Lynn's arm and jerked her around. Hearing and feeling her arm snap, Sari Lynn knew it was broken. Sims pushed her and she fell down a hill and into a creek. As she lifted her head from the water, she saw Sims bent over and breathing hard. He caught his breath then started toward her. Sari Lynn was no longer able to move her left arm at all. Her body was bruised from the beatings and the fall down the creek bank. *Here's a stick. If I can get to it before he reaches me again, I can protect myself.*

Sims was almost at the bottom of the bank when a rock rolled under his foot and he fell. Sari Lynn had a strong hold on the stick. Sims was only three feet away now and getting up madder than she had seen him. Willing herself to wait until the right moment, Sari Lynn swung the stick hard. The stick connected with Sims' face and this time he fell backward. Sari Lynn rose quick swinging the sturdy stick and hitting again, again and again. *How many times* she didn't know. *He's bloody. His head, his arms, he isn't moving. Is he dead? I don't know. I don't care. I've got to get away,* and she ran again up the creek not knowing if she was going in the direction of the town. The only thing Sari Lynn knew was that she had to get away from the evil men that killed her folks. *Oh God they murdered my mother and old Mr. and Mrs. Blount.*

Sari Lynn felt she had gone miles when finally she saw lights. *There's a barn.* She thought at least she could hide there and rest until she could think of what to do. As she entered the barn she saw a horse in the first stall eating oats. Seeing the horse eating reminded her that she had not eaten all day. The next stall was empty. *I can rest here. Then maybe I can figure out what to do and maybe find someone to help me.*

Sari Lynn lay down in the hay. "Just for a minute," she said quietly to herself.

Samuel woke with a start. He didn't plan on going to sleep until after he watered Blackie. "Must have really been tired," he said to himself. It had gotten dark and he would have to use the lantern in his room to lead Blackie down to the creek.

His gelding, Blackie, shared the name of the lamb he had years before. Samuel had never forgotten the lamb. Once outside he saw several houses with lighted windows. "Hello, boy," Samuel said as he stroked Blackie's face. "You finished with the oats? Bet you need a drink of cool water from Lamb's Creek."

The horse was thirsty and drank for some time. After Blackie was through drinking, Samuel brought him back to the stable for the night. As he started to leave, he heard a low moan coming from the next stable. He held up the lantern and saw a bloody girl lying in the hay. She moaned again. *What in the world have we got here*? He went into the stall and in a soft voice asked, "Who are you?" She opened her eyes and started to scream.

"It's okay, miss. I'm not going to hurt you."

Sari Lynn sat upright and scooted back into the corner. She started to cry. There was something assuring about this man's voice yet she was frightened.

"You must be Sari Lynn," Samuel said.

Puzzled, she asked, "How do you know who I am?"

"I buried your mother and the others that were with her. Your mother was still alive when I found her. She told me you had been taken. Before she died she gave me the names of Sims and Paine. But we will talk about all that later. Let me get you inside and cleaned up so we can take care of your injuries."

"My arm is broken. Please help me."

"That's the first order of business. Easy now, Sari Lynn."

Samuel was thinking about what he needed to do to set Sari Lynn's break. He had not wasted his time while in Detroit. Mable had helped him to enroll in a university right away, and he had graduated with a medical degree. Following his studies, he completed an internship at a local hospital.

Samuel carried Sari Lynn to the small bedroom Eli had added to the back of the store, opened his doctor's satchel and removed a small bottle of medicine. "This is laudanum and it will lessen your pain. I'm going to get a lady friend of mine and have her clean you up. I'll be back momentarily."

"Please don't leave me," Sari Lynn whimpered.

"I promise Sari Lynn that you are safe here, and I will only be away for just a few minutes." *It must be getting late, hardly any lights on now. There at the church is a light.* Samuel knocked on the door, opened it, walked in and called out, "Hello, anyone here?"

"Come in, Samuel. Sara said you'd come in this evening."

"Reverend Willis, I need your help." As they walked, Samuel told Reverend Red about the events of the day and the girl in the barn. He asked if Missy or Sara could attend to Sari Lynn.

"You go on back to the store, Mr. Samuel. I'll get some help and be right there."

Samuel barely had time to start heating water when Sara, Missy and the Reverend came running into the back room. When they saw Sari Lynn they couldn't help but cringe.

"Oh, no," said Sara as she knelt by the bed. "How could this kind of thing happen? Poor darling."

"First thing, I have to check her arm. It's broken mighty bad. Sari Lynn, I am going to give you a little ether. It will make you sleep and you won't feel the pain, best that way. One of you ladies will have to help me set the bone. The other, finish heating the water and get something clean to make bandages."

They all looked at Samuel with surprise.

"I'm a doctor, and I know what I'm doing. I'll tell you all about it later."

In a little less than an hour, Samuel had set the arm, Missy had cleaned and treated the cuts and Sari Lynn was sleeping.

"A job well done," Reverend Willis commented. "Never seen any better."

"Thanks Reverend, but there's something I must tell you about. First, do you have a local marshal or sheriff?"

"No, but we have a local militia to deal with trouble makers."

Samuel told them about the burned plantation, the three murder victims, one being Sari Lynn's mother, and the perpetrators dressed as Union soldiers. He relayed Maudey's caution that the men were certainly not soldiers, and that it was Sims and Paine that kidnapped her daughter, Sari Lynn.

"We know the people you're talking about. They're suspected of murder and other crimes. Posing as soldiers is a serious offense in itself and will most likely make these crimes subject to federal prosecution. Your patient there is an eyewitness to murder, and we need to keep her safe. I believe these men are going to be hunting her and will be here before long. First thing at daylight, I'll call the militia together, and we'll be ready when they show up."

"Thanks Reverend," Samuel replied. "How close is the nearest army camp where we can find someone to talk to about the men posing as soldiers?"

"Almost to Chattanooga. I can send a man down at first light to see if they are interested in such a trial."

"Well, everyone needs to get a little sleep. I'll stay here with the patient. She may be in a lot of pain when she wakes up."

"I'll make a pallet for myself and stay here with you and Sari Lynn. You may need some help," said Sara.

"Okay, Sara. That would be fitting. Now let's all get a little rest."

The patient began to moan just before dawn as the laudanum and anesthesia wore off. Samuel gave her another dose of laudanum and soon she was resting again.

At daylight, two men left Lamb's Creek riding south to the military camp. Reverend Willis gathered his militia. They worked to devise a plan for the arrival of Sims and the Paine clan.

Breakfast was prepared and Missy had brought plates to Samuel and Sara. While they were eating, Sari Lynn woke up. For a moment she didn't know where she was or whom she was with. After a few moments, her memory returned. Missy brought her some coffee and breakfast.

"Sari Lynn, you need to eat something. It'll make you feel better," Missy encouraged her to eat.

"Some horrible things happened to you in the past twenty-four hours and we're here to see that nothing else bad happens to you. Try to just relax," Samuel assured.

"Who are you and these other folks? I want to thank you."

"No need for thanks. I'm Samuel Lamb and you're among friends. Like Missy said, you do need to eat and drink. I found you in the stable last night. You were beat up and your arm is broken. Can you tell us what happened? We need to know so we can help."

Sari Lynn shared her experiences. As she spoke, she realized how much her story sounded like a nightmare. "After they shot my mother and the others, they set fire to the house, tied me up and rode all day. I was shut up in a smokehouse. The youngest boy, they call him Junior, seemed to want me for himself and agreed to help me." She explained how Junior barely closed the door so she could get away.

Once Sari Lynn had detailed the events up to the time she found shelter in the barn, Samuel said, "That's enough for now. Finish your breakfast, and we'll check your injuries. Then you must rest."

It wasn't long and Sari Lynn was sleeping again.

"She's still in total shock from the trauma, emotionally and physically exhausted, but she's on her way to recovery with the Lord's help."

Reverend Willis gathered his men and detailed a plan to deal with the killers should they come into town. Five or six men were to stay outside on the porch of the store as if they were visiting or just lazing around. Inside, another three would be shopping and a couple more men would be waiting out of sight until needed.

Nothing happened during the morning and it looked as if they may not come at all. Mid-afternoon one of the militia members walked inside the store and advised Reverend Red that someone had been looking in and around the stables. A little later, five men came down the road and stopped at the store.

"Any of you men seen a bright yella nigger gal 'round here today? My slave run off last night, and we trailed her to them stables behind the store. Funny though cause she ain't there now."

As he was talking, Samuel walked out on the porch to join the militia members. "We found a girl out there last night all beat up and with a broken arm. She might be who you're looking for. You can come inside and take a look. What happened to your face, man? It looks awful. You ought to go see a doctor and get him to examine you."

"Horse just throwed me. I'll be all right in a couple days. Paine, let's go see if this be our gal. You boys sit tight," Sims said. "Won't take but a minute."

Sims and Paine walked into the store with Samuel leading the way to the back room where Sari Lynn and the Reverend were waiting.

"This is the young lady we found. Men, is she the one you're looking for?"

"That's the wench," Sims said. "Come here, girl. I'll teach you to run off like that."

"Wait just a minute," Samuel replied positioning himself between Sims and Sari Lynn. "Sari Lynn, are these the men you were telling us about?"

"Yes, these are two of the men. That one killed my mama and Mr. and Mrs. Blount," she cried as she pointed at Sims.

"Shut your mouth, nigger, and come here. I'll teach you to lie and be disrespectful to a white man."

Reverend Willis moved next to Samuel and said, "Sims and Paine, you are under arrest for murder. Men, tie them up and keep them quiet for a few minutes. Samuel, let's go and get the others."

As they walked out the door, Reverend Red gave a nod and the men who were outside pulled out their guns, held them on the three brothers and arrested them. After they were all securely tied, Sims and Paine were brought out on the porch with the others.

"You can't arrest us. You don't have no authority to do that. That nigger's lyin' and you know it," said Paine.

"We'll let the army decide that," replied Reverend Red. "I don't suppose they'll take kindly to you men posing as Union soldiers."

He turned to his men and said, "I want six of you men to get two wagons and go out to the Jenkins place. See if you can find any uniforms or any items that look like they don't belong there. Also, look around and see if there might be anything that looks like old graves. I have a hunch they may have murdered the Jenkins."

"Bob, I want you to get that youngest Paine boy and bring him back into the store." Reverend Red took full charge of the situation. "Samuel, you come with me. Men, you watch these criminals. They've killed and won't hesitate to kill again. If they try to escape, shoot them."

As the Reverend led Samuel back into the store, he said, "Samuel, if I'm right, I think Junior will be our source for information."

When the men brought Junior into the store, they untied him and led him to the room where Sari Lynn was lying in the bed. When he saw her arm splinted and wrapped and her face black and discolored, he dropped to the floor beside her bed and almost in tears said, "I'm sorry, miss. I didn't know Cousin Sims done this to you. He beat me too last night when he come home. Said you got away. I was glad and told him so, and he beat me again."

Let me see your back, Junior. Take off your shirt," Reverend Red demanded.

"Good Lord," Samuel said as he examined the bleeding whelps all across Junior's back and shoulders. We have to treat this as soon as possible or it may get infected. Come here to this back room, Junior. You probably were beat other places as well."

"Paine, we should have killed that moron son of yours last night. He'll tell 'em everything we ever done," Sims said as they waited for Reverend Red to return.

Samuel treated the wounds that, as he suspected, covered Junior's back, torso and legs. Junior, unaccustomed to any kind of positive attention and upset about Sari Lynn's condition, talked to the men without hesitation. He started with the Jenkins, the family they killed, put in an old dry well and covered with rocks. "Daddy said the old people had the farm long enough and it was time the Paines had it and a few other things."

Junior went on to tell them about others his daddy and two brothers killed and the horrible things they had done to the girls and women before they killed them. The more he talked, the more Samuel could tell that Junior felt a weight lifted. He told the Reverend he was willing to show them where the crimes were committed. Junior observed that when Cousin Sims had come to live with them, the robbing and killing got worse. Sometimes the others had made him go along and sometimes they let him stay home. He explained that he didn't like to go with them. It made him feel bad and have bad dreams. "Please don't make me go back with them and kill and hurt more people," Junior pleaded.

"You will not have to go back with them, Junior. We'll find a place for you to stay."

"Mama told Daddy if he lived by a gun, he would die by a gun. Do you think that's true, Reverend? You think he will die by the gun?"

"He very well may, Junior. Do you remember your mama? What happened to her?"

"Daddy cut her with a knife real bad, and she died two days later. He said she was no good, but I still miss her."

Sammy walked back to the bedroom where Sari Lynn was sitting on the edge of the bed sobbing.

"I'm sorry, Sari Lynn. You must have heard everything," he said. "What a terrible way to bring up a child."

"Oh, Mr. Samuel, what will happen to that poor boy? My heart just goes out to him. He has been treated so poorly."

"That's true, but you're in pretty bad shape as a result of mistreatment yourself. We need to get you well, and Sari Lynn, don't call me mister. People that know me well just call me Samuel."

She wiped the tears from her eyes and replied, "I'll do that, Samuel."

Samuel smiled and said, "I need to get with Reverend Willis and the militia and find a place to keep our prisoners until we can have a trial."

Samuel asked the Reverend if the town had a jail. "No, Samuel, we don't have a jail but we have log chains, heavy-duty locks in the store and men to stand guard over them. We should hear something from the Army tomorrow or the next day. If the Army doesn't want to take time for the trial it will be left up to us. I would guess, however, the Army will want to handle this situation."

The militia chained the four men around four different oak trees by the creek.

Reverend Willis said, "I want four armed men on guard continually until the Army gets here. Don't get within reaching distance of the prisoners. If there are any questions, come and get me. You men rotate in four hour shifts until further notice."

The night went by without incident. The next morning the two wagons and men returned from searching the Jenkins' house and surroundings. The wagons were full of stolen merchandise and ten Union Army uniforms.

"There are at least four or five more wagon loads of stuff in the barn and out buildings, and guess what else?"

"Two bodies in an old well covered with rocks," Reverend Red replied.

"How'd you know, Reverend?"

"We have firsthand eyewitness information. It looks like literally a ton of evidence to me."

The news about the murders and thefts made it around to every house in the area. People came to see the prisoners and the things that had been recovered. Some items were identified, but most were not. The most curious of the onlookers camped along the creek to make sure they would be present for the Army's arrival.

Mid-morning the next day two dozen soldiers and the two

Lamb's Creek militia sent to communicate with the Army came riding into the settlement. Reverend Red stood with the men guarding the prisoners.

"I'm Colonel Roberts out of Chattanooga. I hear you've captured Union soldier impersonators. I would like to question the prisoners. Who is in charge here?"

"I am, sir. Reverend Willis, Colonel Roberts, in charge of the local militia. Right this way, Colonel."

"Sergeant, you and the men dismount and relax. You come with me," the Colonel commanded his staff officer.

The three men walked down to the creek to where the prisoners were chained.

"Men, I'm Colonel Roberts. I have been informed that you murdered and looted while dressed in military dress. Is that correct?"

"Colonel, sir, I don't know why these uppity-up people want to tell lies about us. We ain't guilty of nothin' they say. We just come to get our runaway slave, and they just up and arrested us for no reason."

"Do you deny wearing military uniforms? That is all I want to know and nothing else at this point."

"We wouldn't put on blue or gray uniforms, Colonel."

As the questions were being asked Sims was the only one to answer. The Paine clan was quiet and looked around nervous and afraid.

"I need to talk to you in private, Reverend. Let's walk up to the store."

"Reverend Willis, do you have proof that these men dressed in military uniforms and killed people?"

"Yes, Colonel, we do. We have the uniforms, an eyewitness and I suspect we can find additional witnesses if needed. Let me show you the contraband we collected from the house and barn where they were living. Men, show the Colonel the uniforms."

John, one of the militia, brought out the uniforms and handed them to the Colonel. Colonel Roberts unfolded one of the uniforms and said, "This is a Union-issued uniform for certain. It looks like a bullet hole here in the side." He looked at four more and agreed they were all military-issued.

"I'd like to talk to the eyewitness now."

Reverend Willis led the Colonel into the store and to the back room where Samuel was talking to Sari Lynn.

"Sari Lynn, this is Colonel Roberts. He'd like to ask you some questions."

The officer was shocked when he saw the condition of the young lady. "What in the world happened to you, miss? Looks like you've been beaten near to death."

"I have, sir, by a man named Sims. I watched him kill my mama and Mr. and Mrs. Blount, the family we worked for." Sari Lynn retold the story of that terrible morning that had forever changed her life.

After hearing her story the Colonel asked, "Are you sure they were in military uniforms?"

"I am positive, Colonel. We all thought they were really soldiers."

"The young man, Junior, did he actually take part in the killing and looting that you described?"

"No sir. I don't think there is a shred of meanness in that poor boy. If it weren't for him, I would not be here right now. It's because of him I was able to escape. Sims didn't just beat me, Colonel, he beat Junior badly too for not making sure I was locked up."

"Reverend, I've seen and heard enough to try the four men that you've taken prisoner. We'll begin in two hours. I have to get back to headquarters as soon as I can, but we'll conduct a fair and impartial trial on the porch in front of the store. My men will now take charge of the prisoners. They're no longer your responsibility. Sergeant, cuff the prisoners and bring them here to the front gallery."

"Yes sir, Colonel, right away, sir."

So the stage was set to begin the trial that people in Lamb's Creek would talk about for years. It was one case in many where butchery, looting, and heinous crimes were committed by evil men during and after the Civil War.

A makeshift courtroom was quickly prepared by the soldiers using chairs and tables provided by the townspeople. The prisoners, escorted by the soldiers, were led up the front steps to the store and seated facing the Colonel. A crowd of people, some sitting on the ground, some standing, silently waited to witness the trial. Most of the people knew the Paine clan and were afraid of them. Reverend Red was relieved that the Colonel had so quickly taken responsibility for the prisoners and the proceedings.

Samuel marveled at how perfect a day it was, not a cloud in the sky. The only sound was the rustling of leaves in the wind. A hint of fall was just now showing in the trees.

Luther Paine wondered, *what's with all these people looking at me, my sons and Cousin Sims like we're some kind of freaks? What could we have done so bad to deserve being cuffed and put on display? Maybe we killed a couple people and took some stuff that should have been ours anyway. That's just the way the world worked, right?* In his mind, nothing they had done seemed to warrant the army, especially blue coats.

As the Colonel seated himself, he said, "There is an obvious interest in these proceedings today. I want absolute quiet throughout this trial. The only people to speak will be the ones that I'm speaking to. Any disruptions and I'll make this a closed trial."

Looking down at a small notebook, the Colonel said, "The four men on trial today are Luther Paine, or 'Daddy Paine' as he's known to many, George Paine, Dudley Paine and Ralph Sims." With eyes now fixed on the men on trial, the Colonel continued, "You men are charged with the murders of Mr. and Mrs. Blount of the Rock Mount Plantation and a freed slave woman named Maudey, who lived with and worked for the Blounts. What do you four men plead, guilty or not guilty?"

Sims rose, made one step forward in his shackles and asked, "Colonel, if we say we're guilty, could we just spend a while in jail?"

"Mr. Sims, I mean to be perfectly clear. You are accused of a crime punishable by death. If you confess or if you are found guilty, you will be executed. If you are found innocent, you will be set free. The reason the military is conducting this trial is because you have been accused of impersonating Federal soldiers, otherwise, you would be tried by this community."

"Well, Mr. Colonel, I reckon I ain't guilty." Sims turned to his cousins and asked, "Paine, what you and your two boys got to say to this Yankee?"

"I say not guilty. Me and my boys didn't kill them folks, you did. We ain't takin' blame for what you done."

"Luther Paine, are you admitting to witnessing Sims shooting the Blounts and Maudey at Rock Mount?"

"Yes, he done just that. Me and my boys went in the house to see what we could find and Sims got mad when we couldn't find anything and ups and shoots all three of them nice folks."

"Tell me, Mr. Paine, were you all wearing soldier uniforms?"

"All, but Junior. He didn't. Said he didn't want to be a soldier, didn't want no part in it."

"Sims, Miss Sari Lynn, daughter of Maudey, attested to me earlier that she witnessed you shooting her mother and the Blounts. Now your three partners in crime say the same thing. Do you still deny doing this?"

"I ain't got nothin' else to say, only I thought you boys was my friends. Now, I might tell how you and your kids killed them soldiers so you could have them uniforms, Cousin Luther. I might just do that."

"Men, this will not be a finger-pointing session. You men are being tried today for the murders of the only three people named. I suspect you've killed many more as well as committed many other crimes. There is, however, substantial evidence relating to the murders for which you are on trial for today."

"Luther, George and Dudley, I want you to know that even

though you three did not pull the trigger, you are just as guilty as Sims. Is there anything you would like to say in your defense before I pronounce sentence?"

There was not another word from any of the Paines.

"If not, I, Colonel Roberts, for the murder of Mr. and Mrs. Blount and Miss Maudey, sentence you to death by firing squad."

At the moment the death sentence was proclaimed, people gasped and whispered, trying to make sense of what was about to occur.

"I'd ask that everyone remain quiet and in place. Sergeant, pick ten men and take these four men behind the store. Reverend, you, Dr. Samuel and I will accompany them. The rest of you people will stay where you are."

Soldiers led the convicted men to the rear of the store. They were dazed.

"Reverend, read these men their last rights. Give each of them an opportunity to speak their peace to you and God. Samuel, once they are executed, I will need you to pronounce their deaths."

One by one, Reverend Willis tried to take the men by their hands and asked if they wanted to repent of the evil things they had done. First was Sims.

Sims refusing the Reverend's hand said, "I ain't confessin' to you, and I ain't gonna confess to God. If He don't know what's happening down here, why tell Him?"

Next was Luther.

"Luther, would you like to confess to God and ask forgiveness?"

"I'll say this much, Reverend, I do hate to know I'm the reason my boys stand wrongly accused. I should have left them with their mama. I'm sorry, boys. I truly am. That's all."

Next was the oldest of the Paine boys, George.

"George, would you like to say anything to me or to God?"

"I'm scared, preacher, real scared. Never thought it would turn out like this. I knew I was wrong when I killed and hurt those people. I wish I could tell them I'm sorry. Mama always said if you lived by the gun, you'd die that way. I wish I had a listened to her. That's all preacher."

Last was Dudley Paine.

"Dudley, would you like to tell God you are sorry and ask His forgiveness?"

"Daddy always said there ain't no God. Mama said there is a God, and He sees everything we do. I ain't never knowed it's wrong to do what we did. I reckon though there would have to be a God or everybody would be mean like us. They got some good people like Junior. We used to call him simple or dummy, but I reckon he was the smart one. Would you take care of Junior for us preacher? I do ask God's forgiveness, and I'm sorry I done wrong. Tell them soldiers to shoot straight."

The men were lined up and blindfolded except for Sims. He said he wanted to look at the face of the men who would shoot him.

The soldiers did take care to shoot straight. Samuel pronounced the deaths and noted that the shots put an end to a two-year reign of terror in the Lamb's Creek area of Tennessee.

The day was still a beautiful day. The creek still ran cool and clear over the rocks with a soothing sound and the flowers bloomed in mass profusion with every color of the rainbow. *It made no difference to nature that four men were executed. Time never looses a beat,* thought Samuel. *It just keeps moving on.* How many more he wondered were lying dead on a battlefield on this beautiful day.

Colonel Roberts said his good-byes, lamenting the circumstances that brought him to Lamb's Creek. He charged the militia with burying the bodies, and he and his troops began their trip back to Chattanooga.

"What an awful end to four people's lives," Sara commented as she, Missy and Samuel walked back in the store. "All our lives will be different from now on. Every time we see their graves, we'll think of this day. Why do some people like to do such horrible things to other people?"

"I wish we knew the answer to that question, Sara," answered Samuel as he went into Sari Lynn's little room.

CHAPTER TEN

Captain Eli Roads looked at the barely legible postmark on the letter Sergeant Bill Lions delivered to him. It seemed to be dated the fifth of September 1863, *nearly three months since it was mailed.* "Looks like that letter made the rounds tryin' to find ya," Bill commented.

Eli opened the letter.

Darling Eli,

I received your letter a few days ago, but have just now had time to write to you. Here at Lamb's Creek things are almost unbearable without you, however, a wonderful thing has happened. I will tell you that first. Samuel Lamb has come home. He is so big, tall and handsome, but best of all, he studied medicine and is a licensed physician. Can you believe that? I am so glad he is back.

The other news is that...

Sara went on to write about the Paines and their Cousin Sims and all the events that had taken place up to their execution, not leaving out one single detail.

And darling, it seems that you have been away forever. A night never passes that I don't go outside and look at the moon and say to myself that somewhere you are looking at that same moon and thinking of Roger and me.

I love you Eli, darling. Write soon.

All my love,

Sara

"Bill, I don't know if you ever hear any of the news from back home. You might like to read this letter. It may interest you."

"Thanks, Cap'n, I sure would."

After Bill read the letter, they talked about the events that had occurred back at Lamb's Creek.

"Maybe Orville would like to hear the news. Do you know where to find him, Bill?"

"He's sure to be over at the parade ground wrestlin' with anybody he can talk into takin' him on. That boy is stronger than two young Missouri mules. Never did see such a scrapper. He has beaten most everybody in this camp and some twice. I'll go fetch him, Cap'n."

Eli had, just before receiving the letter, talked to his father-in-law, Major Bruce Darby. They were on stand-by awaiting orders to march somewhere in western North Carolina almost sixty miles away. They needed to get six good men to go before hand to scout the route that the Army wanted to take. The Major asked Eli to pick the men because he knew their skills better than anyone. Eli wanted to know if Bill would head up the scouting party. They were to leave at once.

"Couldn't find that Orville boy, Cap'n, but he'll be here for supper for sure. There's a new group of recruits just come into camp from east Tennessee. Reckon he's over checkin' them out."

"Bill, I just met with the Major and he wants six good men to work as scouts. Would you consider heading up this detail? We need to sit down and discuss the matter."

"Cap'n, I joined up to do what I can and if scoutin' is what you want, I'd be glad to scout."

"We're going to move this camp south to somewhere in west North Carolina. Don't know where yet. Two hundred men are going to leave here tomorrow and two hundred each day until everyone has been relocated. A lot of our field artillery will go with the first group. Needless to say, you scouts are to go ahead, determine the best route for the troops and locate any enemy forces along the way. I'm going to leave it up to you to pick five more men to help you. You need to be heading out by daylight."

"Cap'n, are there any Army regulations for this scoutin' or can we do thangs our way?"

"Bill, I don't think we are going to tell you how to do your job. I'd like to talk to you and your men before you leave to make sure you have everything you need."

"Already know the men I want and I need a fast horse. The one I want is down at the racin' stables. Don't thank he belongs to nobody in perticular though."

"You go tell the officer accountable for the stables that Major Darby needs the horse for a while."

"I'll get my men and horse and supplies together and be back in just a bit, Cap'n."

In less than an hour Bill had his five men, horse and was standing in front of Eli's tent. When Eli walked out, he had a surprised look on his face. He began to grin as he spoke, "Men, I and the Army appreciate you volunteering for this duty. Be careful and God bless." Eli had Bill follow him back into his tent.

"Bill, these men are all the men from Lamb's Creek, and you are all out of uniform. What are you up to?"

"Well, Cap'n, I know these men and they know me, and no tellin' who we might run into. Them southern boys just might not like us if we're dressed in blue. We got our own clothes, our own horses and our own long rifles. Only thang belongs to the Army is the racehorse 'cause we might have to get word to ya fast. I'll send a message back once a day if need be. If there's nothin' else, we'll go chow down and hit the road."

Two hours before dark the scout detail had eaten and were on their way out of camp riding west. The sky was heavily overcast with a cool northwest wind blowing lightly.

"Men, an hour's ride from here is that big cave. The entrance is not deep, but it's large enough for us and our horses. We just might beat the rain if'n we get a move on. Don't ride in no formation. Don't want nobody to thank we're Army so kinda scatter out."

By the time they got to the cave, lightning was flashing all around them but it had not rained.

"Three of you men gather wood, all ya can. You other men help me unsaddle and take the supplies off the horses. Now shake a leg."

The horses were watered and given small bags of oats. A large pile of wood was stacked inside the cave with the horses and a pot of coffee was boiling. The men found places to sit around the fire and commenced talking about home and their folks while waiting for the coffee to finish brewing.

"Boy, you be the first to stand watch after coffee. Each one will take two hours accordin' to age, youngest first. Up to you to figger out your ages."

"Sarge, why do you always call me boy? I'm seventeen and I got me a name, it's Hiram."

"What kind of name is Harm?"

"It's not Harm. It's Hiram, H-I-R-A-M, not boy or Harm. If you don't want to call me Hiram, you can call me Tater. That's what everybody back home calls me. I'm sure you can remember that."

"Well, I be doggone. I didn't know ya had a name and now ya got two. You just full of surprises. Why do they call ya Tater?"

"Because I ate so many growing up. Sweet taters, Irish taters, fried or baked taters. As far as I'm concerned taters are about the best thing the Lord give mankind to eat. The next would be squirrel brains. What about you, Sarge? Where you from? Where'd you grow up?"

"Well, we won't get into that right now, but I'll tell ya, it's time to get your rifle and go watch."

As the men were sitting around the fire sipping coffee, the earlier conversation had Bill thinking of bygone days growing up on a little farm down in Mississippi. His daddy grew up in the beet fields in Colorado. When he was old enough to go out on his own, sixteen years old, his daddy drifted down to Mississippi where he went from one job to another. At eighteen Bill's dad met a beautiful Cherokee girl. They married and settled down to sharecropping for a wealthy landowner. A little over a year later, Bill was born. Things went fairly well for five years then his daddy had some trouble with the landowner and was let go.

The small family moved up to Tennessee and again moved from place to place. When Bill was eight, his family moved back to Meridian, Mississippi, where he attended school for five years. All the moving didn't bother Bill but his mama was never able to adjust. She always said she would like a home of her own, "*Not a large one, a small one would do with a little white picket fence and flower garden.*" She just couldn't seem to make it happen. His parents got into an argument one night about moving again. His daddy wanted to go back to Colorado, but his mama refused to go. She suggested he go and get a job and then send for her and Bill.

Bill's daddy left mad and said they'd never see him again. He was a man of his word. They never saw him again. Bill, almost fourteen years old, quit school and got small jobs trying to earn a little money, but no one would give him a real job. His mama got a job working in a hotel restaurant as a cook. She was a real good cook for sure but it provided for just a mere existence.

Then, a Mr. Nobles, who was staying in the hotel on a business trip, asked if she would be interested in moving to Nashville and cooking in his restaurant. He agreed to pay their fare and expenses and supply a small two-bedroom apartment. Her salary would be twice what she was earning. Bill recalled it was the best move they ever made.

"Sarge, you mighty quiet. Something on your mind?"

"Not really, Johnny. Just thankin' on days past. Guess I shouldn't pick on Hiram so much. I knowed his name but didn't know they called him Tater."

"Sarge, he likes you to pick on him and would do anything in the world for you."

"Men, we better get some shut-eye. Mornin' will be here afore ya know it."

"It's been almost two hours, Sarge. I'll go relieve Tater."

The night passed with little rain and morning broke with cool temperatures and bright skies. The trees were showing such bright colors that Bill thought the scene seemed almost unreal.

"Alright men. The next few days we have to be mighty careful. Could be enemies anywhere along the road. We have to ride slow and easy. The first two hundred soldiers will be here sometime this evenin'. We'll leave one man here. The other five will move on ahead scountin' a couple miles each side of the road. I figger the troops will cover about fifteen miles a day or less. They have a lot of artillery to move. The scout that's left here will join the troops that arrive this evenin'. Me or someone will bring news back before dark."

"Johnny, you stay here and keep a lookout for anyone who might be movin' around. I'd stay outside the cave if'n I was you. Don't want to get caught in here. Just stay hid somewhere with your horse close by."

"I'll ride the road first. Two of ya ride on my right, the other two on my left. Ride slow and under cover as much as possible. Every two hours meet me back on the road. Any questions or suggestions?" All were quiet, so Bill said, "Let's go then, men."

After the first two hours, three of the outriders met Bill back near the road and after a while the others showed up. The scouts saw no one so they rode out again. Bill rode off the road a little ways so he wouldn't leave tracks for anyone to see.

The rest of the day was carried out just as Bill had commanded. No other people were seen. At two o'clock, Bill and the scouts made a fire and quickly cooked a meal. After eating Bill said, "Men, go a couple more miles, make camp, then scout the area two or three miles around. No fires after dark. I'll be goin' back to camp and see that everthang's on schedule. Should be back here mid-mornin' tomorrow. As little talkin' as possible."

Bill saddled the big racehorse that was raring to go and left their camp at a gallop. The miles slipped by in a hurry and in a little over two hours he came upon the front guard of the moving troops.

"Where can I find Cap'n Eli Roads, Lieutenant? I'm Sergeant Bill, a scout for Cap'n Roads. I have a message for 'im."

"Just a little way back, Sergeant. You can't miss him."

Captain Eli and the scout, Johnny, were riding side by side in front of the artillery.

"I see ya made mighty good time, Cap'n. Didn't figger you'd make it this far."

"The men were in a hurry to change scenery and the horses were eager to move. Give us a day or two. They'll slow down."

"My men are camped about fifteen miles ahead, Cap'n. Ain't seen nobody all day."

The front guard and scout unit found a good place to set up an overnight camp. Tents were quickly erected next to a small stream and plenty of grass for the horses.

"Reckon you made a good eighteen miles today, Cap'n. Won't take no time to get where we're goin' at this rate. Hope it don't rain. Sure would slow us down movin' these cannons if'n it gets muddy."

After a meal and discussions about upcoming plans, Bill and Johnny decided to turn in early so they'd be ready to leave at daylight.

With an early breakfast, they left camp just as it began to lighten in the east. The weather had turned much cooler during the night with a slight sprinkle of rain.

"Better put on that slicker, Johnny. Don't want to catch cold right now. We got us a lot of ridin' to do."

A couple hours brought them to where yesterday's camp had been. They slowed their pace and found where the scouts had spent the night. They were nowhere to be seen.

"You go about fifty yards off the road on that side. I'll do the same on this side and we'll ride ahead slow. They won't be far ahead."

"Saw you coming, Sarge. We've been waiting for you. We found a small patrol a couple miles east of here. Guess they might be a scouting party like us."

"How many? You sure they Rebs?"

"Counted about sixteen at daylight this morning. They were still in their bedrolls. Sure enough Rebs. You want to see if we can capture them, Sarge?"

"No, one might get away and that's all it'll take to cause a whole lotta trouble. We need to make them move away from here."

"A couple of us could go and lead them away."

"No, I don't want them to know anyone's around. Plus, someone might get hurt or captured and we don't want that. I thank I'll just go and talk them boys into goin' away. You men can go a ways with me but stay outta sight. I may need your help if'n I get in trouble."

So the Union scouts rode up close to the Rebel camp and hid while Bill rode into the camp. "Hello," he called out, "got any extra vittles? I'm kinda hungry."

Startled, everyone grabbed for their guns. They had not posted any guards. A Lieutenant came forward.

Bill said, "Howdy, Cap'n. I sure would like to have a bite with ya. Ain't eat much the last few days."

"Who are you and what are you doing here? You a Union man? Get off that nag. Men, tie his hands."

"You ain't no more friendly than them soldiers I saw yesterday. At least they let me ride off. Folks in these parts of the country ain't the least bit sociable, but I could still eat some of that food."

"You never answered my question. Who are you?"

Bill told him that he was Bill Lions and had come looking for his uncle and five cousins who had come from Mississippi to join the Rebel army. He had been looking for them for six weeks. "They just seemed to disappear. Went east almost to the ocean. Would you have met up with them maybe? While we talkin', I could sure be eatin."

"Jones, get the man some grub."

"And coffee would sure go good too, Cap'n."

"I'm not a Captain, Mr. Lions, just a Lieutenant and how do we know you're not a spy for the North?"

"Well, reckon you don't, Cap'n. All I can tell ya is yesterday them blue coats like to hung me and now you gray coats thank I'm a spy. This ain't a very healthy place to be. This cookin' sure is good though. Been a long time since I had this kind of vittles."

A Sergeant from the Rebel troops asked, "Lieutenant, can I talk to this man?"

"Why not, Sergeant. I can't seem to get through to him."

"Where did you say you're from, Lions?"

"I was raised up in Meridian, Mississippi, Sarge. Daddy was a sharecropper for a good long while till he got in trouble and lost his job. Then we moved around a lot."

"Did you know Mister Taylor, a wealthy landowner?"

"That's who my daddy worked for. How do ya know him? You from there yourself?"

"Lieutenant, this man is no Yankee. He must be telling the truth. We both know the same people. Tell me about them Yankees you saw yesterday. Where were they and how many were there? Were they camping or were they on the move?"

"I come across them early yesterday mornin'. Looked like they was campin'. Reckon about sixty or seventy, maybe. They let me go after some questions, and I took off before they changed their minds. Rode hard all day and most the night. Poor ole hoss is about done in."

"Where did you say they were camped, Lions?"

"They were east of here. However long it takes to ride pretty fast all day and most the night."

"Thanks, Lions, for the information. Sergeant, get the men on the double. We need to check this out. Our information must have been wrong when they said the Yankees were this far west."

"Could I maybe have one more cup of coffee, Cap'n? Don't know when I might get some more."

"Sergeant, give this man a pound of coffee. He's been a big help."

The Rebel soldiers broke camp and pulled out, leaving Bill sitting on a log drinking his coffee.

As the scouts came out of hiding, Hiram asked Bill, "Sarge, what'd you tell them Rebs to make them take off so fast?"

"Well, I told them that I had five of the meanest men hidin' in them bushes and if'n they didn't get, I was gonna call ya out. I guess they believed me," Bill said with a big grin.

With the Rebel soldiers going in the opposite direction the six scouts continued scouting the way for the Union Army moving southwest. Nothing of consequence happened the next couple of days, and the troop made good time on their march.

"One more day, Bill, and we ought to be in the area of bivouac. General Atwood and the Major will be there. Something's brewing around Chattanooga, and I expect we'll see a lot of action in a few days. You can feel the tension in the air. I don't like it at all."

"Cap'n, when we get there do ya want me and the other scouts to continue or do ya have another job for us?"

"We'll decide that after I meet with the other officers," replied Captain Eli.

The next evening, the first of four groups of men entered the camp area already housing three hundred soldiers with nearly six hundred more on the way.

"Bill, the Major said for you to get your scouts together and wait. We won't know anything until General Atwood gets here, but there's something about to go down, so be ready."

"My men are waitin' by that wagon over there where Orville's fixin' to meet his match. Ole boy from Kentuck. Bet he's over three hundred pounds. Thank I'll have to watch this Cap'n. Just holler if'n ya need us."

"They call me Big Coon where I come from, boy. I ain't never been whupped yet, and I don't expect you big enough to do it. Will it be fists or wrestlin'?"

"My name's Orville. I've only had one person tie me, but I got him the next day. He was bigger than you. I could probably beat you with just one arm. Let's wrestle, Coon."

Before Bill could say scat, Orville pinned Big Coon on the ground. Orville let him get up and Coon kicked him on the hip. As Orville turned, Coon tried to hit him in the face, but a fast move caused him to miss. Orville countered with two left-rights to the mid section. As Coon was trying to catch his breath, Orville pounded his face and head with multiple blows. Coon went down and didn't move. Big Coon's friends could hardly believe their eyes. Their idol lay unmoving on the ground.

"Didn't want to do that fellas, but he gave me no choice. I'll check on him tomorrow. Hope he ain't too badly hurt. No hard feelings."

Eli, arriving as the fight was over, said, "Bill, get your men together and come inside the tent. We need to talk."

As the scouts gathered inside with the Major and Eli, Bill relayed the events of the match between Orville and Big Coon in detail.

"If'n we had one company of men like him, the rest of us could go home."

"Men, the Major said we're going to experience some heavy fighting in the next few weeks. The enemy has taken over the Chattanooga area with hundreds if not thousands of troops, and the big brass say we must move them out. A large order if you ask me. We have about eleven hundred men here or will have when the rest of our troops arrive in the next three days. We need you scouts to leave in the morning and scout for enemy units between here and that part of Tennessee. We will need a daily report. It's not settled yet when we march in that direction. We have fifteen hundred troops marching this way from Alabama and a number coming south. It will be devastation when we all meet, but it just may help bring the war to a close. Good hunting, men and the Lord bless."

Bill said, "Well, there it is. No more laying around on our backsides, boys. Go find ya somethin' to eat and try to get some rest. Lord knows when you'll get another chance."

It snowed all afternoon. It was the first snow that winter in the area, a heavy, wet snow that covered everything with a white blanket.

The next morning before daylight the scouts were in Captain Eli's tent sipping coffee waiting for breakfast when they heard what sounded like all heck breaking loose. It sounded like hundreds of mortar projectiles were blowing up throughout the camp. Caught completely unaware, no one knew what to do for a moment. Then as quickly as it started, it ended. The camp was in disarray when Eli and his scouts went outside. The Major was asking why this had happened, was no one on guard for this kind of thing? Why had the patrols not seen this coming? He viewed it as a severe act of incompetence.

"Cap'n, we'll check it out. Be back shortly."

Bill and his scouts hit their saddles and reined their horses north, the direction from which the mortars had come. About five hundred yards out, they came across three mortar cannons that had been blown up.

"These are our own cannons, men. What do you thank happened here?"

Hiram, circling the area said, "Looks like about a dozen horses went this way, Sarge. Want we should follow?"

"No, not now. Could be waitin' for ya in ambush. Let's ride back the way these cannons come from. See what we find."

They didn't go far before they saw a soldier stumbling toward them.

"Looks like you run into trouble, soldier. What happened?"

The soldier looked at them and could only point back. He said nothing. Bill said, "You men go a little farther. You'll probably find the other artillery soldiers. I'll take this one back to camp. He looks badly hurt."

The men lifted the wounded man up to the front of Bill's saddle and they rode back to camp. The soldier never uttered a word.

Bill took him to the hospital tent jammed with wounded men,

both dead and dying from the attack.

"Here's another one, Doc, found him on the road. He looks to be hurt kinda bad."

With that, Bill turned his horse and rode back to Captain Eli's tent. The Major was still raising cane, so Bill motioned Eli to come outside.

"Our own cannons, Cap'n. Looks like the last three was hijacked and used against us. About a dozen horses headed east on the run after blowin' up our cannons. I found a wounded man on the road. He's at the hospital now in bad shape. My men are hunting the other cannon troops and I can guess what they'll find."

How in the world can things get so out of hand so fast? Eli wondered.

As they uncovered information, all the pieces of the puzzle fell in place. The last three cannons got farther and farther behind as the snow muddied and slicked the road. All but the last three cannons had been in the front of the column where they had help if needed. After nine cannons, two hundred men, horses and wagons passed, nothing was left of the road but a deep mud that caused exhausted men and horses to fall behind. A Rebel recon unit had followed them and found their chance to kill the nine men with the last three cannons. Guns were positioned within firing distance and the gunners waited for daylight to open fire. The last cannons were destroyed so that they could not be used again.

"Well, that clears that part up, Bill, but why do you think no one was sent back to help them? I need to tell the Major what you just told me. Let's go talk to him," Eli said.

When the Major heard the story, he fell back in his chair and sat with his head in his hands. "Good Lord. Some heads will roll over this."

Bill said, "Major, one side can't have all the breaks," as he turned and walked outside with Eli right behind.

Hiram's report worked out about like Bill had guessed, eight men were found dead only half a mile from the cannons. They hadn't stood a chance.

"Cap'n," Bill said, as he looked him straight in the eye, "this is all a part of war. If'n them politicians and big shots in Washington who started this dang war had to get out here in the snow, sleet and freezin' weather and risk their lives, there wouldn't be no war. They don't care about us out here. We're expendable. Just so's they got their power and money, they're happy. That's all, Cap'n. I'm through talk'n. Want we should go scountin' now?"

"Yes, and send me back a message before dark. And, Bill, for what it's worth, I feel the same way."

So Bill and his little detachment of scouts went in two directions examining the countryside. For the first few hours not a word was spoken. They met up at two o'clock as planned, made a fire, brewed coffee and ate cold biscuits.

"I'll be a ridin' back to camp after we eat," Bill said. "Be back in the mornin'. I'll catch up to ya sometime. Just be careful and use your heads."

Bill made it back to camp just before dark. "Didn't come across nobody today, Cap'n. It sure is fine country west of here. Some pretty high hills, too. How far you want us to go? Be kinda hard to send somebody back every day when we get out a ways."

"Bill, we might try letting you stay out three or four days at a time unless you run into something we should know about. Try and stay within about thirty or forty miles of here. Don't know yet when we'll start to move toward Chattanooga. By the way, that man you brought in is doing good."

"That's good to hear. Thank I'll turn in early, been a long day. I'll see ya in the mornin' before I leave."

Bill went to his tent where he and his men had been staying since they arrived. It was quiet as he undressed and lay on his cot. He thought about the shelling of the camp that morning and all the men that were killed and wounded. *Could it have been the men that I tricked and sent in the wrong direction? Should I have handled it in a different way? What about my men? I should have told them to be careful, but they knew to do that,* and as he began drifting off to sleep, he thought about his mother. *She sure had it hard most of her life. I was thirteen or fourteen or – no matter, when we moved to Nashville to Mama's new job at that fancy restaurant. She was the best cook the restaurant ever had Mr. Noble had said. "More new customers coming in every day to eat your food, Mrs. Lions. Guess I'll have to pay you more money." It was the first time we had more than we needed.* Bill recalled that it was also the first time in a long time that his mother began to laugh and be happy.

After they were in Nashville over a year, he and his mother were talking one Sunday after church. "Mama, we're doing pretty good, ain't we? You got a little money in the bank. I've been makin' a few bucks and we seem to be right settled, but Mama, I feel a need to see other places. I'm a little restless."

"Oh, Bill, my baby. You sound so much like your daddy. You

are just a child. You need to get back in school, son."

"Mama, I can read and write and figger well enough. I know it ain't too good, but I reckon I can get by. I feel it's the thang I gotta do."

"Bill you are not but fifteen years old. I don't know what I would do without you here with me."

"Mama, you don't need me. You got a good job. You got lots of friends and I promise to write. I'll just go for a little while and come back. I promise."

It was then that Bill caught his first train going west, but as he promised his mother, he came back in two months with stories of his adventures.

Seemed like he had just closed his eyes and the morning bugle call was sounding. *Can't believe it's mornin' already, but it's gettin' daylight outside. Better go check in with the Cap'n.*

Eli was writing a letter to Sara. "Bill, my son, Roger, is going on ten years old. Man, it has been a long time since I've seen them."

"Cap'n, I'll go to breakfast then come back and take your letter to the mail tent on my way to my scout detail."

So, Eli wrote a quick letter to Sara leaving out the details about the war.

Darling Sara,

I think this camp will be moving out in a few days going to the Chattanooga area. I expect we will face a large force of resistance. I am not looking forward to what is to come, but it can't be avoided.

As I move through my days, they are filled with a longing

for you and home. I hope to see you and Roger very soon.
Your loving husband,
Eli

"What a beautiful morning," Sara said to herself as much as to Roger. "I just love this time of the year." Little patches of snow were visible up and down the valley that flowed through Lamb's Creek. As she and Roger stepped out the door a feeling of fear about the war overcame her and she said, "I sure wish your Daddy was here with us. I hope everything is alright with him and your grandfather."

Each day Sara found that she would have fleeting moments of peace and tranquility followed by disturbing thoughts. "It's a strange feeling to have our men gone so long," she said as she and Roger walked towards the store. She slowed her walk as she continued along thinking to herself. *This is going to be a special day in my life. Could this be a premonition? Good I hope, but what if something has happened to Eli. I've got to think of something else.*

Roger ran ahead and was waiting in front of the church for her to catch up. "Mom, I'll see you at lunch." Missy was the schoolteacher as well as the pianist at church.

"Good morning, Missy. Do you need help today? Looks like you have a room full."

"We have six new ones this morning. The Hinsen children are here. If I need your help, I'll let you know."

A half block from the church was the store and Sari Lynn was sitting on the porch bench in the sun. "You sure are looking chipper, Sari Lynn. You must be feeling better," Sara said as she sat down beside her.

Her bruises were mostly healed and the splints had been taken off. "Miss Sara, I want to help you in the store. I need me something to do. I have been idle long enough and I am a fast learner."

"Sari Lynn, I would be glad for your help, but don't you think it's too soon? What does Dr. Samuel say?"

Sari Lynn blushed and said, "My doctor said I could do anything I wanted to do."

Everyone in the community knew there were feelings between Sari Lynn and Dr. Samuel Lamb.

"Sari Lynn, would you do a favor for me and go tell Samuel that I would like to see him? Can you stop by on your way and tell Reverend Willis the same? I'll be here in the store." Sara's feelings of anxiety were becoming stronger than ever. She began to be frightened. *I'm sure there is nothing to this. I just need to relax.*

"Of course I will, Sara."

"Good morning. You wanted to see me?" Samuel asked as he arrived at the store.

"Yes, Samuel, let's go inside. There's something I would like your opinion about. It may just be my silly imagination."

"Hello, Samuel. Hi, Sara. Isn't it a beautiful day outside this morning?" the Reverend asked.

"It sure is Reverend, but I'd like to talk to you and Samuel about something. I really don't know how to explain it, but I feel there may be something going to happen to Eli. Samuel, with your studying medicine do you think people can have these kinds of thoughts and they be more than just imagination or melancholy?"

"Sara, I minored in the field of psychiatry and it's an area that's highly discussed these days. Not much is known about the mind but there are many theories. Tell me about your morning and what it is that's weighing on your mind?"

"This morning I got up happy and in a good mood. The day started out fine. I thought, *this is a perfect day,* and then in almost the same moment I was sure Eli and Daddy were in real bad trouble right then. These feelings are getting worse, Samuel, almost overwhelming. What is this I'm feeling?"

"Sara, some call it intuition, some a sixth sense. Of course there are many that say there is no truth to it."

"What do you say, Samuel? Is there something to it?"

"I don't know how to answer that. Just try to relax. What do you think, Reverend? Do you have some insight from the scriptures?" asked Samuel.

"None I can put my finger on right now. I do believe God in some cases gives people a special insight into what's going to happen, but I cannot say this is one of those cases."

Their thoughts were interrupted by Sari Lynn's voice, "Sara, here's the mail. The mail rider just came by." Sari Lynn gave Sara the small stack of mail for the community.

The store served as the post office for Lamb's Creek. Sara quickly flipped through the letters and laid them on the counter, all but one. It was from Eli, dated only ten days ago. None of his previous letters had been delivered within so few days. She felt weak. Her hand holding the letter began to shake. "It's from Eli," she said in a faint voice. Samuel caught her before she hit the floor.

They brought her to the bed where Sari Lynn had been sleeping for the last few weeks and bathed her face with a cool wet cloth. She slowly opened her eyes and then sat upright on the edge of the bed.

"You fainted, Sara. You saw that the letter was from Eli and fainted. Are you all right? How do you feel?" asked Samuel.

"Yes, I think I'm alright. As for how I feel, I'm having difficulty understanding it myself. Samuel, would you read the letter to me?"

Samuel read the letter and watched her as he read. "I cannot see anything in the letter out of the ordinary. I think you may be under too much stress."

"No," Sara said, almost too loud. "Eli's in trouble or will be soon. I know it for sure. I have to go and find him. Can't you see he needs me, Samuel?"

"Sara, wait a day or two and see if you view things differently. I'm going to give you a sedative and you'll be able to rest. When you wake up, you might feel better."

"I will try it your way, Samuel, but if I don't feel different, I must go and find Eli."

After sleeping for four hours, Sara woke. She started to get up but felt too weak. She lay back down and was instantly asleep again.

"Must have given her a big dose, Doctor," Reverend Willis said. "She's been asleep for six hours. What are we going to do if she insists on trying to go find Eli?"

"I don't know. She just might be right. She may see something that we don't. Now it's our turn to wait and see."

Mid-afternoon Sara got up still groggy. "I can't tell how I feel, Samuel. My head feels muddled. What time is it?"

"It's two o'clock. You need to eat and drink something. That will help you feel less groggy."

Roger was out of school and Sari Lynn had prepared a hearty meal. As they ate, Roger asked, "What's wrong, Mama? You look like you don't feel good. Can I do something for you?"

"No, I don't need anything. I'm just a little woozy. I'll be all right in a bit. If you all will excuse us, Roger and I will go home and rest. I know I will feel better tomorrow. Can someone watch the store the rest of the day?"

"Yes, we can do that," Samuel said, "but maybe Sari Lynn should stay at your house with you tonight."

"No. We'll be all right. We will get a good night's rest and see you in the morning."

By dark, Sara had made up her mind. She would go and find Eli and she would take Roger with her. He was only ten years old but she felt he was capable to make the trip. She couldn't let the others in town know what she was doing or they may try and stop her. She would leave a note telling them what she was doing. *We will go tonight.* Sara wasted no time. She caught the old plow horse and bridled him. Eli had taken the good riding horse, but Old Gray would do just fine. There was no saddle so Sara folded two blankets and tied them on. *We'll need more blankets, coats, clothes, and food... Lord, where will I put all the supplies we need? The wagon is a two-horse wagon so that won't work. A travois, that'll work.* She and

Eli had a travois and she was familiar with how it worked. Working frantically, she hitched up the travois and loaded all their supplies and woke Roger.

"We're going on a trip, Roger, to find your daddy. You can ride Old Gray and I will walk. We'll take turns. Just don't go to sleep and fall off."

"Mama, do you know where to find Daddy?"

"No, son, but I think he's somewhere near Chattanooga. I believe we'll have help when we need it. It will take a week maybe longer. Just pray with me that we will stay safe."

At ten o'clock that night, Sara and Roger left Lamb's Creek in search of her husband. The night was cool but not freezing. She put extra clothes on Roger but knew she would stay warm walking. *Lord, I know you are telling me to go and I pray for your guidance and direction. Please keep Roger and me safe and watch over Eli and Daddy. I thank you, Lord.* "Get up, Old Gray. Let's go."

At last Sara was on her way and she knew she was right.

CHAPTER ELEVEN

"Cap'n, me and my men ain't come across no Rebs at all the last three days. We thought we'd come in and see how thangs are goin' and if'n you got some new orders. Maybe catch up on eatin' some vittles, too."

"We do have new orders. We'll be leaving this camp in the morning. We'll break up into three companies. It'll be easier that way. You and your men go to the chow hall, get something to eat and rest up a little while. After you've rested, we'll go over our plans for you and your scouts. And Bill, if you see Orville send him to me."

"Right, Cap'n. I'll send my boys around to find him."

They found Orville and Bill relayed the message that the Captain wanted to see him.

"Boy," Bill said to Orville, "there might be some hostile days ahead. You stay close to the Cap'n and watch out for him but don't tell him I said to, okay?"

As they were walking to their tent to rest up a while, Hiram said, "Sarge, you must expect to see a lot of shooting at us in the days to come. Reckon it might be kinda bad?"

"I reckon it will, boy. I want all you men to be careful and don't do anything foolish. Wanna bring you all back home to Lamb's Creek."

After a couple hours of rest the scouts walked over to Eli's tent where he, the Major and Orville were waiting for them.

"Bill, Orville will be information runner between the Major and me on this excursion. I want four of your scouts to scout ahead of our company and keep in constant contact with us. Each company has their own scouts. You men need to get together so you will know the scouts in each company. We want no upsets. Orville, your first assignment is to go to each company and give them a request in reference to this excursion. I'll write you an official request in a minute. Bill, we have no communication with Washington at present so I want you and one of your men to ride north with a message that I'll give you. I don't know how far you will have to go before you can get an open line. Do you remember the camps as we came through them?"

"Thank so, Cap'n. Them Rebs cut the lines again?"

"They must have. We've had no contact for the last twelve hours. Bill, who do you want to ride with you?"

"Reckon I'll take the Tater. Somebody needs to watch out for 'im."

"You four men can go to your tent. I'll have the scouts from the other companies to meet you there. Orville, here's the request. Go to the other two commanding officers and let them read it. You're dismissed."

"Now, Bill, I don't want to write this message down. You and Hiram will have to remember it. You are to somehow get this message to someone in authority. Mr. Lincoln if necessary. We don't have enough ammunition, food, clothing or medical supplies to fight a skirmish let alone a full-scale battle. I feel the South is as bad off as us, but we must get these supplies. Tell them this request is from General Atwood, and we need these things on the double. They will know where to send them. Any questions?"

"Cap'n, that's a long ride on horseback if'n I have to go all the way to Washington. Reckon the lines are open?"

"Don't know. They may be when you get a little farther north."

"We made this request two weeks ago and the supplies may be on their way, but we need to make sure they know what kind of shape we're in."

"Bill, this whole camp will move out in the morning so when you deliver your message, head back the best way you can towards Chattanooga. We will try and save a little action for you and Hiram. Be alert."

Bill and Hiram rounded up two fast horses each, gathered necessary supplies and headed north at a gallop. Bill said, "We've got us a long way to ride, boy, keep ya eyes open."

Sara and Roger were headed toward Chattanooga over a hundred miles away from Eli. "Mama, it's starting to get daylight. It's your turn to ride. My bottom's getting numb. Old Gray is a little bony."

"Let's continue on until we find a stream. Then we'll stop and rest a while and cook some breakfast."

A little ways further they found a small stream, stopped, unhitched the horse and staked him out where the grass was plentiful. Roger built a small fire and gathered more sticks while Sara began breakfast. After eating, they lay on a blanket to rest and both went to sleep.

Sara woke to the sound of Roger's voice. "Mama, Mama, Old Gray is gone. I'll go see if I can find him."

"Oh, Roger, we should not have gone to sleep. You go up the creek. I'll go down. If you don't see him in a little ways, come back. Don't go too far."

Around the first bend Roger found Old Gray with his picket rope tangled in a bush. He called out, "Mama, here he is! I found him."

Sara felt a great relief when she heard him call out. She turned and walked back to camp. "We have to be more careful," she said as he came into camp leading Old Gray. "If we lose our horse, we'll be in big trouble. We have to have a system."

"I guess it's about noon. We must have been asleep five or six hours. Let's pack up and go a little further then camp for the night. Let's not try to travel at night. It's too dangerous."

"Mama, we can't go much further today before it get's dark, can we? Just wait till morning. You said we were in no hurry and I think Old Gray could use more of this good grass."

"Well, I don't think it'll hurt anything. That may be a good idea, but let's make sure this time the picket pin is deeper in the ground."

Roger gathered wood for a fire so Sara could prepare and afternoon meal. He and Sara talked. She told Roger about the anxiety she had the day before, the letter from Eli and her decision to try and find him. "It's like some great force is compelling me to make this journey."

"Mama, do you think Daddy is alright? I hope he isn't hurt."

The Union troops had been on the go for five days with only slight resistance, mostly small roving bands of gray-clad soldiers who were trying to get out of the way.

Johnny was now in charge of the scout detail. Late on the fifth day, he rode into camp just as they were setting up small temporary pup tents. He found Eli and stepped out of the saddle saluting. "Rode in Captain Eli to let you know there's a lot of cannon fire about fifteen miles ahead. We started to go closer but I thought you might want to know about it this evening."

"You did right, Johnny. It'll be dark in an hour or so. Are your scouts out of danger?"

"Yes sir. They are well hidden and waiting for orders."

"You stay the night here, and we'll talk strategy after supper."

The entire camp of two hundred men was more like a ghost camp than one of living, breathing soldiers. The men were awed to silence by the sounds of cannon fire and the sight of flares from explosions lighting up the western sky.

"Must be quite a battle over there," someone said. "Be our turn next," someone else replied, and then no one spoke for a long time.

"Captain, what are my orders? Should I go out tonight?"

"No Johnny, our orders are to move out at first light. Get up early and go to your men. You should scout around towards the fighting. Stay well back and avoid contact if possible. We should be there about noon. You come back and meet us at nine or ten with a report, then we'll go from there."

Two days after Bill and Hiram left camp with their message, they returned to their previous campsite. Only half a dozen tents were set up. A guard halted them as they rode up to the tents.

"We're scouts from General Atwood's army, boy," Bill said to the guard. "There be any officer here?"

"We have a Sergeant in the last tent, but he's hurt."

The two scouts went to the tent where the Sergeant lay on a cot his leg in a bandage. "Is there a telegraph here, Sarge? We got a message to send."

"Nope, another fifty miles I would say if it's working."

"Thanks, we're in a hurry."

"You game for a midnight ride, boy?" Bill asked Hiram.

"Game as you are, Sarge. Let's change horses and get."

As they rode, they changed horses every couple hours. By mid-morning they were challenged as they entered a large camp by a river.

"We are scouts from General Atwood's troops and need a telegraph."

The guard called for the Corporal of the Guards. "These men say they're scouts from some General and are asking to use a telegraph."

"Come with me. You can talk to Captain Charles." They were introduced to the Captain in charge of communications.

"Do you have a workin' telegraph? I have to send a message to Washington."

"Yes, we do. Let me see the message."

"Nope. Can't do it. It's not writ down and it's for Washington from me."

"Sergeant, who do you think you are talking to like that?"

"Cap'n, my name is Bill Lions. I'm a Sergeant and a scout sent direct by General Atwood with a unwrit message to President Lincoln in Washington. You want to question that? We been ridin' nigh on two hundred miles with an urgent message. I demand to see somebody who can help me. Now."

"Follow me, soldier. We'll see about that. You can stay here, Private."

"No, Cap'n. He's part of this. Come along, boy."

The Captain was fuming as he turned and walked briskly toward headquarters.

"Stay here until I see someone inside."

The two scouts did not stay but followed the Captain inside the tent.

"Major, these simpletons come here demanding to send a message to the Capitol and even to the President. I tried to tell them..."

"Bill, Hiram, what are you doing here?" Major Darby asked smiling.

The Captain's eyes revealed shock and his mouth hung open.

Bill said, "Cap'n, best close ya mouth. You might swaller a bug."

"Dismissed, Captain Charles," the Major ordered.

"Glad to see you two men. How are things? How is Eli?" Major Darby asked.

They explained their mission to Major Darby and that they were ordered to personally see a message was sent to someone with authority to respond."

"Men, it seems you made an unnecessary ride. The needed supplies should be in their hands as we speak. Atwood's troops may get one-fourth of what they need. Chattanooga is about to explode. Men are being sent there from wherever they can find them. Some don't even have guns, just grenades or whatever they can arm themselves with. The Rebs are in worse shape. Many go without weapons, without even shoes on their feet. It's a real blood bath with thousands dying on both sides."

Major Darby opened the flap at the entrance of the tent and called on Captain Charles. "Go on over to the mess hall and tell the cooks I have two special guests for dinner. I want the best for my friends." He turned back to Bill and Hiram, "Enough talk of the war now. Let's sit down to a meal and some conversation."

"The Captain gave you a hard time, didn't he?" asked Major Darby. "He's trying to make an impression. His daddy is a Major, same as me, a real good friend. The boy just needs a few more lessons in humility. I think you might have helped him out with that."

After supper they talked of old times, of Lamb's Creek, experiences they had building the community and of hopes for the future.

The next morning, Major Darby said, "Tell Eli hello for me and I hope to be going that way in about a month. Good luck, men, and may God bless you two."

After handshakes, they left camp. Captain Charles scoured at them as they rode away, still not fully understanding what had happened. Bill looked dead in the Captain's eyes and said, "Cap'n, better watch these scouts. They could be Generals in disguise," and laughed heartily as they rode out of camp toward Chattanooga.

The sky was turning pink in the east when Sara opened her eyes. She saw that Roger was still asleep, rolled in a blanket. Her thoughts immediately went to Old Gray. She looked towards the creek and the horse was standing with his eyes closed. "We must have driven the picket pin deep enough this time, Old Gray. You're still with us," she said softly.

Sara made a fire and put water on to boil. "Time to wake up, Roger. You can help with breakfast." Cooking and eating didn't take long and by the time the sun was up, Sara and Roger were on the way south.

"Mama, how do we know where to go to look for Daddy?"

"We don't know for sure. The letter he wrote said he and his men were going to be sent to Chattanooga and Reverend Willis said that was south. So we are going south until we find someone to talk to."

They rode to near sundown stopping twice to rest and let the horse graze a few minutes. *The country is beautiful,* Sara thought to herself. The hills were getting much higher here. "There is no way we would be able to go far without the trails through these mountains," she told Roger.

When it was time to stop for the night they passed through a narrow opening between two ridges. Once through the ridges, the land opened up to reveal the loveliest valley Sara had ever seen. "This reminds me of Lamb's Creek," she said.

"Mama, someone must live here. There are cows everywhere. Maybe we can find out where we are. Let's go a bit farther and see."

There was a draw off to the right, a cabin with smoke rising from the chimney and a good-sized barn with horses in the corral. Someone was walking from the barn towards the house.

They nudged Old Gray signaling him forward.

"Hello," Sara called out, as they got closer to the house.

A woman stopped and shaded her eyes with her hand, then walked towards them. "Land a notion. Where'd you two come from? We never have anyone come from that direction. Who are you? I'm sorry, don't mean to be impolite. I'm just surprised. You must be tired. Come in. Then we'll talk."

A tall, skinny black girl stepped outside as they neared the house. "Winnie, take these folks' horse to the barn and tell your daddy to unhitch and feed him. We're going to have company for supper."

"Name's Claire Allen. My two hands and I live here. We hardly ever get visitors."

"We don't want to impose, Miss Allen. We're just passing through and saw your place. We don't know where we are for sure and thought you might tell us. We are trying to get to

Chattanooga. Are we going in the right direction?" Sara introduced herself and Roger to Claire hesitant to offer too much information about why they were traveling to Chattanooga.

"I want to tell you right off, Sara, that you and your son can't go there right now. There are a lot of people dying between here and there. A war is going on and that's where most of it is happening. A dozen or so Rebel soldiers came through here yesterday. This morning twenty Yankee soldiers came through trailing them. They said the Rebs have been raiding through the area, stealing livestock. The soldiers are starving is what they told me. Said, 'I better not try and stop them if they come back to get my cattle. They might just burn me out.' I have two sons in this war, Sara, one wearing blue, the other gray. Tell me what kind of sense that makes. None at all to me."

Claire and Winnie cooked a meal for their guests. Sara and Roger hesitated to take the food under the circumstances. Claire insisted that they eat and conversation went on for what seemed like hours.

"No close neighbors around here and it gets mighty lonesome since my boys left home. Almost thirty miles to Chattanooga," Claire said, "and no other house less than fifteen miles. This area is sparsely settled with too many hills and not many valleys large enough for farming and cattle."

"I bet you two are getting tired. Guess I talk too much. There are two single beds where my boys used to sleep. Just go in there and make yourselves at home. We'll talk more in the morning."

Sara and Roger were exhausted, thankful for bed. They fell asleep moments after lying down.

The following morning, Sara woke to the smell of bacon frying and coffee dripping. Roger was already up and had walked down to the barn. Old Gray was eating corn and seemed content.

One of Claire's hands was pitching hay to the horses in the corral and singing something to himself.

"This sure is a fine place," Roger commented. "How many cattle do you have?"

"Don't know but we's got plenty to care for," answered Old Mo. I think they's callin' you. Breakfast must be ready."

Roger walked back to the house with Old Mo. "Wash up and come eat," Claire said, "before it gets cold."

Claire, Sara and Roger ate at the table in the dining room and Winnie and her father ate in the kitchen. Roger thought it was strange for them to eat at separate tables.

"Can't I talk you into not going any further south? I'm telling you it will be very dangerous."

"What we are doing is most important to us, Claire. We do appreciate your hospitality and concern but we must go on."

After breakfast Claire told Winnie and Old Mo to go and hitch up Sara's horse. After good-byes, Sara and Roger continued on their mission.

About one o'clock Roger wanted to stop and take another turn at walking. That's when they heard the first cannon fire. "What was that, Mama? It shook the ground."

"I guess we found the war, Roger. That was a cannon."

Having lived with her father who was a career soldier, Sara had been on military training bases and knew the sound of cannon fire. This, however, was no training mission. Six loud booms followed the first fire and more answered from another place.

"Mama, I'm scared. They aren't shooting this way, are they?"

"No, they are not shooting this way, but they aren't far off. Picket the horse, but don't unhitch him. I am going to climb that hill to try and see what is going on. You can come if you want."

Sara and Roger slowly climbed to the top of the hill while the cannons continued to blast away. "Mama, I can see them. Look!" They looked down on a wide meadow with trees on either side. From their vantage point they could make out shadows of soldiers in the trees.

Sara quietly told Roger, "They shoot each other with cannons first if they have cannons, then they charge each other."

"What a stupid thing war is," said Roger.

What was unknown to Sara, Roger and the soldiers was that half a mile away someone else was looking down on the same valley from the top of another hill, watching.

A little while later, the cannons stopped. "Maybe they are going to charge, Mama. Can I watch?"

They sat, waited and nothing happened. After a while Sara said, "They may not charge since it's getting so late. They may wait till morning to continue and if that's the case, we may be able to go see if Eli is here somewhere." Hurrying, they made their way to the bottom of the hill and pulled the picket.

"Roger, get something white. We'll make a flag."

The only thing he found white was his long handle underwear. Sara found a stick and they made a flag as they went around the hill that separated them from the battle. Sara led the horse. Roger sat on its back and waved the flag.

When they were close, someone called out loudly, "Hold your fire," and on the other side, the same thing, "Hold your fire, men."

Sara held her breath as she, Roger and Old Gray slowly walked to the middle of the meadow and stopped. Roger continued to wave the flag. Soldiers on both sides stood and walked to the edge of the meadow. An officer in a blue uniform left the line and started towards her. Then, an officer in gray did the same.

The men approached Sara and she found herself unable to speak. She waited until the man in gray said, "Ma'am, do you know what you are doing? Are you all right?" The one in blue said, "Can we help you, ma'am? People are dying here now on both sides. What is it you want?"

Sara's throat was very dry, and Roger was still waving his long-john flag.

Finding her voice she said, "I'm looking for my husband, Eli Roads. Is he here?"

"You're what, ma'am? Did I hear you right?"

"I'm looking for my husband, Eli Roads. Is he here?" She almost screamed.

The officer in gray said, "Well, never in a thousand wars could this happen. I'll have to live to tell this story even though no one will believe it."

"Ma'am, what color does your husband wear?"

Sara had to concentrate on what he was saying. "Blue. He's wearing blue."

"He's not here," the Union officer said.

"Oh, Lord," Sara said. "I risked Roger's life for nothing."

"No ma'am, for your husband. I wish my wife loved me that much. Hey Reb, now that we've been stopped by this young lady, how about a truce for the rest of the day?"

"Sounds like the thing to do. Thank you, ma'am. You must be an angel from above."

There was a wild yell from both sides. Sara saw that the men had walked out into the meadow and were able to hear their commanders agree to a truce.

"Ma'am, would you like to take a break and visit a while?" The officer in blue asked.

"No, thank you so much. I must find my husband," and she and Roger walked on through the meadow with the men calling, "We hope you find your husband."

CHAPTER TWELVE

Two soldiers dressed in blue uniforms heard cannon fire and rode their horses to the top of a hill east of the firing. Under cover they watched the battle as each group fired with a deadly accuracy, trying to destroy the other.

"Answer me a question, Sarge."

"What do you want to know, Tater boy?"

Hiram looked at Bill so surprised that he almost forgot his question. "Sarge, you just called me by my name. I didn't think you remembered it. Can't believe it, Sarge."

"What's the question, boy?"

"Oh, yeah. Why do men like those down there try and kill each other? They don't even know one another."

"Somebody up in Washington told them to, so they do it. Just like you and me. We take orders from them that take orders and so on till it reaches the top. The ones at the top is the ones to blame."

All at once, the firing ceased.

"Reckon they fixin' to charge each other, Tater. Hold on."

"Sarge, do you see what I see? That's a boy waving a flag and a woman. Is that what you see?"

"Yep, right through the middle of a battle. Look at them officers walkin' out to her. Well, dog my cats, that beats all."

"Sarge, look at them blues and grays mingling together and not shooting. This can't be happening."

"Well, boy, we just seen us a miracle. What next? Look, the woman's comin' this way. Let's watch and see where she goes. This might be interestin'."

They followed Sara and Roger from cover, not wanting to reveal themselves. As Sara and Roger rounded a bend, Hiram in a low voice said, "Sarge, these people are being followed. Look, two blue soldiers are sneaking up on them. Going to be trouble. No doubt about it."

Sara and Roger were talking about what had just happened when two soldiers stepped from behind a large boulder.

"Missie, hold on now. Ain't no need to be in such a hurry. We just seen what you did back yonder. You are quite a gal, yep, quite a gal."

Sara moved to step in front of Roger.

"Now, you just hold on, missie, we just want to talk."

"Mister, we don't want any trouble. Just leave us alone. We don't have time to talk," Sara said, trying to keep her voice steady.

"I say you going to take time. Willie, shoot the kid if she don't do like I say. Now, you just come over here and don't cause no fuss."

As the man reached out to grab Sara, she heard another voice say, "Soldier, if you as much as touch that woman, the top of ya head is gonna disappear. Now, just back away."

The soldier looked to the voice and relieved to see blue uniforms, smiled and said, "Well, lookie here, another Yankee. You just have to wait your turn, mister, we saw her first."

"Do I have to tell ya again? This lady's husband happens to be my good friend, and if'n you and your friend don't get outta here mighty quick, you won't be leavin' at all. Now get before I change my mind."

The two men turned around and at a brisk walk, almost a run, went back the way they had come.

"Bill, thank God! You just saved our lives. What are you doing here? Where is Eli? Is he here? Oh, tell me he is."

"Mrs. Roads, we need to hurry up and get away from here. Those two men just might get some of their buddies and come back. We'll talk along the way."

Bill answered Sara's questions, explained his and Hiram's orders and talked about the recent visit with her father. They told her the Major was doing fine. Then Bill had questions for Sara. He wanted to know what she and Roger were doing here in the middle of a war. Sara explained her concern for Eli and that there was no question she had to find him.

"You just can't go 'round stoppin' battles like ya just did. You was lucky, Miss Sara, mighty lucky."

Hiram moved ahead of the small group to scout the trail. "Don't want no surprises," he said as he rode off. He came back a little while before sunset. During his scouting he found a good camping place less than a mile away from where Bill, Sara and Roger rode. "It's just off the trail, Sarge, but well hidden with water and grass for the horses."

Before dark, camp was made, wood gathered and Sara was preparing supper. The task helped her deal with the anxiety she felt from the day's events.

"I want to thank you again for being there this morning to help Roger and me. This proves to me there is more to this than just going to find Eli. I know we will find him. I know he needs us, too," Sara said.

As the Union Army continued to move west, the terrain became more and more hostile. The hills became mountains, the passes and trails fewer and smaller. Johnny and Captain Roads were talking while taking a break.

"Captain, when we get on the other side of this mountain, it opens up a bit, but it will take some doing to cross over the mountain. We've managed the terrain thus far, but half a mile ahead there's a rockslide to be moved to make the path passable for the cannons and wagons. Sir, two of those rocks are as big as the wagons. You might want to ride ahead and take a look."

"Johnny, is this the only way you scouts have found to cross this mountain?" asked Eli.

"Sir, we went north and south twenty miles and this is it. In fact, the other companies might have to come this way if they can't find another route. Scouts from the other companies are supposed to let us know if they do find another way. So far, we've heard no word on optional routes."

As they talked they rode to the rockslide. Once there, they

climbed the slide to the other side and saw that it was impossible to pass unless the boulders were moved. Eli said, "Johnny, go talk to the artillery Captain and have him bring up two of the cannons. We may be able to blast them two boulders. I think it's worth a try."

The cannons were set in place. The blasts were loud but didn't seem to do much good.

Eli ordered the artillery Captain to charge the cannons with as much powder as was safe and try again.

"Give it another try," the artillery Captain told his men, "but this time move the cannons a little further to the side." The big guns sounded again and one of the boulders crumbled. With another round, the other boulder was gone.

"Okay," said Eli. "Get some men and horses up here and get this mess cleaned up."

"Mighty good thinking, Captain Roads. This rockslide is slowing us down a bit, but once we get through, we should be able to make up a little of the time lost," Johnny said.

Three hours later they were on the move again.

"We've been making good time the last few days, Johnny. A couple more days will put us close to where we need to assemble all our troops."

"In the morning you and your scouts need to move ahead of us, check out the terrain and look for enemy troops."

"The men are already doing that, Captain. I'll head out now if it's all right and find out what's ahead. Be back in touch as soon as I find out."

"All right, Johnny, be careful. Without a doubt, we're nearing the Rebel army. They'll have their own scouts and patrols out."

The next day about noon Johnny found his men.

"When we saw that big roan horse coming through the woods without you on it, we got worried. Where were you, Johnny?" one of his men asked.

"I didn't want to get shot. I saw you boys but didn't know for sure it was you. I circled around and came up behind. Did you find anything we need to tell the Captain about?"

"There are about a thousand southern boys thirty or so miles ahead. They seem to be waiting for somebody or something. Can't tell what, maybe food, supplies or ammo. Some of them boys don't even have shoes on."

"We'd better start back to Captain Eli and tell him what you found. It's probably important," Johnny stated.

The scouts rode into camp just as the sun was setting. The sun shining on clouds gave them a blood red hue. "Not a good omen," one of the scouts said. "Not at all."

The four scouts and Eli sat around a campfire eating supper and talking about the Confederate troops they had spotted.

"They didn't seem to be too concerned, Captain, just looked to be resting or waiting for something."

"Did you see any cannons? Were they dug in?"

"Didn't see any and didn't look like they expected the Union Army to be anywhere around. Didn't see any signs of scouts. Do you suppose they even know we're near?"

"I would bet on it, Johnny. Don't ever underestimate the enemy. You say there are about a thousand? And they're thirty or forty miles ahead?"

"That's a fair assessment of the situation, Captain. Are we going to confront them?"

"Our orders are for the three companies to reassemble, move on to Chattanooga and take possession of the Confederates."

"I think you four scouts need to split up, two go north, two south, locate the companies we're to assemble with and come let me know where they are. Make sure to tell them what's going on with us."

"We have sufficient supplies to confront a force their current size but not enough for several thousand."

The next morning at sunup the four scouts moved out on their mission. Thirty minutes later Eli and his company moved out west toward the Rebel army. Eli's troops made twenty miles with no resistance.

Eli was puzzled over the lack of enemy forces. One expected this close to the enemy to navigate around scouts and recon patrols. Eli expected more intelligence once his scout patrol returned.

Eli, his troops and the other two companies were unaware that the Confederate Army watched as they split their forces and marched west.

The Rebel troops were luring the Yanks into a death trap. They had nine hundred troops camped out in a long valley while the larger group moved into the trees and hills out of sight. After the Union scouts left they moved the nine hundred men down the valley to the west making tracks that could easily be followed.

Eli's new inexperienced scouts were duped into thinking there were only nine hundred poorly-armed Rebels. They reported to

Eli that the Rebel troop of about a thousand had departed. "Everybody's gone, Captain. The troops had been there for sure, but they must've been called back to Chattanooga."

Eli was not convinced. Something was troubling him. *Why did the troops leave just now? I sure wish Bill and his scouts were here. I wonder why he and Hiram haven't returned. I hope they're all right.*

That night Eli could not sleep. He was tired but sleep would not come. He finally decided to write a letter to Sara. He would mail it as soon as he was able.

Darling Sara and Roger,

We are not too far from our destination point of Chattanooga. We haven't come in contact with the enemy as of yet, but I have to believe that we will soon. I'm unable to sleep tonight and thought it a good opportunity to write to you. The moon is big tonight just like the last night we were together. There are no moonflowers, but tonight more than ever I feel your presence near me. I cannot wait until we are together again.

I love you with all my heart, my love.

Eli

Eli thought of Sara as he drifted in and out of sleep. He could not know then how things would soon take a turn for the worst. By seven o'clock the next morning, Eli's troops were on the move. When they were about five miles from where the Rebel camp had been seen, Eli, riding next to Orville said, "Orville, I want you to stay close today. I may need to send a message. In fact, go tell Lieutenant Donaldson to take a platoon of men up front and help with the artillery. Tell them to move slow and be watchful. Then you come straight back to me."

A little farther into the valley, Eli called a halt. He rode up to where the cannons were in line and told the Artillery Captain to wait a few minutes while he sent a scout unit ahead to see what was over the next rise. "Be ready with those big guns, Captain. Something's not right here."

The scouts galloped their horses over the rise and a little later returned saying, "Captain, the tracks show the Reb army still moving west. We scouted several miles out. Nothing up there, sir."

Orville looked at Eli and said, "What's wrong, Captain? You look mighty nervous."

"Something's wrong, Orville. I can feel it. Move slow and keep the cannons at the ready."

Slowly the company moved forward into the valley. *The trees,* Eli thought, *had the scouts checked the woods on each side of the valley? Surely they had.* "Orville, ride to the front of the column, stop them from going any farther. Send the scouts back to me. I need to talk to them. Now."

A few minutes later, the scouts returned with Orville. "What's up, Captain?"

"Did you men check out the woods and beyond on each side of this valley? If not, go do it now. We'll wait here until you do."

Before the scouts could turn their horses, a cannon blasted a deafening sound to their rear. Then, pandemonium broke out from all sides.

"The trees," cried Eli, "shoot into the trees."

Their cannons roared back at the Rebel troops. Men fell.

Others maintained their ground and shot back at an unseen enemy. "To the woods, men," became a repeated yell. "We're sitting ducks out here in the open." Eli watched in horror as the Union Army was cut to shreds. Somehow many of the men ran toward the woods. Mortars had reached their cannons.

Oh, Lord, Eli thought as he tried to pull the wounded to cover in the woods. *How did I not see this in time?*

Orville was at Eli's side yelling, "Let's go, Captain. We have to find cover." Before they made three steps, the shell hit that ended the battle for Eli and Orville. They lay among the devastated artillery unit and the hundreds of dead and wounded men. Some had made it to the trees only to be met with more Rebel troops firing at them.

After what seemed a lifetime, in reality only minutes, over eight hundred Union troops were dead or fatally wounded with two hundred taken prisoner. Three hundred Confederate soldiers were dead and many more severely wounded.

One of the Federal Officers, a Washington observer, was overheard saying, "Good fighting men. This is a successful day. I'm proud of you men, mighty proud. I watched it all from the top of this hill. Yes sir, a mighty good day."

The evening before the battle, Sara and Roger caught Bill up on the happenings in Lamb's Creek since he had been away. Sara talked about the Paine family and Sims, the court marshal and firing squad, and Samuel Lamb's return home. "There hasn't been any trouble since the trial and execution."

"Always knew they'd end up like that," Bill said.

"Mama, is that the kind of moon you told me about the last night Daddy was home? Look how big and bright it is. I wonder if he might be looking at it right now. I'll bet he is."

"I suspect he's looking at it as we speak and thinking of us."

"Miss Sara, I reckon you and the boy better get some rest. It's been a long day. Tater and me will clean up the dishes and take turns on watch. In the mornin' we'll figger out what to do."

"Sarge, where do you suppose Captain Eli is now? Think they ever made it to Chattanooga?" Hiram asked. "It can't be too far from here."

"Maybe they've made it to Chattanooga if he ain't run into the Reb Army. You take the first watch, boy. Wake me in three to four hours."

The sun was already up when Sara and Roger woke the following morning.

"What are you and Hiram going to do now? Are you still scouting for the Army?" Sara asked.

"Yes, we are, ma'am. Reckon we'll try to find our outfit and see what Cap'n Eli wants us to do. What are you and Roger going to do? You still goin' to try and find the Cap'n?"

"Yes, we are. I still feel he's in trouble and needs our help."

"Well, ma'am, being we going the same way, we might as well travel together. Be safer that way."

"Thank you, Bill. After what happened yesterday, I will feel safer traveling together."

Breaking down camp took only a few minutes and they were

on their way. A heavy frost was on the ground but where the sun shone on the ground it had started to melt. Sara thought it strange that everything could appear to be so serene and quiet on the surface. The only sounds were the soft sounds of their horses walking and the birds chirping.

"It doesn't seem that only yesterday we heard cannons firing and a full scale battle going on. It's so peaceful today," Sara said.

"Ma'am, it can change mighty quick. One minute peace and quiet and the next minute people dyin' all around you.

"Tater, why don't ya ride on ahead and take a look-see what's up there. Got me a feelin' all of a sudden. Don't want to get caught unawares. We oughta be gettin' close to our people or the Rebs. We'll just go along slow."

An hour later, Hiram came back with a report. "Sarge, the place is crawling with Rebs. I haven't seen that many in one place, ever. Looks like they have at least twelve to fifteen cannons. They're just sitting around not talking or moving. Just waiting for something."

"Can't be good, ma'am. We got to find you and Roger a place to hide till we know what's goin' on. That little holler back a ways might be what we're lookin' for. Let's check it out. We can't be out in the open. Some of them Rebs might come ridin' back this way."

They crossed the creek and rode back to the holler. They found an overhang that offered a good place to hide. A group of cedars concealed most of the opening and Bill thought that unless someone was looking for the entrance they would just ride on by.

"Ma'am, you and Roger just stay right here till me and Tater check out the situation. We oughta be back in a little while."

After leaving Sara and Roger under cover of the overhang, the scouts galloped back the way they had come. Before they could see the soldiers, the loud blasts of cannon fire shook the ground. The gunfire that followed was an unceasing sound.

"Somebody's in a peck of trouble, Tater. Let's ease up a little and see if we can tell what's goin' on."

"Maybe we can see better from the top of that hill, Sarge."

The two scouts tied their horses and climbed to the top of a hill overlooking the battle zone. They could barely see the men the Rebel soldiers were shooting at but they could see literally hundreds of Rebel soldiers. The Union cannons fired in return and Union soldiers began returning fire and running to the woods directly into the line of Rebel fire. Soldiers dressed in blue and gray fell, but the Union troops were out-numbered and in a relatively short time overcome by the enemy. Those that survived were quickly surrounded, disarmed and taken captive. The scouts watched as hundreds of dead and dying soldiers covered the meadows and Confederate troops advanced from the trees on both sides of the meadow.

"Caught in a cross fire," Bill said in a weary voice, "never had a chance."

"Think that may be our unit out there, Sarge?" Hiram asked. "If it is, there aren't many that survived that battle."

"Don't know, Tater. Can't make out a thang. We sure can't go down there now. It might be cleared out by mornin'. Then we'll see. Better go back and make sure Sara and Roger stay put. She just might try and ride right into the middle of this mess."

The two scouts untied their mounts and without a word rode

back to where Sara and Roger were hiding. They thought that she and her son were gone until they rounded the group of cedars and saw them standing together. Fear was evident in their faces. Once Sara and Roger recognized Bill and Hiram they relaxed a bit.

"We heard you coming, but couldn't know for sure it was you. We have been so frightened, Bill. Tell us what happened. There was so much shooting. Was it Eli and his troops out there? I so hope not. It sounded so horrible."

"Don't know ma'am, couldn't tell who it was, only that it was a useless slaughter. Probably three or four thousand Reb troops caught our soldiers in a crossfire and not too many survived. Those that did were taken prisoner. God help their souls."

"I have to go and see if Eli is out there, Bill. Come on Roger we have to see."

"Can't let you go, not now, Miss Sara. You wouldn't have a chance. Battle fever's ragin' down there. They would shoot ya on site, woman or not. We'll have to wait till mornin'. They might be gone by then. If not, their fightin' blood might be cooled down."

"If he's down there, Bill, I know that God will watch over him. Oh, why do people have to kill one another? Why aren't the ones that want this war out there fighting? The spineless cowards."

"Mama, Daddy may not have been in that battle. He's probably somewhere else."

"I sure hope you're right, son, but even so, just think of all those men killed and injured. They're all someone's son, husband or father. Their families will never see them again. Why, tell me why, Bill, did these hundreds of men need to die?" and Sara let herself cry.

"Can't give ya a good reason, ma'am. Guess there's a lotta reasons, but none of them will justify all these deaths."

"Bill, what if Eli and Daddy are out there dead or injured? Why can't we just go take a look?"

"Ma'am, like I told ya, them Rebs or Union Soldiers, makes no matter the color of the clothes, are celebratin' a victory over the enemy. It'll take 'em all night to calm down. Won't do to go down there now. Tater and me are goin' out a ways and make sure nobody comes around without us knowin'. We'll be back about dark. Won't be long now."

They had all been close enough to hear the cannons exploding round after round, rifles popping and Sara could imagine men falling in piles literally covering the ground. *I have to stop thinking about this,* she thought to herself. *I have to think of something else.*

To get her mind off the horrible thoughts of war, Sara said, "Roger, come and sit by me. Let's talk of the good times when we were all at home together. Remember when we would be at the community store and people would come by and bring something to trade for the things they needed. Then others would come by and trade for those things. No one had much money but money's not needed when people share what they have with others."

Sara hardly slept that night, thinking about the possibility of Eli and her father being on the battlefield suffering from injuries. Before daylight she was up. She nudged Roger and said, "Time to wake up, son. We have a lot to do today." Bill and Hiram came walking into camp as Sara was hitching up Old Gray.

"Ma'am, it won't be light enough to see for another hour. Tater, you build up the fire and make some coffee. We'll leave by first light."

Sara was anxious to get started but she realized that Bill was right. They couldn't see anything right now anyway.

"Now ma'am, we can't just go tearin' down there. We gotta go slow 'n easy. Might still be snipers waitin' for those that may come to pilfer around."

Sara said, "Lord, be with us today and keep us safe and if Eli is out there, help us to find him." After she prayed, she felt a calmness that she had not felt in a long time. Sara had faith that God would answer her prayer.

The sun was beginning to shine when they reached the west end of the valley where the battle had been fought. Sara saw there was a light fog that the sun only penetrated in rays here and there. Smoking holes, where the cannon balls hit and exploded, added to the eerie feeling of the scene. As they neared the valley the smell of death, blood and gunpowder overwhelmed her.

"Wait a minute," Bill said, "before ya walk out there. Roger, find that white flag you had the other day and we'll tie it to your horse so it can be seen if'n somebody's watchin'. Now, Miss Sara, Tater and me can't ride out there with ya so we'll travel alongside ya in the trees. Take it slow. Ma'am, maybe the boy oughta go with us. There's some awful sights out there."

"No," Roger said. "I have to go with Mama. We have to find Daddy if he's here."

Sara and Roger slowly walked out on the field of battle and as they moved from one body to another, they witnessed firsthand the devastation of war. Some men didn't seem to be wounded at all. No signs of being shot. Looking at the open eyes of the dead caused Sara to shiver. *They seem to have wanted to say "mama" or "darling" or "why am I here?"* Sara thought. Some were blown to bits, only parts of their bodies remained. Some were just boys seemingly no older than Roger. Sara recalled a conversation with Bill when he said a boy can pull a trigger easy as a man and the bullets were just as deadly.

"Mama, this man is still alive. He's trying to say something." Sara ran to where Roger was kneeling beside a soldier. One of his legs was blown completely off.

"Roger, go get the canteen off the horse."

"No need, ma'am," the wounded man said in a barely audible voice. "I'm already dead. Just can't seem to let go. Now that you're here, maybe I can. Thanks for coming," and he died.

"Mama, how can we find Daddy in all of this? Suppose we don't recognize him even if we do see him?"

"We'll know when we see him," Sara assured.

Sara and Roger weaved themselves back and forth through the carnage looking for Eli, the husband and father they loved and had not seen for almost a year and a half. As they moved through the bodies, someone would moan in pain and they'd try to find who it was. Mostly, they could not, but when they did, they'd give them water and talk to them.

"Do you know if Captain Eli Roads was in this company?" Sara asked. No one was able to give her confirmation to the question. So on and on they moved looking, hoping to find Eli.

"Mama," Roger yelled, "come here quick! I think this is Orville." Sara dropped the reins of Old Gray and ran to where Roger stood. Another soldier was lying across his chest. When they managed to pull the body off Orville, they saw that his left arm was blown away.

When Sara saw Orville she started heaving but had nothing left inside. She had already done that several times.

"Mama, I think he's dead. He isn't breathing."

Sara tried to locate a pulse but could not. Feeling helpless she started to weep saying, "If Orville is here, there's a good chance Eli's here too." Then she knelt next to Orville's limp body and prayed, "Help us, Lord, to find Eli." They moved slower and with more caution back and forth through the bodies.

Sara saw a reflection of something bright. It was on the neck of a soldier that was lying facedown. The shiny object was hanging from a little chain. She walked over and saw that it was a silver dime and she knew that she had found Eli. It was the lucky dime that Samuel Lamb had found when he was a child. Samuel had saved the dime and given it to Eli. Eli cherished the coin and Roger had put it in Eli's hand the day before he left to join the Union Army. "It'll bring you good luck, Daddy." Sara didn't have the strength to call out for Roger. She just knelt beside Eli and cried.

Roger saw his mother crying and ran to her side. "Is it Daddy? Have we really found Daddy?"

"Yes. See the dime around his neck? Help me turn him over, son."

Instead, Roger ran to where Old Gray was and took the flag and started waving it. Bill had said to wave the flag if they found Eli and he and Hiram would come to help. Roger led the horse to where his mother was and in a few minutes, Bill and Hiram were there beside them.

"Bill, we've found him, but I can't feel a pulse. See if you can. Oh, please let him be alive."

"Miss Sara, I can't either. Let's wrap him in blankets and strap him on the travois. We have to move outta here as soon as possible. The medical core and burial detail will be here in a little while escorted by a guard unit. We can't be here when they arrive."

A short time later they were back in the woods under cover, moving back the way they had come.

"Bill we have to stop and really check Eli. Maybe he's not dead but unconscious. We didn't check him for wounds. It won't take but a few minutes."

"All right ma'am, but don't get ya hopes up. I didn't feel a pulse. He has a bad head wound and the front of his shirt is stained with blood."

"Tater, you build a fire and heat some water. I'll help Miss Sara check the Cap'n's wounds. We need to clean him up anyways. Ma'am, we gotta undress him down to his shorts, wash him up and clean his wounds. I have a small medical kit in my saddle bag."

Eli had a serious head injury and several places on his body where shrapnel penetrated and burned his skin.

"Bill, I cannot feel a pulse nor can I tell if he's breathing, but I think he may be alive."

After taking care of his injuries and bathing him, they again wrapped him in blankets and moved out. It was late afternoon when they decided to stop. "We'll make an early camp this evenin'. I know you and Roger are tired. I'm kinda tuckered out myself. Guess we travelled at least fifteen miles. You and Roger sit and rest. Tater and me will do the fixin'. Tater, you thank you can catch a mess of fish for supper?"

"Reckon I can, Sarge. You taught me everything you know and catching fish is one of the things. Roger, you want to join me on a fishing trip?"

They moved Eli under a huge old oak tree. Sara dipped a pan of cold creek water and used it to make a cold washcloth for Eli's forehead. Again, she felt for a pulse and found none, nor could she tell if he was breathing.

"Bill, there's a farmhouse we should reach by tomorrow evening. We'll stop there overnight. Maybe we can borrow another horse or a wagon. If we can, it'll make travelling easier."

After a fish supper the two scouts cleaned up while Sara and Roger planned their journey home. Sara continued to put cold towels on Eli's forehead.

"Mama, what if Daddy's not alive? What if he doesn't make it? Will we take him home and bury him?"

"Yes, son, that's the least we can do for him. I can't stop thinking of all the soldiers we saw this morning. Bill said all the bodies will be put in one long ditch and covered up. Their loved ones may never know what happened to them or where they are buried. At least we'll know where your Daddy's grave is, and I think he would like that."

"Bill, would you come here? I need you to check something. Does Eli's hand feel warm to you? I have been checking his pulse and even though I can't find any, his hand feels warm."

Bill felt Eli's hand and neck and reached under the cover and felt his foot. "Ma'am, you're right. He's gettin' warm. He must have a fever. See if you can get a spoon of water in his mouth. He has to have water."

Sara could not move for a few seconds and then she screamed with joy, "Thank you, Lord. Thank you." Everyone in the camp was cautiously optimistic.

"Loosen the blanket a might," Bill said, "but not too much. Don't want him to get cold, just cooled off a bit. Not much water at a time, just a few drops. Don't want him to strangle." Then he looked at Sara and said, "We need a doctor. Maybe he's got a chance now."

"Samuel Lamb is a doctor. He's back at Lamb's Creek, but that's forty miles away."

"Tater, you thank you up to a long ride? You can take my horse."

"Thought you would never ask, Sarge. Be there and back as soon as I can."

"Wait. The farm I was telling you about is north of here. It's on this trail, Claire Allen's place. They have several horses if you need another one. I want you to stop and tell Claire what has happened and to send a wagon with a bed. We'll meet them on the way."

The moon was bright and Hiram left camp at a trot leading Bill's horse by the reins.

"Ma'am, Old Gray is kinda tired, but if we take it easy he'll be all right. Roger and me will pack up. You keep gettin' a little water in Cap'n Eli."

"Boy, don't put out the fire yet. We need to make up some

medicine. You know them willows down by the creek? Go cut me some limbs and brang 'em here."

Roger ran to cut some willow limbs. Bill got out a small pot and put about two cups of water in it and held it over the fire. He added a couple spoons of sugar. Roger brought the willow limbs and Bill peeled a handful of bark off and put it in the pot to boil.

"Let's finish loadin' up while this stuff cools off."

When Bill's brew cooled off, Sara got a small bit of it into Eli. They strapped him on the travois and slowly started north. The moon was big and full and there was a chill in the air. No one felt like talking. Sara was praying, *"Lord thank you for helping us find Eli. I always knew that we would, and Lord, watch over him and if you can see fit, make him well again. Thank you, Lord."*

Roger also was asking God's blessing on his father.

As Bill was leading Old Gray, he also felt compelled to talk to God. *"Lord, I don't rightly know if'n you have time to listen to one like me. I've always been sort of a rascal, but Lord, I don't try to be hurtful to other folks. I just can't seem to be what I oughta be. I enjoyed the time I went to church and heard preacher Red Willis talk about ya and what your Word says and I seem to come up short. I'm not askin' for myself but for Cap'n Eli and Miss Sara and Little Roger. A bunch of men died yesterday in that battle and a lot of 'em probably were good men. Somehow Eli is still alive and I believe it's because of you. It would be a shame to take him now, Lord, 'cause his family done got their hopes up. I'm tryin' to say would ya see fit to give Cap'n another chance at life? I'll be thankin' ya, Lord."*

The miles began to fall behind them as they continued to tread up the trail stopping every hour to let the old horse rest a few minutes. About four o'clock in the morning, the wagon from Claire's farm arrived. They transferred Eli to the wagon that Claire had prepared with a makeshift bed. They continued on the way to the farm.

As the sky was turning pink in the east, the wagon pulled up to the house and Claire and Winnie ran out to greet them.

"Sara, let's get your husband into the house. We'll put him in the room where you and your son stayed the other night."

"We need to dress his wounds right away, Claire."

"Winnie, hurry and heat some water. Warm the broth we made earlier. I'll get some clean bandages."

"Miss Sara, here's a jar with the fever medicine we made. Try and get some down him. It'll help him," Bill offered.

"Bill, I still cannot find a pulse and I can't tell that he's breathing, but his body is hot with a fever. The good thing is he doesn't choke on the liquids, the bad thing is that his injuries are looking worse."

"I have some salve," Claire said. "It's supposed to be for open sores."

After cleaning and treating his wounds, they gave Eli some of the fever medication a few drops at a time and then a little of the broth. After covering him they went into the kitchen and ate a breakfast of bacon, eggs, biscuits, homemade jelly and coffee. After eating, Roger went back to sit with his father and Sara told Claire what had happened since they left her house a few days earlier.

"Mama, Mama, quick. Come quick, its Daddy," Roger yelled.

"Oh, Lord. Don't let it be," Sara cried as she ran into the room.

"Daddy's eyes are open. Come quick."

Sara stopped at the side of the bed and saw that Eli's eyes were open. She let out a cry as she knelt beside him. "Eli. Oh, Eli," she whispered as she reached for his hand. There was no response from him as she held his hand.

Bill and Claire followed Sara into the room. Claire quietly walked over to where Sara knelt and sat on a chair beside her. "Honey," she said, "he's alive. That's enough for now. He needs time to rest now. This is a good sign."

Sara placed her hand on Eli's forehead and he closed his eyes. "His fever is coming back. Get me a towel and some cold water and loose the covers a little. Let's see if we can cool him off. Oh Claire, I'm so happy. Maybe Doctor Samuel will be here about dark. He'll know exactly what to do."

PART V

The Homecoming

CHAPTER THIRTEEN

About mid-morning the day Eli was carried to Claire Allen's farm, Hiram rode into Lamb's Creek at a gallop. He rode to the store and quickly dismounted. As he stepped up on the porch, Sari Lynn met him at the door.

"Where's the doctor? I have to see him right now."

"He's over at the church talking to the pastor."

Hiram turned and started for the church when he saw the two men coming toward the store. Reverend Red Willis, waving, said, "Hiram, it's good to see you. Is everything all right?"

"Reverend Red, I need Dr. Samuel and I'm in a hurry."

"What's wrong, Hiram?" Samuel asked.

Hiram relayed the story about Sara and Eli.

"Don't know if he's alive or not, Doctor, but Bill should have gotten him to a farmhouse by now about forty miles from here."

"I have a horse in the stable around back of the store. There's a couple extra. You saddle them while I get a few things together."

Hiram took his horse to the stable, saddled Samuel's horse and another and brought them out front. He was talking to Reverend Red about the bloody battle when Samuel walked out of the store with his satchel.

"I don't know what I'll find, Reverend, or how long I'll be. Just remember Eli and the rest of us in your prayers. Let the people of Lamb's Creek know what's happened. See you when we get back." They mounted their horses and rode off.

Eli didn't open his eyes the rest of the day although Sara continued every couple hours to give him broth, water and medication for his fever. About eight o'clock that night the two riders from Lamb's Creek rode into the yard at Claire's ranch. Everyone went out on the porch to greet them.

Samuel said, "Sara, I need to examine Eli and then we'll talk. Everyone but Sara will need to wait outside his room."

As they entered the room, Samuel asked for another oil lamp to be brought in. First, he checked for a pulse and lifted Eli's eyelids then listened for a heartbeat. He removed the bandages and asked for some hot water. As they waited for the water he asked Sara what she had been doing for him. Sara explained that Eli was able to keep down water and broth, that Bill had made a medicine from willow bark and Claire had helped her treat Eli's wounds with a salve. Claire brought in more light, hot water and clean bandages, and then left the room. Samuel began the process to clean the wounds and asked Sara if there had been any noticeable changes in Eli since they found him.

"This morning he opened his eyes for just a few moments, but didn't seem to see or be aware of anything. Can you tell me what you think, Samuel? Will he be all right?"

"Sara, I have to tell you the truth and it might not be what you want to hear. Eli has a severe concussion and that alone is life threatening. He has several bad wounds from shrapnel, but there doesn't seem to be any shrapnel still lodged in his body. You've done a good job of cleaning the wounds. The wounds will heal if we can keep down the infection. The head wound is what I'm most worried about. I cannot tell at this point if he has any damage to his brain. We will only know the extent of injury to his brain with time. His breathing is barely detectable and his pulse is very weak. We in the medical profession have found, through trial and error, that germs can often be the greatest killers in cases like this. Whoever changes his bandages and feeds him needs to wash their hands in a disinfectant like I did before tending to him. Because he opened his eyes, I have greater hope."

"Sara, your health is also very important. You have to get your rest so you can continue to care for Eli. If you'll permit me, I'll give you something to help you sleep. I will sit with Eli until morning. You get ready for bed and I'll be back as soon as I tell everyone what I believe to be true about Eli's current condition."

Samuel gave Sara something to relax and make her sleep. He went into the next room where all anxiously awaited his report. Samuel shared the same information he had given to Sara and ended with, "All of you have done your best, now it's up to God. The best thing for us all is to get some rest and see what tomorrow brings. I'll sit and watch over our patient tonight. I'll see you all in the morning." With that, Samuel returned to Eli's room to begin his vigil.

The next morning Samuel examined Eli and changed his bandages before Sara began to stir. When Sara came into Eli's room, Samuel said, "As soon as you can wash and disinfect your hands, feed him as you normally do. He looks the same but his heart beat seems a little stronger."

When Sara had washed her hands, she began to feed Eli some of the warm broth slowly from a spoon. Samuel watched as she gave him water and medication the same way. She was wiping the dribble from his chin when Eli opened his eyes.

"Look, Samuel, he has his eyes open," Sara said as she grabbed his hand. Samuel stepped in front of Eli but he seemed not to see either of them. "Eli, this is Samuel. Can you hear me? Can you see me? If you can, squeeze Sara's hand." Eli faintly squeezed Sara's hand.

Barely able to feel it, Sara said, "Samuel, he did, he squeezed my hand. Oh, darling Eli, you are going to be all right. Thank you, Lord."

As they watched, Eli closed his eyes again. A minute later he opened his eyes and his lips moved as if he wanted to speak but there was no sound. He closed his eyes and that was all.

"Sara, you prayed for a miracle. This is it. Let's go tell Roger and the others," Samuel beamed.

Samuel and Sara walked in the kitchen where everyone was assembled. The smile on Sara's face let all know that something good had happened. "He opened his eyes and tried to speak," Sara blurted out.

A light snow had started during the night.

"I only just now noticed the snow. It is so beautiful," Sara said through tears. "This is one of the best days of my life. Thank you, God."

Claire Allen hugged her and Sara said, "And thank you Claire for all you've done."

Nothing changed until late in the afternoon. Sara was helping Samuel clean and dress Eli's wounds when he opened his eyes and smiled at Sara and Samuel. "Sara, my love, are you real or am I dreaming?"

"I am very, very real. I thank God that you are able to speak. This is Samuel, Eli. Do you remember him? He's a doctor now."

"Yes, I remember Samuel. What's happened?" Eli asked. His voice was very faint. "I vaguely remember cannon fire, nothing more."

Sara, trying to remember every detail, recounted what had happened since the battle. That was almost five days ago.

Samuel asked Eli if he thought he could eat. "Your body needs nourishment for strength."

"I feel like I could eat a bear, maybe two."

"We don't have that but we can find something for you in the kitchen."

The reality was that Eli could eat very little. "Your stomach has shrunk," Samuel said, "but it'll get better with time. Just take it easy for now."

Sara called everyone into Eli's room and introduced Claire. "She was here when we needed her, couldn't have made it without her. Bill and Hiram are here also."

"Good to see ya doin' better Cap'n. You had a scary time."

After a short while, Samuel said that everyone needed to leave the room so Eli could get some rest. "Rest is what he needs most of all. You all can talk to him tomorrow."

So everyone including Sara vacated the room to let him rest.

Eli, feeling much better, tried to remember what had happened before the battle but was soon asleep. A little later, Sara came and lay down in the other bed and prayed. "I thank you Lord for giving him back to me."

Two days later Eli seemed to Samuel to be a new man. After breakfast he wanted to sit outside in the sun. The light snow had melted. There was no wind and Eli enjoyed the bright sunshine. He asked Bill and Hiram to sit with him. "I want you to tell me what happened out there, Bill. I can't remember anything before or after the cannons."

Bill told Eli that he and Hiram were on their way back from their mission north to ask for more supplies for the company when they met Sara and Roger on their way to find him. "That sure is a spunky gal ya got there, Cap'n," Bill said. He told of Sara stopping the battle the same day they found her, hearing the cannons roaring, climbing the hill, seeing the whole Union company in a deadly cross fire that killed most of the Union troops. He also told Eli that about two hundred men had been taken prisoner. Bill ended with details about Sara and Roger wading through the masses of dead and dying soldiers the next morning hunting for him.

"Cap'n, they seen a lot of terrible stuff out there. They come across Orville. He was dead with his left arm blowed off. Don't know exactly where the Major is now. We left him further up north a few days before the battle."

"I wish that I could remember, but I just cannot. Samuel says some memories may come back to my mind some day."

"Cap'n, what do ya want me and Tater to do?"

"I don't know what to tell you, Bill. I can't seem to think too straight and don't want to tell you wrong."

"Well, Cap'n, we'll just stay around till ya can thank a little straighter. Thangs might come to ya in a day or two."

Eli was taking a nap in the afternoon when Winnie came running into the house yelling, "Somebody's stealin' our cows, Miss Claire. Some sojers are taking our cows!"

"Where they at, girl?" Bill yelled as he and Hiram grabbed for their pistol belts and rifles.

"Out past the barn aways on horses."

Bill and Hiram ran out the back door toward the barn. They saddled their horses in record time. The horses were rested and ready to go. The men rode out the barn toward the back pasture. In moments they reached six soldiers herding cattle toward the fence where another soldier had cut a gap and pulled the barbed wire open.

The two scouts yelled at the soldiers as they came into hearing distance. "What ya thank ya doing? You trying to steal our cows, boys? We don't take kindly to rustlers 'round here," Bill said as he and Hiram rode their horses between the cows and the fence.

The man that had cut the fence threw down his wire cutters and cursing, said, "We're commandeering these cattle to feed the Union Army. What are you two soldiers doing here?"

"We are here with Cap'n Eli Roads, Sarge. I reckon ya better come on up to the house with me before ya get in a lotta trouble. The rest of ya boys better start fixin' that fence. If one cow gets out somebody's gonna answer to this man I got here with me. Tater, ya make sure they do it right. Sarge, ya gonna come talk to Cap'n

Roads."

"And what if I refuse?"

Bill leveled his rifle at the Sergeant and said, "I reckon the next in charge will do just as well as you then."

The Sergeant mounted his horse and he and Bill galloped up to the house and dismounted. "Ya stay right here, Sarge, while I go and talk to the Cap'n." Bill started to go into the house when Eli opened the door and asked what was going on. "This Sergeant and his men are tryin' to steal our cows, Cap'n. I believe his words were 'commandeer them for the army'."

Eli was dressed in his Captain's uniform. He turned to the other soldier and asked if this was so. "Sir, we were sent out to find and collect what food we could and bring it back to camp. The men are starving, sir. We can't get any supplies from up North. We don't have hardly any ammunition left. Just as well walk off and go home."

Eli asked where there camp was and who was in charge.

"Major Alexander is in charge, sir, and there are about two hundred fifty men there. Many of them are wounded and unable to travel. We have had several skirmishes the past couple of weeks and are unable to withstand any more. We're camped about ten miles northeast of here."

Claire had walked outside and heard what the soldier said. "Captain Eli," Claire said, "you can let these soldiers have half of the cattle. That will give me plenty left to tend. I can't rightly let all those boys starve when I can help. My own sons may be in the same situation. Just let these men have them." She turned and went back into the house.

"Okay Sergeant, half the cattle are yours. Have your men drive them through the gate and on to your camp. Don't be cutting any more people's fences."

"Yes sir. Thank you, sir." He rode back to his men. They drove the cattle through the gates, down the trail and were soon out of sight.

Eli and the scouts went into the house. "That was a wonderful thing you did, Claire. A lot of men will not have to go to bed hungry thanks to you."

That evening Eli talked to Samuel about going to try to find his father-in-law, Major Darby.

"Absolutely not," Samuel exclaimed. "You are not as well as you think you are. You could relapse and be worse off than you are now. You lost a lot of blood that your body has to replenish, and I'm not yet satisfied that your concussion will allow you to safely travel. You could go into a coma and that would be bad, maybe even fatal."

After three more days of rest, Samuel could see that Eli was getting anxious and decided that he could travel if he would consent to ride in the wagon on a mattress. Eli agreed and the next morning after an early breakfast the six of them left Claire's farm and started the trip to Lamb's Creek.

"Thank you so much, Claire," Sara whispered as she hugged her friend. I don't know what we would have done without you and all your help. Please come and visit us when you can."

"I'll try and do that this spring, Sara. It would be nice."

The air was cold but the sun was shining bright. All were in good spirits.

"Probably take two days to get home if'n all goes well. You tell us if ya need to stop, ain't no need to hurry," Bill said.

The group stopped twice the first day and that evening Eli was overly tired. He ate very little supper and immediately went to bed.

Sara and Samuel washed their tin bowls in a small creek near their camp. Sara said, "Samuel, I hope Eli is alright. He sure seems tired."

"I think he's fine, Sara. He lost a lot of blood from his wounds. He's weaker than he thought. We'll let him sleep in if he wants. It's only about six hours more until we get home."

Eli was first to rise the next morning and was making coffee when the others began to stir. "What's the matter with you loafers? You going to sleep all day? We're burning daylight, you know."

"Well, well, I thank the Cap'n's pullin' rank on all of us includin' the civilians. Want we should stand at attention and have role call, Cap'n?"

"No need for all that, Bill. We better cook up breakfast. I'm starving."

After eating Eli got Bill and Hiram to hitch up the team to the wagon and said, "I'll be driving the wagon for a couple hours this morning. I need to start doing a little of the work. Sara, you and Roger can ride in the wagon with me if you don't mind."

Bill and Hiram rode in front and Samuel behind the wagon at a brisk but non-tiring pace.

"Eli, I'm so glad you're doing well now. I was worried while you were unconscious. We couldn't tell if you were even alive. God surely answered our prayers. What are your plans now?

Surely you can't go back to war."

"Not now, Sara, not until I can get my memory back or until I know what's going on. From what Bill says, my troops were nearly all killed or captured. I don't know where to go or to whom to report. I think I will send Bill and Hiram back out to scout around and see if they can find out anything."

The weather was warming and the sun was almost hot. As they stopped to rest the horses, Eli explained to the two scouts what he had in mind.

"You men need to visit with your families a couple days and then see if you can scout out any of our Union forces. Try and find out where the Major might be and let him know what's happened. See if he has orders for me."

"Ain't got no family 'round here, Cap'n. My mom lives in Nashville as you know. Guess I'll go see her when this war's over."

"I'll go visit with my folks a couple days," said Hiram. "You might as well come and go with me, Sarge. Then we'll hit the road."

After a while they loaded up and started on the last leg of their journey. A couple hours brought them to the community store. By the time they tied the horses, half the towns people surrounded them with shouts of welcome. Missy wouldn't let Sara's hand go, holding on and telling her how much she had missed her. "I will never let you out of my sight again."

Samuel led Eli to the little bedroom in back of the store and asked that he lie down and rest for a while. "You are not fully recovered yet, Eli."

Reverend Red said that things had been mostly peaceful, just a few minor situations. The militia had taken care of things and done a good job in their absence. He was anxious to talk to Eli. It had been a long time since he left. Samuel motioned Reverend Red to the side and explained that Eli had suffered some bad injuries and needed a lot of rest. In time, Eli could tell the people when he wanted them to know. He explained it would be best to let Eli talk about things in his own time.

Most of the people had gone to their homes when Eli woke that evening.

Sari Lynn had cooked supper for the few that had lingered. As they ate, Sari Lynn couldn't keep her eyes off Samuel.

After they finished eating, Eli, Sara and Roger walked the couple blocks to their home. Someone had built a fire in the stone fireplace and the house was warm and cozy. Eli sat in his chair in front of the fire and let out a big sigh.

"Seems like forever since we've been together like this. Thank you so much for coming to find me. If you hadn't, I would not have made it. You and Roger saved my life. I love you both with all my heart, and never want to leave you again."

"Something made me go to find you. It was as if I had no choice in the matter. Some great power compelled me, I just can't explain. I knew you were in trouble, and that I would find you. God answered our prayers."

The next morning Eli slept in and when he got up Sara and Roger were talking in the kitchen. Roger said, "Good morning, Daddy. I'm going out to feed the chickens and look around. Seems like forever we were gone."

"O.K., Roger, but stay close to the house. I might need you to run an errand for me in a little while," Sara said.

Roger went out the door with a skip in his step and headed for the barn. As he rounded the lilac bushes to the gate, he saw Mr. Hinsen and his oldest son drive a milk cow into the lot next to the barn. Roger ran back to the house and into the kitchen where Eli and Sara were talking.

"Daddy, Mr. Hinsen and his son just drove a milk cow into the calf lot. They are coming this way now."

Sara went to the front door and onto the porch. The Hinsens were dismounting their horses when Sara asked them to come in. "Eli is in the house. Come join us for a cup of coffee. I'm sure he will want to talk to you."

Eli stood and asked them to sit as Sara poured their coffee and offered them something to eat.

"Coffee will be fine, Mrs. Roads. We've already had breakfast. One of my milk cows got out this morning and we found her down by your pasture. Would it be all right if she could stay here until we have time to take her home? My son will come and milk her if you don't mind. We have four more at the farm."

"You can leave her as long as you want, Mr. Hinsen," Sara said, "and I can milk her myself. Fresh milk will be good for a change. Would you care for more coffee?"

"No thanks. We have a lot of work to do. It's good to have you back, and if we can help in anyway, let us know."

The Hinsens left and Sara looked at Eli and said, "You know that he made that story up about his cow getting out. They know we need the milk and butter. The folks here are all so wonderful. I am so glad we're home where we belong. The pantry is full and someone hung a few hams and bacon in the smokehouse. There's enough food for weeks."

"It's very touching how the people treat us, and like you, I feel so blessed. Let's clean up the kitchen. I have to walk down to the store and talk to Samuel and Reverend Red."

The three of them left the house and started to the store. As they passed the church where Missy was teaching school, Roger said he was glad to be going to school again. "See you this afternoon, Mom and Dad."

As he entered, the one-room building exploded with excitement. All the kids yelled, "Welcome home, Roger." Missy hugged him as she waved to Eli and Sara.

Reverend Red came out of the parsonage as they passed and joined them as they walked to the store. Samuel and Sari Lynn met them at the door as they walked up the steps.

"Got a job for you, Rev," Samuel exclaimed as he looked at Reverend Red. "There's going to be a wedding. Sari Lynn said that she would marry me and I feel ten feet tall. Is that how everyone feels?"

They all looked at each other and back at the couple and began to laugh, hug and shake hands with the soon-to-be bride and groom.

"We all knew this was coming, Samuel. Just didn't know when. Have you set a date?" asked Reverend Red.

"No, I just asked her ten minutes ago. Sari Lynn, I guess we got a lot of planning to do and need a place to stay until we can build a house. Someone give us some suggestions, will you?"

"If you two are going to get married soon, you can have the

room in back of the store. It's small but it will do until we can build you a house. If you want to wait four or five weeks, we can…"

"No," Sari Lynn interrupted, "let's get married soon. The room in the store is big enough. We don't need a lot of room or a lot of things now. That will come later. Oh, Samuel, I am so happy."

"You heard her, Reverend, the sooner the better. Today is as good as any. Good Lord, Sari Lynn, are you sure you're ready for this? It's so sudden."

"I'm not going to give you time to back out," Sari Lynn said jokingly and they all laughed, all but Samuel. He was scared, real scared.

All things were put on hold so the community could prepare for the wedding. The first since Eli's and Sara's wedding more than ten years earlier.

Sara worked with Missy to prepare notes for the school children to take home. Once school was out, the children took notes home inviting everyone to the wedding at six o'clock in the church. Missy and Sara made a cake while others came early with dishes prepared for a wedding dinner.

Sara got out the dress that she and her mother were married in and with only minor repairs, fit it for Sari Lynn.

"Oh, Sari Lynn, you are so beautiful," Missy said as she buttoned the back of the dress. "Are you as excited as I am? You don't look nervous at all."

"I'm scared to death. I hope I don't faint."

At six o'clock in the evening, the church was filled to capacity.

Those unable to find a seat stood outside looking through the windows. Samuel and Reverend Red were standing together and Missy was at the piano playing softly. The Reverend gave a nod to her and she began playing the wedding march. Eli and Sara walked first. Sari Lynn, escorted by Bill Lions, walked slowly down the aisle where the men stood. Eli, Sara and Bill went to the front row where three seats were saved for them. Sari Lynn and Samuel stood facing Reverend Red. The wedding march ended and the only sounds that could be heard were the sniffing sounds that came from tears of joy among the ladies of Lamb's Creek.

"Are you, Samuel Lamb and Sari Lynn, sure you want to enter into this ceremony of marriage?"

"Yes," both said in unison, nodding their heads.

"Does anyone here have reason that these two should not marry?" asked the preacher. After a brief pause, "If not, we will continue. God himself instituted marriage between man and woman when he created Eve and gave her to Adam to be his wife. God still sanctions marriage between man and woman. Samuel, do you take Sari Lynn to be your wife and promise to love and care for her, to honor her all the days of your life?"

"Yes, I surely do promise."

"Sari Lynn, do you take Samuel Lamb to be your husband and promise to love and care for him, to honor him all the days of your life?"

"I most certainly do."

"By the power vested in me, I now declare you to be husband and wife. You may kiss the bride."

As Samuel kissed Sari Lynn, people outside began to whistle

and yell, "Hip, hip, hooray," at the top of their lungs. All were in a festive and happy mood, and then the wedding feast and celebration began.

Tables had been set up outside the church and were filled with farm-raised foods of all kinds. Another table had pies, cakes and other assorted sweets.

"Eli, I have never witnessed such a turnout on such short notice and look at all the food. Don't you think that the wedding was just divine?" Sara asked. "Sari Lynn just glowed it seemed."

"Eli, here comes Mrs. Lewis. I haven't talked to her since we came back. Oh dear, I have to tell her about Orville. She shouldn't have to go through life not knowing what happened to him. This is going to be so hard for her. Pray that God will give her the strength she needs to hear the news and go on with her life."

Mrs. Lewis hugged and greeted Eli and Sara warmly and welcomed them back home.

"I wanted to come over and say thanks for all you folks do around here. I heard about Eli's terrible tragedy, and I am so sorry. I'm glad to see you are able to come to the wedding, Eli. Can you tell me anything about Orville?"

Sara knew she had to tell Mrs. Lewis the truth and didn't know just how. "Mrs. Lewis, there isn't any way to make this easy. Your son is dead. Orville was killed in the same battle that Eli was wounded in. I saw Orville just before I found Eli. There were over a thousand soldiers killed in that battle and many were just young boys. Oh, Martha, I am so sorry. I should have come to see you sooner."

Mrs. Lewis simply smiled at Sara and said, "Thanks, Sara. I

know telling me was hard for you. I truly thank you for the truth. I guess he died doing what he liked to do. I do wish though I could bury him here in Lamb's Creek."

Mrs. Lewis reached for Sara's hand, gently squeezed it and said, "Thanks again, Sara. Come and visit sometime," and slowly turned and walked away.

After Mrs. Lewis left, Bill and Hiram walked over to where Eli and Sara were standing.

"Told her about Orville, I reckon. Seen her sad in the eyes. She's a strong woman, Miss Sara. She'll be all right. They say time heals all wounds. Talkin' about time, guess it's about time Tater and me here get back to duty, Cap'n. What ya thank we oughta do?"

"Bill, you and Hiram come by my house in the morning and we'll discuss matters then. Now, just go and enjoy yourself."

The party lasted until after midnight. No one noticed when Samuel and his new bride left the festivities earlier for their little room in back of the store.

Sara and Eli let Roger leave with the Hinsen family to spend the night.

"No trouble at all," Mrs. Hinsen said to Sara when Roger asked to go with his friends. "One more child makes no difference when you already have eleven. We will be glad for him to come."

Sara and Eli left about ten o'clock. Eli felt worn and tired. "We should have left earlier," Sara said as Eli leaned back in his chair with a big sigh. "I didn't realize you were so tired."

"With a good night's rest I'll be as good as new. Wasn't that a fine wedding? I think Sammy was as scared as I was when we got married. We have had a good marriage I think, don't you?"

"Yes, darling, we have had a wonderful marriage, and I think having God in our lives has made the difference."

Eli slept deeply that night. He dreamed of his and Samuel's adventures during childhood. What a good time they had until the tragedy took his parents on their journey to Nashville. Eli's dreams faded and he slept.

Sara quietly left the bedroom a little after daylight and closed the door not wanting to wake Eli. She dressed and built a fire in the stove wanting to get the chill out of the kitchen. Filling the kettle, she put it on the stove to heat. Then with the milk pail in hand, she went outside to milk the cow in the barn. It was colder than she had thought it would be and it had snowed during the night. The cow was eagerly waiting to be milked and fed. After tending the cow, she pitched hay down into the manger and went back to the house. It was beginning to snow again. When she entered the kitchen, Eli had already dripped coffee and was sitting at the table with a steaming cup in his hands.

"How is the milking going? Is she a good milker?"

"The best I've ever seen. We can never use all this milk. I'm sure we can find someone who needs it. It's starting to snow kind of hard and I hope Roger won't have trouble getting home. Do you think I need to go get him?"

"No need for that. The Hinsens will take care of him. Don't worry about that."

A couple hours later there was a pounding on the door. Sara opened the door and Bill, Hiram and Roger were standing on the porch, snow covered and shivering.

"Get yourselves in this house before you freeze. Don't you know better than traipsing around in a snowstorm? You men!"

"Had to bring your youngin' home, Miss Sara, and this could hardly be called a snowstorm. Where I'm from it snows this much in July. This would just be a nice warm day. Is the Cap'n in?"

"In here, Bill. You men come stand by the stove and warm up. I'll pour up three cups of coffee."

"Daddy, can I have a cup of coffee?"

"I said you three men. I was counting you, too."

"Gee thanks," Roger said as he proudly picked up his cup of hot, steamy coffee. "First time I get to drink with the other men. Tastes great, Daddy."

"Bill, you and Hiram better stay here until this weather gets better. No use going out in this. When it does break, I'd like you to try and find out where the Major is stationed. I want details about our company. I know you said that most were killed and captured, but our unit was only a third of the company. Find out what you can about the other two units and let me know. Also, I'd like you to check on Miss Claire and her ranch. She's sitting right in the middle of this mess."

The next morning there was a white blanket covering everything. The sun came out and the sky was a brilliant blue.

"Be a good day for trackin' rabbits, Tater, but we've no time to do that. Best be doin' some soldierin'. Let's go by and tell the Cap'n we're movin' out."

After speaking to Eli and with the Roads' good wishes, the two scouts headed south towards Claire's farm. Bill wondered about what was yet to come.

CHAPTER FOURTEEN

The snow lay in deep drifts along the trail. The sun reflected off the snow making it hard to see. Bill and Hiram had ridden about ten miles when they decided to let the horses rest and paw through the snow for forage.

"Bill, what do you think will happen to Captain Eli? He doesn't seem to be himself. I sure worry about him."

"I talked to Dr. Samuel a few days ago. He said it might take a long time for Eli to get over that concussion. The other wounds are healin' up good. Said he might never be the same as he used to be. If'n it weren't for his wife, he wouldn't even be here. Ya know somethin', Tater? A man couldn't find a perttier place to settle down than in this here country. After this war, you could find yourself a little filly and raise a family. You could farm, hunt and fish these streams and be your own man. Don't that sound good?"

"You talking about me or yourself, Bill?"

"I'm talkin' bout anybody that had a hankerin' to live that kinda life."

"Bill, she's too old for me, but not for you."

"What you talkin' about, boy? I ain't called no names."

"I saw you couldn't keep your brown eyes off Miss Claire the other day. Don't deny it, Sarge."

"Well, she sure is a looker, but I ain't ready for that. I got ramblin' blood like my pa, boy. Can't seem to take root nowhere. Need to see what's over the next hill, then the next. Somethin' draws me."

"When you find the right woman, you'll change, Bill. Look what happened to Samuel. We were all surprised by the suddenness of his wedding."

"Reckon we done talked enough. Better get movin'."

The scouts stopped early that evening when they rode up on a grove of cedars in a little draw off the main trail.

"Ain't expectin' company, but no one can come up on us in these trees without us hearin' them. Can't be too careful. You remember that."

The heat of the sun had practically melted the morning snow. The men made coffee over a small fire and ate biscuits and bacon that Sara had prepared and packed for their journey.

"Bill, what you said about your daddy today is the only thing I've ever heard you say about your parents. You never talk about yourself, where you're from or anything. I don't even know how old you are."

"Son, where a man's from don't matter. It's what he does and how he acts that matters. Treatin' people right and bein' honest counts, too. We lived from pillar to post ya might say. Movin' here and there. Never in one place very long. Pa couldn't keep a job, didn't want one. Just drug Mama and me here, there and yonder. Grass was always greener over there. When he decided to go to

Denver where he grew up, Mama told him to get a job and send for us once he got settled. Well, he went but never sent for us. Don't know what ever happened to 'im. Reckon I'm about thirty or thirty-two. Lost track somewheres. That's enough talkin' for now. Let's get some rest. Don't guess we need to stand guard since it's just you and me. Sleep light."

The next morning about a mile before reaching Claire's farm, they come across fresh cattle tracks headed northeast.

"Looks like we got us some trouble, Tater," Bill said as he circled around examining the tracks. "Bout six riders takin' the cows on a fast run. Probably Miss Claire's cows. Let's go check on her then we'll get them cows back."

They reached the ranch in record time skidding to a stop at the front gate. Claire opened the door with her double-barreled shotgun pointed at the two riders.

"Hold on, Miss Claire. It's Bill and Tater. We seen the cattle tracks and knew somethin' was wrong. What happened here?"

Claire recognized the scouts and pointed the gun in another direction. Bill realized that she seemed relieved they were there.

"Those soldiers came back yesterday evening and stole the rest of my cattle. They killed Winnie's daddy, Old Mo. We were just going out to bury him when I saw you two riding up."

"Do you know for sure it was the same men?"

"Winnie and Mo were in the barn when they rode up. Mo went out to see what they wanted. The Sergeant shot him. Winnie saw it all take place from where Mo told her to hide in the loft. I didn't even hear the shot."

"It was the same sojers. I seen them plain. It was them for sho.

They didn't have to kill my Pappy," Winnie said wringing her hands.

"Miss Claire, show us where ya want to bury him. Me and Tater'll dig the grave."

"We don't have a coffin, Bill. We didn't know how to build one."

"We can do that, too. Just tell us where the lumber is."

"There should be some in the loft of the barn. The tools are in the tool room in the barn as well."

Bill and Hiram built the coffin. They buried Old Mo on the same knoll where Claire had buried her husband years before.

After the funeral, they all went to the house where Claire prepared lunch. They ate in silence.

"We'll try and get ya cows back, Miss Claire," Bill said as he helped gather up the dishes. "Won't be hard to track them in the mud. They got a good start, but we can ride faster than they can herding cattle."

"No. Those cows are not worth you and Hiram taking a chance getting hurt or killed. I'll get some more cattle after this war is over."

"Ma'am, these men are killers. They have to be stopped or they'll keep on killin' innocent people. We'll just take a look see and follow them a ways. They must plan on sellin' them cows somewheres close."

After assuring Claire that they would not take unnecessary chances, they left the farm and started on the trail of the rustlers. Before sundown, the scouts stopped and made camp. They unsaddled the horses and staked them out.

"We'll catch up to them tomorrow, late I reckon. They done slowed down. We'll just follow and see where it is they're takin' them animals."

"Bill, I can't understand how some folks can just shoot someone like they done Old Mo and steal a woman's cattle. She had already given them half of what she had. It makes no sense."

"I call them kind of folks leaches, Tater. They don't care if a man works his whole life buildin' somethin', if they want it they kill 'em and take it all away, like Sims and the Paines. They kill and take. Makes them no never mind."

The next morning they got started at first light. The day was breaking clear with a chill in the air. After an hour's ride, the hills became fewer and the land was more open with one wide and long valley after another. The scouts took to the trees that lined both sides of the valleys. The strategy insured that if someone was watching they wouldn't be easily detected. Just after noon the scouts rounded a bend and saw the cattle grazing five hundred yards ahead. Most of the soldiers were lying around and two were on their horses watching the cows.

"They must be waitin' for somebody, Tater, or they would be drivin' them cows. Whoever it is must be comin' from the other direction. I don't thank they comin' behind us. Tell ya what, let's circle around and see if'n we can see them before they get here. Maybe we can do somethin' with whoever's coming. I'm kinda curious."

The scouts maneuvered around the cattle camp and hid in the woods a mile ahead of the waiting rustlers.

"Let's change into our civilian duds, Tater. Don't thank it wise to be in uniform. I'll bet it's the Rebs buyin' them cows. Be mighty careful, son."

The scouts had almost given up when a lone rider came easing along near the tree line. He was a Confederate soldier, a Lieutenant riding a dapple-gray horse. He passed not forty feet from where the scouts were sitting behind a rock.

"Howdy there, soldier. That's a mighty fine lookin' horse. You lost or somethin'?"

"Man, you scared the daylights out of me. What are you men doing here? Don't you know there's a war going on?"

"Reckon we do but our little ones gotta eat. We out tryin' to shoot a deer. Ain't seen any so far. 'Bout dark they start movin' some. There's some soldiers with a few head a cows that way 'bout a mile, but they dressed in blue instead of gray like you. Counted six men."

"They're the ones I'm looking for. I need to buy the cows. We need them to feed our men. Good luck with your hunting."

"Wait a minute, officer. Could ya use help drivin' them cows? We sure could use the work."

"These soldiers are supposed to drive them up close to our camp. Maybe you could help drive them on in the rest of the way."

"I'd be mighty thankful for the work. Let me talk to my brother here. See if he can ride with us. Wait just a minute and I'll ride with ya."

Bill talked to Hiram and told him to stay under cover but follow them within rifle shot of the soldiers and close enough to hear them talk.

"You might have to shoot the Sergeant and if ya do, don't miss.

This is life or death. Shoot to kill."

"Bill, I haven't missed a shot since I was eleven years old. I only missed then because my horse jumped."

"Well, don't sit ya horse then. We'll play this by ear. It'll be touch and go."

Bill mounted his horse, which he had tied in the timber. "My brother'll meet us when we move them cows. I'll go with ya and see if they might can pay me and my brother a couple dollars for helpin' drive."

The two rode together talking about the war. The small troop of three hundred men had not received supplies for four months and was in bad shape. A few weeks before, the same soldiers sold them twelve head of cattle, but that was long gone. The Lieutenant said, "This time they are suppose to have about thirty head which would last a couple of months."

When they came to where the cattle and men were, the Sergeant asked, "Who you got with you, Lieutenant?" He did not recognize Bill in his civilian clothes. Then one of the other soldiers jumped up cussing and said to the Sergeant, "This is the man that messed us up getting all the cattle the first time we came for them."

In seconds Bill had his rifle aimed at the Sergeant and his Russian forty-four pistol aimed at the Reb soldier.

"Don't do anything dumb, Sarge. You either, Reb. I got men with rifles pointed at you boys. One stupid move and ya won't ever move again."

"He's bluffing, men, ain't nobody but him," the Sergeant said as he reached for his pistol. They all froze when Hiram's rifle sounded and the Sergeant's head was ripped apart.

"Anyone else want to try? Now, I want each one of ya to slowly put ya weapons down and back away. You can just hand me your revolver, Reb. I sure hate that I had to trick ya, Lieutenant. I really like ya. These cows was stole from a good friend of mine, and we're goin' to see she gets them back. Sorry about your troops. Maybe some supplies will make it to them yet."

Hiram rode out from under cover and over to where Bill sat on his horse with his weapons still pointed towards the men. It was two or three hours before dark when Bill and Hiram decided to get the cattle moving toward Claire's farm.

"What are we going to do with these men, Sarge?"

"Well, son, these men drove these cows out here and they can drive them back home."

"But suppose they try and run? Do we shoot them?"

"Yep, but let's make it hard for them to run."

The five Union soldiers promised to peacefully help drive the cows. The Rebel soldier wanted to know what they were going to do with him.

"Don't know yet, Reb. Depends on how ya act."

"Hiram, I'm goin' to show ya an old Spanish trick. Get me some rope. Can ya make horse hobbles? Cut pieces just long enough so they can step out good, but not long enough for them to run. Put them on the front legs. Then we tie the soldiers onto their horses. Tie their hands to the saddle horn and their feet together under the horse's belly. Then if'n they run, shoot 'em."

"You can't do that to us. We're Union soldiers. You'll be shot for something like that."

"Just ya wait and see what we can do, boy, and we'll just see who gets shot. Tie them tight, Tater. Don't take no chances. We'll ride till we get there, boys. The moon's bright and the cows know the way. They'll not try and run, just ride easy."

They put the cows on the trail towards Claire's home with the soldiers in a group behind them. Bill and Hiram brought up the rear. They had a little over an hour of daylight left when they started and by the time it was dark, the cattle knew they were going home. A little later, the moon came up and the going was easier.

The men were complaining that the ropes were too tight and they needed to stop and rest.

"Tater, did ya ever see grown men act so much like little kids? I swear. Do ya thank they're real men?"

The night passed with no incidents other than the complaints of the men, all but the Lieutenant. He spoke not a word.

At daylight, they were less than three miles from Claire's. Everyone was tired, even the cows, but when the animals neared the farm they began to low and pick up speed.

Claire heard them coming. She and Winnie had the pasture gate open and the cattle filed through the gate, glad to be home.

"All present and accounted for ma'am. Even got us some guests. Thank we can get a bite to eat? Been ridin' all night. I thank our soldier boys are a little tired."

"Winnie, go put more coffee on and it looks like we need to prepare to feed an army," Claire said smiling at Bill. "Are you and Hiram all right? How did you do this? Oh, I want to know everything that happened."

"We'll get it all said ma'am. It'll just take a while. First, we need to secure these men. They're prisoners, Miss Claire. Don't get around them. They're dangerous. Tater, untie their feet and get them off their horses. Let them walk around a bit. Check their hands and see if'n the ropes need to be loosened."

"Take these ropes off, man. You can't treat us like animals," one of the soldiers barked.

"I don't trust none of ya. You act like animals and I'll treat ya like animals. You sit or lay down under that tree and rest while breakfast is bein' cooked, and Tater, keep a sharp eye on them. If'n they give ya any trouble, shoot 'em in the leg first, then in the head. I'm goin' in the house a little while. Reb, you come with me. If I untie your hands, do ya promise to behave?"

"As an officer and a gentleman, I promise."

"By the way, Reb, what's ya name? Mine's Bill Lions."

The two men stopped before going through the gate and looked at each other. Their eyes probing trying to figure out what the other was thinking. "My name's Bob Yates," the Rebel soldier replied, "and I come from McMinn County, east of here a ways. Look, Bill, I got into this with my eyes closed. I didn't know these cattle were stolen, not from a woman anyway. Our men are hungry with a lot of them wounded. Hardly anyone has shoes or sufficient clothing. This war has been hell. I'm one of the senior officers, believe it or not, and only a few of the men knew of this cattle deal. A sergeant in my command was a friend with the man Hiram shot yesterday. They made the last deal and this one."

"Well, Bob, I was here the last time they tried to steal all Miss Claire's cattle. We caught them red-handed in the act. They said they were for their company of troops who was also starvin'. Miss

Claire went and give them half of her cows then. I thought that was mighty good of her. Three days ago the same men came here and killed Old Mo. He was the only help Miss Claire had on the place aside his little girl, Winnie. When they killed Old Mo, they stole the rest of her cows. I had to try and get them back any way I could. Now, Miss Claire don't have no help at all."

"I'm truly sorry about all this, Bill. I didn't know. What are you going to do about me?"

"That's what I gotta figger out. I don't know ya Bob, but I kinda trust ya. I thank if'n ya give me ya word you'll keep it. There's two thangs rollin' round in my mind and we gotta settle it with Miss Claire. One, you can stay and work for Miss Claire six months. Or two, I can take you as a prisoner of war with me and turn ya over to the Union Army. Take ya pick."

"That's not a hard decision for me to make, Bill, but how do you know I won't slip off when you leave? You don't know me."

"No, I don't know ya, but I'm a good judge of men. If'n ya tell me your choice is to stay and help out, I'll believe ya. If'n ya don't do what ya say, I can find ya again. Miss Claire has to make the decision if'n you stay or not."

The men walked on to the house and knocked on the door. Claire told them to come inside, that the coffee was ready.

"Miss Claire, can I talk to ya just a minute in private? I thank it's important. Bob, you can wait on the porch." Claire and Bill walked into the kitchen and Bill sat at the table as she poured them each a cup of coffee. "What do you have on your mind, Bill? You look serious. Is something wrong?"

Bill rose from the table pacing back and forth as he laid out his thoughts about his prisoner. Every now and then, he would stop and just look at Claire and kind of shake his head and walk and talk some more. Bill looked at Claire again nervous-like and said, "Miss Claire, on second thought maybe this ain't the thang to do. He might not be the man I thank he is. If'n he does somethin' he oughta not, I would be responsible. No, we better not do this."

Claire just looked at Bill. It seemed to her that his eyes were big as calf eyes. She had never seen him indecisive and nervous, and it didn't take her long to realize what he was thinking. She was sensitive to her own feelings for Bill and got up from the table and walked over to where Bill stood.

Taking him by his hands, Claire looked up at Bill and said, "I've been thinking of your well being, too, Bill, ever since the other day when you rode off to find those blasted cows. I was hoping and praying that you would come back." She stood on her toes and kissed him lightly on his cheek and went back to the table and sat down.

Bill stood, looking at Claire as if he couldn't believe what had happened. He was thinking, *did this beautiful woman just come over and kiss me? No, couldn't have, not Miss Claire.*

Claire brought him back to reality when she said, "Bill, come sit down. Your coffee is getting cold."

"But, Miss Claire…"

"Bill, you don't have to call me Miss. When two people feel like we do about each other, you don't say Miss or Mr."

"But Claire, this changes thangs. We can't have an enemy staying here with ya. I'll have to take him with me."

"You don't have to do anything of the kind, Bill. Just a

moment ago, you felt you could trust him. I still do. This war has made many good men do things they otherwise would not have done. He's a good man and I don't want to see him a prisoner of war. Just think about it. What would you want if you were in his place? Let's call him in and talk to him."

After the three talked it over, Bill felt better about the arrangement. Bob Yates was to stay at the farm and work for Claire. After six months he would be free to go.

"One thing, Miss Claire, we need to straighten out now," Bob Yates said. "Most of the cattle you gave the Union soldiers went to feed my men, and I need to pay you for them. We got twenty-five head. Here's three hundred dollars if you think that would be adequate."

"No, I gave them to feed hungry men and that's exactly what happened. Even if most went to the Confederate that doesn't matter, Bob. I have two sons, one wears blue and one wears gray. I would give food to either or both sides. I don't need or want any pay, but I thank you just the same."

"That's a mighty good thang you tried to do, Reb, mighty good. One more thang ya need to know, Bob, before we finish talkin'. Miss Claire is spoken for, and I just want ya to know that."

As he spoke, Bill looked at Claire, smiled a big smile and poured himself another cup of coffee.

Claire asked Bob to take food to the others outside.

"Be careful, Bob. Them's mean men," Bill warned.

After the food was taken out, Bill told Claire that they were on an army mission to try and find out where the Major, Sara's father, was and about the condition of their own outfit.

"Claire, I don't know how this thang happened, but I'm glad it did. I never thought anybody could ever care about me. It's mesmerizin'. Now I know what's been the matter with me the last few weeks. I'm in love with ya, Claire. Ole Tater knew the whole time. He said as much." As he said the words, Bill was compelled to take Claire in his arms and kiss her like he had seen Samuel and Eli kiss their wives. "Sure gonna be hard to leave ya now, Claire, but I'll be back. You can count on that."

About noon Bill, Hiram, and the five prisoners mounted their horses and rode south to try to find Major Darby and his troops.

Hiram noticed that Bill had a different look about him as he left the ranch. He seemed to sit taller in the saddle. He kept eyeing him for a while and then with a big grin, said, "You finally came to your senses, didn't you, you old goat? Did you ask her to marry you? I bet you did."

"You got that right, ya mind reader. How'd ya know?"

"It's easy to tell when someone's in love, Bill, even you."

"Okay men, tell me where we find your outfit," Bill said.

"We won't tell you anything. You turn against your own side and help out them Rebs. You ain't nothin' but a traitor."

"Suits me just fine. We'll keep ridin' around lookin' while your hands and feet fall off from them ropes. They ain't comin' off till we get to where we're goin'."

A little later they turned to the west. The soldiers realized Bill was going to keep them tied until they reached their destination about fifteen miles away.

About four miles from the Union camp the party stopped for the night. The men complained about being tied and sleeping on the hard ground instead of a cot.

"You'll make it, boys. Enjoy it while ya can. It's only gonna get worse."

All during the night, the prisoners moaned but what bothered them most was what they didn't talk about. What would happen to them when they reached camp?

CHAPTER FIFTEEN

"Halt. Who goes there?"

"Easy there, soldier." We're scouts with Cap'n Eli Roads' outfit, with prisoners. Need to talk to the commanding officer."

As they were talking, the Sergeant of the Guard came and escorted them to General Martin's tent, the highest-ranking officer in the camp.

"General Martin, sir, some of Captain Eli Roads' scouts are here to see you."

"At ease, Captain. Send them in."

Bill asked the Captain to have the prisoners guarded until the General made a decision about them. General Martin remembered the scouts from almost two years before when they had come from Lamb's Creek to join the Army.

"How is Captain Eli, men? I heard the unfortunate news about his unit being almost wiped out, terrible thing that was. Someone said they couldn't find his body and that he wasn't in the group taken prisoner."

"He's toleratin' his injuries, sir, but still in bad shape."

Bill shared the story with the General about how Sara and

Roger found Eli on the battlefield barely alive. He explained what Dr. Samuel Lamb had shared with him about Eli's injuries and concussion.

"It's a miracle alright, men. I've never heard such a story in my military career. When you see him again, please relay my personal thanks to him for his loyal service. He should stay home and get well. He has done more than his share."

"Sir, there are a couple more thangs I want to talk to ya about. One is the Major, sir, Major Bruce Darby. Cap'n Eli wanted me to find his whereabouts."

"Major Darby is still stationed in Washington. You know they wanted to raise his commission and he said no. Everyone knows him as the Major. He said Major is his name to most folks back home and to change it would mess up everything. The folks in Washington don't understand it, but they don't know the Major. He's quite the man. What is the other thing you want to know, Sergeant?"

"Sir, I have five prisoners outside I need to tell ya about. They're Union troops, General."

"Well, tell me what this is all about."

Bill explained the killing, cattle rustling and selling cattle to the Confederate Army. He explained that he and Hiram had to kill the ringleader of the group in self-defense.

"These are serious charges, Sergeant. Are there any witnesses other than you?" asked General Martin.

"Tater here, sir, was a witness along with the woman who owned the cows and the black girl who works for her. Sir, there's also a Lieutenant in the Rebel army who was goin' to buy the cattle. He can verify my story."

"Bill, this is getting more confusing all the time," the General said as he rubbed his forehead.

So Bill explained about the Rebel soldier and the decision they had come to about him working for Claire. "Thought it best, sir. Miss Claire needs the help and ya don't need more prisoners to feed."

"That part is true, Bill. We need to get this thing settled today if we can. I have to leave in two days for Atlanta for an important meeting. Can you be here in my tent in two hours?"

"Yes sir, General, I can. Oh, there is one more thang that Cap'n Eli wanted to know. What happened to the other two units of his company after they split into three?" Bill asked.

"It was explained to me the southern unit came through without much conflict, but the northern unit got beat up pretty bad. They lost half their men. We're working on prisoner swaps now. That's what the meeting in Atlanta is about. If that's all, I'll see you in two hours."

Bill and Hiram were exhausted from the last two weeks on the go without much sleep. They were ready to rid themselves of the prisoners and head back to Lamb's Creek for a little rest and relaxation.

"Hope this hearing don't drag out too long," Hiram commented as they walked out the tent.

"I thank the General is goin' to hurry this thang up. He's in a mood to get outta here. Don't thank he wanted to have this come up right now," Bill replied.

The two sat under an oak even though it was a little cool in the shade of the tree. It was just a short way from the General's tent. Hiram asked Bill if he and Claire were going to get married and if so, when?

"Don't know 'bout that, son. Just have to wait and see what she wants to do. Now that I've had time to thank, I wonder if'n we doin' the right thang."

About an hour and a half later an escort of guards brought the five prisoners to stand and wait until the General and four officers assembled to start the hearing. The prisoners gave the two scouts dirty looks as they waited. The officers entered the tent from the rear and a Sergeant came out and motioned the scouts to come into the tent. The area inside was large enough to conduct staff meetings. The officers were sitting behind a long table and returned the salutes of the two scouts. The General asked Bill to tell the story as he had related it to him earlier. "Tell us the entire story, Sergeant. Include the part about the Confederate officer whom you captured." After hearing the story again, the General asked the four other officers if they had any questions they wanted to ask Bill. None had questions at that time and indicated they may later.

"Sergeant, I want you to go outside and separate the prisoners. Don't let them talk to one another. Bring them in one at a time." The Sergeant brought in one of the men and stood him in front of the officers.

"Soldier, you are charged as an accomplice to murder, with cattle rustling and trying to sell stolen cattle to the enemy. What do you say to this charge? Remember, you are under oath and if found lying, there will be a charge of perjury as well."

The man was so shaken up that he could hardly be heard as he answered. "It was our Sergeant, sir. He shot the slave. We didn't know what we were doing. He forced us to help him steal the cows."

"Was this the second time you tried to steal these same cows?"

"Yes sir, I think so."

"You don't know for sure?"

"Yes sir, it was the second time."

"Who did you sell the cattle to the first time?"

"Most of them were sold to the Rebs, sir."

"Soldier, would you like to say anything to these officers and myself?"

"No sir, General, I guess not."

"Sergeant, take this man out. Don't let him talk to the other prisoners. Bring another one in."

One by one the prisoners were questioned and their answers corroborated the story relayed by the first soldier. After all prisoners were questioned, General Martin asked the other officers if they had any questions for Sergeant Lions and Hiram.

"One question," one of the officers spoke up, "Sergeant Lions, do you think you made a wise decision concerning this Confederate officer?"

"Yes sir, I do thank so. I believe him to be an officer and a gentleman, just as you men are. He was in the wrong place at the wrong time, sir, and got caught. He needs to pay somethin' for his actions. Makin' him a prisoner of war means we gotta feed him, sir, and Miss Claire lost her help in this mess and needs his help. I figger everybody wins this a way."

"I guess you got a point, Sergeant. There's a first time for everything. Everyone wins but these rustlers."

"Bill, you are dismissed. Go and take care of Captain Eli Roads and let him know that I wish him the best. And Bill, take care of Miss Claire. She probably needs you more than she needs that Rebel soldier. So long men. God bless and thank you for your service in the Union Army."

The two scouts saluted the officers and walked out of the tent.

"What do you think they are going to do with those men, Bill? Court martial or maybe firing squad?" Hiram asked.

"Don't know, son, but I'll bet ya a cool drink a water that they'll live to regret what they done. Let's go home."

The scouts, greatly relieved the hearing was over, mounted their horses and were riding through the camp when they saw a crowd of men yelling and taking bets.

"Let's check it out, Sarge," Hiram commented as he reined his horse in that direction. "I think it's a fight."

"Here we go again," Bill said as he followed Hiram. There was a small man literally beating a larger man almost to death.

"Fight, you yellow dog," the men were yelling. "We thought you could whip anybody. You can't even whip this little squirt."

"He won't even try and fight to protect himself," someone yelled. "Squirt is going to beat him to death."

Bill and Hiram stopped their horses just outside the ring of men and could see that the larger man was knocked out and someone was holding him up while the smaller man kept pounding him.

"My Lord, Tater. Tell me that ain't who I think it is. Look, he's just got one arm. Can it really be Orville?" Bill jumped off his horse, pushed through the crowd, grabbed the little man by the shirt collar and jerked him around. "That's enough, boy. It's over. He's whipped."

"They say he's whipped everybody in camp with one arm tied behind him. I say that's a lie. Let me go. I'm going to kill him. My buddies got bets on that."

"Boy, you make one more pass at this one-armed man and I'll jerk you over my knee and spank ya like a baby. Now, I say it's over."

The crowd quieted as Bill finished talking and the sound of Hiram's pistol being cocked drew attention. The crowd quickly began to dissipate and Bill and Hiram grabbed Orville and led him to a nearby tree.

"Lord, he's a mess," Hiram said as they eased him down.

"Get ya canteen and a rag, son. Let's see if'n we can clean him up."

They washed the blood off as best they could and Orville began to mumble and move his arm trying to push them away.

"Easy boy, it's us, Bill and Tater. We gonna help ya get on that horse. We have to find the medical tent."

"It's two rows over, Bill," Hiram said. "I seen it when we came in this morning. Let's hurry. Orville needs help bad."

"Don't need a horse then, Tater. We'll pack him if'n we have to."

The doctor saw them coming and helped put Orville on a cot. "Is this what the ruckus was all about, another fight?" the Doctor asked.

"Afraid so, Doc," Bill answered.

"This one is in rather bad shape. I believe I know this boy. Yes, this is Orville. He lost his left arm a few weeks ago. I didn't think he would make it. Real depressed, he was. You men know him?"

"Yes, Doc," Hiram replied. "He's from the same place we're from. Can you fix him up?"

"I'll do my best. Now stand aside and we'll see." The doctor cleaned and dressed Orville's wounds and turned to Bill and shook his head and said, "This boy will get over his beating all right. Think he has a couple ribs that are bruised pretty badly which will be painful. It's what's wrong inside his head that worries me, not physical mind you, but mental. Losing his arm has caused a deep depression. In his mind, he's not a man anymore, maybe something even worse than that. He seems to want to punish himself for some reason. This blamed war has affected most everyone in this country. Most of the folks living through this tragedy will never be the same as before."

"Doc, do you know where I can get a horse? I want to take this boy home."

"Are you the men who brought the rustlers in?"

"Yep, guess that would be us."

"Just one minute. I'll get you a horse." The doctor spoke to a young boy just outside the tent and turned back to Bill and Hiram. "He's going to fetch one of the rustler's horses. From what I hear they won't have any need for the horses after all."

A few minutes later, the boy returned with a big Roan horse already saddled and ready to go.

"Good luck men, and take it slow. Orville needs a lot of care.

Like I told you, he's not well."

"We will, Doc, and thank you for everthang you done to mend Orville." They managed to get Orville in the saddle and positioned on either side of him, they rode through the camp and toward home.

"Tater, don't ya get us involved in anything else. You just mind ya own business. You gonna get us killed or worse."

"Now Bill, don't get fired up. If we didn't get involved back there Orville would have been beaten to death."

"I know that, son. I'm just talkin'. Boy, won't Mrs. Lewis be surprised when we show up with her son. She thanks him dead. She'll probably just keel over."

With the sun still high they found a little meadow off the main trail next to a wide, fast running creek.

"Let's take care of Orville first, and then we'll catch us a mess of fish for supper. Ain't had none in a while. Tater, that boy's face looks terrible. His eyes are plum swelled shut. Sure took his self a beatin'. Wonder why he didn't fight back? He coulda thumped that squirt over with his finger. The mind's a wonder."

They managed to settle Orville on a couple of horse blankets and covered him. The air was turning colder. After the horses were staked, Bill and Hiram went down to the creek with fishing lines and worms they found under a rotted log.

They fished in silence and strung their supper on a string before heading back to camp. Orville seemed to be sound asleep. Hiram built a fire, cleaned the fish and packed them in mud as Bill had done many months before.

"That is the best way I know of to cook fish. It's so easy and no skillet to clean up."

After supper, before it was fully dark, the two men fixed their bedrolls and were sound asleep. The next morning Bill awoke to the smell of brewing coffee. Hiram was up before him, which was unusual.

"You going to sleep all day, old man? You sick or something? It's almost sun up."

"Don't get smart with me, boy. Didn't your mama learn ya to respect ya elders? Just for that, you can brang me a cup a that joe and then shake out my boots."

The voices penetrated Orville's sleep, and he opened his eyes as much as was possible. He looked from Bill to Hiram but did not speak.

"You awake, sonny? Guess ya can't sleep with Tater's big mouth a goin'. Brang him a cup a joe, Tater."

"Thought I was dreaming but I guess I'm not. I knew it had to be you because no one else carries on so. Where are we? How'd I get here? I'm really confused, and I hurt all over."

"Found ya yesterday gettin' the tarnation beat out of ya. Doc fixed ya up and we takin' ya home, boy."

The three sat in near silence not knowing what else to say. Along with the coffee, Hiram brought out four-day old biscuits that Claire had sent on the trail with them.

"Better if ya soak 'em in the coffee first. Otherwise, ya might break ya teeth. Know'd a man once, said his wife's biscuits was so hard you had to beat 'em with a hammer before ya could eat 'em. That was when they was fresh."

Orville never cracked a smile as if he hadn't heard.

"Better hit the saddles, boys. We'll be to Claire's 'bout noon."

Hiram and Bill saddled their horses and Orville just sat in a daze not moving, just staring.

Hiram looked at Bill and Bill nodded toward Orville's horse and he quickly saddled him. Bill walked over and caught Orville by the arm and Orville stood and walked to his horse and quietly mounted.

The scouts were concerned about Orville. The swelling in his face was better and he didn't seem to be in any pain, but he seemed completely unaware of what was going on. As they rode, the temperature dropped and the riders encountered a few snow flurries.

"We better get there soon, Tater, or we may be in for a big snow storm. I figger we got about three more miles."

About one o'clock they rode their horses into the barn with the snow so hard their visibility was limited to ten feet. Bob, the new hand, was in the barn cleaning stalls when Hiram opened the door and the men brought the horses into the barn.

"Put your horses in the first three stalls," Bob said. "They're all ready finished. If you want, I'll rub them down and give them some grain. You men go to the house. Miss Claire has a large pot of chicken soup hot on the stove. She said this morning you might be riding in."

The snow was really coming down but Bob had strung a long line from the barn to the back door. "Good thankin'," Bill said as he and the others held to the rope and walked to the house. They stepped upon the porch knocking snow off and Winnie came to the door.

"You mens come in. We's just talking about you. Miss Claire," she yelled, "they's here."

Claire came to the door and hurried them inside. "You men sit down at the table, and I'll fix you some hot soup. There's fresh coffee on the stove. Winnie, pour them each a cup."

"We're gettin' your floor all wet, Claire."

"No matter, it'll dry. Just sit."

All three men were starving, even Orville, whom Bill introduced to Claire and Winnie.

"Orville and his mom are part of our community at Lamb's Creek."

Claire could see there was something wrong with him and whispered to Bill, "We'll talk later."

After they ate, Claire took Orville to the spare bedroom and left him to undress and get into bed. A few minutes later, she went in to get his clothes and hung them behind the stove to dry.

"You men get into some dry clothes and I'll wash these. I have some I think will fit you two."

After changing, Claire and Winnie washed and hung the wet clothes on a line they put up in the kitchen where it was warm.

Bill asked how the new help was working out and talked to her about Orville and the hearing that had been held for the rustlers.

"Bob stays busy and the farm is beginning to take shape again," Claire said. "He eats here with Winnie and me morning and night. Other than that, I rarely see him. He has fixed up Old Mo's room in the barn nice and cozy with a small stove I had stored. Bill, he's a hard worker. Thanks for letting him stay here and work for me. I had no one to work this place but Winnie and myself. Old Mo was good help, but he was getting old and couldn't do much, bless his heart."

Claire and the two scouts passed the afternoon talking.

"My gracious," Claire said looking at the wind-up clock on the counter. It's already five o'clock. Winnie," she called, "it's past time to fix supper."

"You don't have to cook no more, Claire. We're still full from dinner. We can skip supper."

"No, we'll make biscuits and fry up some ham. Bob will come in about six. We usually eat supper at that time. That's how I always did with my husband and sons when they were here, an old habit."

Winnie came in and started frying the ham and Claire made the biscuits. As predicted Bob Yates came in at six o'clock with a pail of fresh milk.

"Smells good in here, Miss Claire. Want me to strain this milk for you?"

"No, Mr. Yates. Winnie can do that. You just sit with the men and we'll set the table."

After supper Bob went back to the barn.

Claire wanted to know if she should wake Orville but decided to let him sleep. He needed the rest. "Bill, you sleep in the room with Orville and we can make a pallet on the floor here in the kitchen for Hiram. It's the warmest place in the house."

Bill talked to Claire about how they had found Orville beat up and the doctor's diagnosis about his mental health.

"Claire, can we stay here a few days? I don't want Orville's mother to see him with his face all beat up. You know she was told that he'd been killed in the same battle that Eli was injured in. She'll be really surprised when he walks in."

"You men can stay as long as you want, Bill. It's nice to have you here with me."

"Do you think we should go to Lamb's Creek and get Dr. Samuel?" asked Hiram.

"Let's give him a couple days and see how he does. Maybe he'll improve on his own."

After the kitchen was cleaned and dishes put away, Claire fixed Hiram's pallet and they all called it a day.

"Mr. Yates will be here about sun up with the morning milk, so be up then, Hiram."

"Seems like all we do 'round here is cook 'n eat 'n drank coffee. I'm not complainin' though. I kinda like it. Night folks," Bill said.

Claire gave Bill a lamp. She took one for herself and all went to bed.

The next two days it snowed off and on. The snow was over two feet deep.

"Ain't seen a snow like this in several years," Bill commented as he and Claire stood by the large kitchen window. "Claire, there's somethin' I want to talk to ya about."

"I know, Bill, I feel undecided about everything we spoke about when you were here last. I can tell it's bothering you. You are a kind and loveable man, and I would not hesitate to marry you if that was what you wanted. I can tell you're having second thoughts though. You just aren't ready yet."

"Claire, you are one in a thousand. I was wonderin' how I was goin' to explain to ya about thangs. You are ahead of me every step. It's not that I don't want to marry ya. I just gotta make sure of some thangs." Bill explained about his own dad never settling down and how he, himself, had a wandering spirit.

"It's all right, Bill. I understand and I love you the more for being honest. If it's to be, it will happen and if not, so be it. We'll still be close friends."

Bill went on to tell Claire about his mother in Nashville. Her employer wanted to marry her, but she said she already had a living husband. Although she loved him she couldn't marry him. "I have to go to Denver and find my father if he's there. He'll have to give her divorce papers so she can marry the man she loves. I know he's declared legally dead, but not to Mama. She has to know for sure. Claire, that Reb ya got workin' for ya, now he seems a stayer and a hard worker. Might thank about him."

"Bill Lions, you trying to find someone else for me to marry? Shame on you."

Orville showed signs of physical improvement. He had started conversing with the others although he was never the one to initiate a conversation. Claire and Orville sat alone on the front porch one afternoon enjoying the warm sun. The snow had almost melted except in the drifts. Bill and Hiram were out in the corral helping Bob put in some new posts. Claire wanted to talk to Orville about losing his arm, thinking it may help him to talk about what he had experienced.

"Orville, losing your arm doesn't make you any less a man than you were before. It may slow you down a bit until you get accustomed to not having it, but it won't take long to adjust."

Orville stopped rocking and just sat still for a minute. He turned his head and looked at Claire thinking about how to say what was on his mind. After some hesitation Orville finally said, "Miss Claire, losing the arm really don't bother me so much. It's that I think God is punishing me for being such a headstrong braggart. I use to wrestle and box for the mere fun of doing it, and I was good at it. So good that most times I could whip any man with one hand behind my back, and I did. I had never been beat, Miss Claire. Oh, I was so sure of myself. But in that battle and with all of my assuredness, I let my Captain and best friend get killed. I didn't take care of him like I should have. God probably said, 'Well, if you don't need that arm, I'll just take it away.' So He did and I don't blame Him. I'm sorry I was such a fool. I'll never fight or wrestle again. I can see now it was wrong."

Claire got up from her chair and hurried over to Orville. She hugged him the way she hoped to hug her own sons again. "Oh my dear boy, you don't know. No one has told you. Eli wasn't' killed. He was badly wounded but is doing much better. Sara, Roger and the scouts brought him here a few weeks ago and Dr. Samuel came here and tended him. He is back at Lamb's Creek."

Orville again didn't know what to say. Claire took his hand and lifted him to his feet. She put her arms around him and squeezed him. "I guess no one thought to tell you about Eli. I think you are wrong about God punishing you, Orville. There are a lot of men that lost limbs that never wrestled before. So many have lost their lives. I think you are punishing yourself and you shouldn't. The effects of this war will be with us all for a very long time. Oh, I'm so glad we talked. You must feel better knowing that Eli is alive."

Tears ran down Orville's cheeks. He was silent. Claire reached up and wiped the tears away with her thumbs. "It's all right to cry, Orville. You'll feel better if you do. Now you can heal your mind and your heart. How about we go in and I'll make us a treat, just you and me. I think a cup of hot chocolate is what we need." The two of them went into the kitchen and Claire made the best cup of hot chocolate Orville had ever had.

"Didn't thank to tell him 'bout Eli. Figgered he knew. Ain't it strange the way thangs work out? Reckon it's time we be leavin', Claire. Need to get Orville home so his mama can tend to him. Soon as I handle my business, I'll be back and we'll talk if'n ya feel there's somethin' to talk about."

The next morning while saddling their horses, Bill motioned Bob Yates aside and spoke to him. "Ya know Reb, since ya got a long time to work for Miss Claire, I expect ya to stay here till your time's up. And one more thang, Bob, I no longer have claim to Claire. If ya thank you can win her with ya southern gentleman ways, she may be open to ya. Just so's ya know, ya better not mistreat or take advantage of her in any way or you will answer to me for it. Be seein' ya in three or four months."

Hiram and Orville were already in their saddles waiting for Bill to finish his talk with Bob Yates.

"You know something, Orville? I think old Bill is getting feebler every day. He used to be the first to mount up. Now I have to saddle his horse and still wait on him to get going."

"You just go ahead and talk boy, but you'll never see the day ya can out do old Bill."

"Bill, you do know don't you, that leaving that young, good-looking southern gentleman alone here with that beautiful Miss Claire is not the smart thing to do. He'll sweep her off her feet before winter is over. I'm telling you, it's going to happen."

Bill had said his goodbyes to Claire away from the others. As Bill rode away he felt an overwhelming loss and expected that Claire felt the same. He thought about how much loss Claire had experienced in her life. She was the only woman that he had ever felt something for and she had made him feel at ease. *She even agreed to marry me. I must be the biggest fool in the world,* Bill thought.

Claire was full of her own thoughts as she watched Bill ride away. The feelings she had for him were stronger than those she'd had for her husband, the father of her sons. *He may come back. And again, I might never see him again. There are so many places he's never seen. Well, I have a farm to tend and Bob can't do it all by himself. I promise myself that in one month I'm going to see Sara and Lamb's Creek. It must be some place. For now, I'm going to stop thinking about Bill, saddle Pearl, and ride the farm to check things out. It's too pretty a day to be sad.*

Claire put on her riding clothes and went to the barn to saddle Pearl. Bob saw her start to bridle her horse. "I'll do that, Miss Claire. Where are you riding today?"

"I plan to ride over my entire property. Want to come?"

"It's a fine day to ride. It'll take me just a minute to get my horse." Bob hurriedly saddled the dapple gray. As they started, Bob said, "It's going to be spring before you know it, Miss Claire."

As Claire rode, she began to feel a release of the sadness that overcame her as Bill rode away. She smiled and remembered a time when she, her husband and their two little cotton-headed boys arrived at this valley fifteen years ago. Her husband had died, but she managed to keep the farm and at least half the cattle. She watched Bob as he rode ahead of her, *that man sure is a hard worker and not a bad looking guy either*. Well, Claire, she thought to herself, *time will work out all matters of the heart, happy and sad.*

CHAPTER SIXTEEN

"Bill, why don't we put these horses in high gear and get to Lamb's Creek about dark? I'm anxious to see my folks."

"No, son, I'm thankin' we don't need to ride in after dark. It might make people nervous with three riders comin' into town that late. They might call out the militia. Be best to get in 'bout mid-mornin'."

Hiram agreed with Bill and they camped about fifteen miles out of town. At sun up they were in the saddle again.

"Now Orville, ya Mama thanks ya dead. Me and Tater here might oughta be there when ya see her."

"No, Bill. Just let me go in by myself. It will be all right."

Mrs. Lewis' house was outside of Lamb's Creek right off the main road. When they came to her lane, Bill and Hiram rode on and Orville galloped his horse up to the front gate. Mrs. Lewis was sitting on the porch swing peeling potatoes. Orville dismounted, opened the gate and started toward the porch. Mrs. Lewis couldn't believe her eyes. She dropped the pan of potatoes and ran towards her son. "Oh Lord, my son," she said. *I knew he wasn't dead*, she thought.

"I'm home, Mama, at least most of me. I'm so sorry that I left you here all alone. I'll make it up to you somehow."

Mrs. Lewis, shaking uncontrollably, wrapped her arms around Orville and said, "Son, you don't have anything to make up for. I just couldn't believe that you were dead when Sara told me about seeing you on the battlefield that day. She found Eli, but I knew she was mistaken when she told me that you were dead. I thank God that you're home, Orville, right where you belong."

"Mama, I have to go see Eli. I have to apologize to him. Let's walk to the store since it's such a pretty day. I'll put my horse in the stable and be right back."

Mother and son walked the quarter mile in the warm, bright sunshine greeting others that had already heard the good news from Bill and Hiram. Eli, Samuel and Reverend Red were on the steps of the store with big smiles and hearty welcomes when Martha and Orville arrived.

Orville immediately apologized to Eli. He said he was sorry he had not taken better care of his Captain. "I knew I was supposed to, but I failed you."

"Orville, first, as your superior officer it was my job to take care of all my men and second, you did not let me down. Now, I want you to forget that nonsense." Turning to Mrs. Lewis, Eli said, "This is cause for a celebration."

"Yes," said Mrs. Lewis. "We sure have a lot to celebrate and be thankful for."

Sara hugged Mrs. Lewis and through tears said, "Oh Martha, we should never have left that battlefield without Orville."

"Sara dear, what happened to Orville is not your fault. It's a miracle that he's home and its time for all of us to rejoice," Martha said.

"Hopefully, things will be getting back to normal in a little while," Eli said to Sara. "The community should plan a get together, maybe a picnic on Sunday after church."

"Yes," answered Sara, "it can be a welcome home party for you, Orville, Bill and Hiram. The townspeople are so glad to have you four back. I can only hope the others will return soon." Word spread throughout Lamb's Creek about the celebratory picnic on Sunday. People busied themselves with preparations for the picnic.

As Orville watched his mother prepare, he said, "Mama, I'm not going to that picnic. I won't make a spectacle of myself in front of the entire community."

"Orville, the people just want to show their appreciation for what you and the other men did for the nation. They aren't coming to gawk at a one-armed man. You have to get out sooner or later."

"I can't Mama, not now."

"Well, think about it. You might change your mind. It's still almost a week away. I have to go to the store. Do you want anything?"

"No. I'll stay and work some in the garden."

On his way to the garden shed for tools, Orville remembered when he and Reverend Red built the shed years ago, when he was just a kid. *A kid maybe* he thought, *but a kid with two arms and a body able to beat any man in a wrestling match. Now I don't even know if I can hoe a garden. Why did I have to be so stupid?*

After cutting down a few of the vegetable plants along with the weeds, he had the urge to throw the hoe across the fence. Orville stopped himself and said aloud, "I have to take my time and be patient. I can learn to use one arm." Then, he remembered all the men he had out wrestled using only one arm. He smiled to himself and thought, *if I did that, I can't let this hoe get the best of me.* Orville tried several different techniques with the hoe and after a while he was able to control the tool a little better.

Mrs. Lewis went to the store not to buy anything but to talk to Missy. *Maybe,* she thought, *Missy could talk to Orville and do some good.* "Missy, I need your help but most of all Orville needs your help. He refuses to go to the picnic on Sunday. He's afraid of what the people will think of him having only one arm."

"I don't know, Mrs. Lewis. He has not even spoken to me since he's been back, and he never used to pay me any attention."

"He doesn't know what to do around you, Missy. He likes you so much and always has. He's always talked to me about your beautiful voice, your talented piano playing and how pretty you are. Your beautiful red hair has always fascinated him. The reality is Missy, he has always had a crush on you."

"Sara and I used to talk about Orville and wonder if he would ever grow up. Maybe he has. He has such a wonderful voice too, Mrs. Lewis. I loved to hear him sing when he led the singing in church. Do you think that he would consider doing that again?"

"I don't have any idea. I think we need to take it one step at a time. You come to my house in an hour or so like you do on Saturdays to help me clean house, and we'll see what happens."

Should I make out like losing my arm makes no difference? Orville thought as he worked in the garden, *if I accept it as it really is, maybe others will. I know sooner or later I'll have to accept it. You lost your arm dummy, get over it.* As he worked, the hoeing became easier as the morning faded into mid-day.

A voice jolted Orville from his thoughts, "Orville, time for a break, how about a cool glass of lemonade?" *Lord, that's Missy. Of all people, not her, not now,* Orville thought.

"I come to help your mama clean house today. She wants you up to the house for something to drink. Wow, it's hot out here. How can you stand this heat? Better come up to the house for a few minutes."

Orville was still trying to deal with the fact that Missy was standing there. *Too late to run, I may as well go with her or she'll keep hounding me.*

"Yeah Missy, I'll take a break. I thought you helped Mama out on Saturdays."

"Usually I do, but the picnic is on Sunday. Saturday I'll have a thousand things to do. By the way, I expect you'll be leading singing at Sunday services again since you're home. We have been having a heck of a time since you were away, Orville. Thank heavens you're back. Come on let's go get something to drink."

"I cannot lead the singing in church any more, Missy, not with one arm. I don't think I can go to the picnic either." Orville said.

Missy turned around with hands on hips and eyes drilling into Orville, "What do you mean you can't lead singing with one arm? One is all anyone needs to do that, and you'd better show up at the picnic on Sunday. It's for you and the other men who fought in the war. What would it look like if you didn't show up? Come on. Let's go to the house." Missy turned and walked ahead of him up the steps. "Sit down and I'll bring you something to drink. Your mama is worried about you working in that hot sun."

"What got her all fired up?" Orville mumbled to himself. *What right does she have to boss me around?*

"Here's your lemonade, Orville Lewis. Now sit down. We have stuff to talk about. Not on the steps either but in the swing by me," Missy said as she handed Orville the glass of lemonade and took a seat in the swing.

Orville, taking the glass was just about to take a seat on the steps but turned and walked over to the swing to sit next to Missy.

"Now tell me why you are being so hard on yourself about losing your arm. You should be thankful you made it back home. So many men didn't. Don't you know that the town is glad to have you back home? It doesn't bother anyone here that you only have one arm. You are still Orville Lewis, our hero."

Orville was beginning to mellow a little as Missy's voice became more pleasant and soft. Again he thought as he looked at Missy sitting in the swing next to him, *she sure is a beautiful girl, fiery like her hair, and beautiful.*

"I don't know. I guess I just can't get use to being a cripple."

"You are not a cripple, Orville," she said softly as she placed her hand on his arm. You are as handsome as you ever were and a lot more grown up. Promise me you will at least come to church and the picnic on Sunday. We'll talk more about you leading singing again later."

"I can't promise, but I will think on it. Missy, can I come by and call on you this evening?"

"I'll fix supper tonight about six o'clock, so I will be expecting you," and with that, Missy went inside to help Mrs. Lewis with her housework.

"I don't know how you changed his mind so fast, but thank you, dear."

"He just needs a little encouragement, Mrs. Lewis, that's all."

Orville felt better as he walked back to the garden to work. *Did I make her a promise just now? I don't think so. No, I told her I would think on it. I did make a date with her for this evening. Now why did I do that? I've never called on a girl before in my life. What will I talk about? Not wrestling. Oh no, not that. I'll think of something.*

The plans with Missy gave Orville something else other than his missing arm to think about. As the time ticked by, Orville got nervous. He couldn't eat when his mother called him in for lunch.

"No, Mama. I'm going to Missy's house for supper and I want to be hungry. What will I talk about? Suppose I can't think of anything to say?"

"Don't worry about that, Orville. Missy will find plenty to talk about."

Orville went back to work in the garden until four o'clock in the afternoon. He took a bath, dressed in his Sunday clothes and waited in his room until it was time to go.

"I'll be home early, but don't wait up for me." *Gosh* he thought as he opened the yard gate, *I should have picked some of Mama's flowers for Missy. Well, too late for that now.*

Missy had prepared a pork roast with all the trimmings and a lemon pie that Orville thought melted in his mouth. He had seconds and both the conversation and the food were good. "Never had such a good meal," Orville stated just before he took his last bite of pie. "I'll help with the dishes."

"No, I'll do the dishes," Reverend Red said. "You two go and walk the meal off."

Without any argument, Missy kissed her father on the cheek and motioned for Orville to follow her out on the porch.

"Let's sit on the porch swing, Orville. You must be tired from all that garden work. It's beginning to cool off a little now in the evenings. Let's just sit and talk a while."

"Missy, you sure are pretty this evening. I was going to bring you some of Mama's flowers, but I forgot to pick them."

"That's alright, maybe next time. And, thank you for the compliment."

"You want to know something? I thought that same thing nine years ago, the first time I saw you."

"You sure are full of surprises, Orville. I didn't know you even remembered that night."

"I sure do. That was the night we lost a wagon wheel just outside of town. We saw the light in Eli's window and got soaked walking to it. Samuel got us each a blanket and we wrapped up while our clothes were drying on a line hung in the house near the fire. Eli and Samuel went for the wagon and while they were gone, you and Reverend Red brought us some of the best hot tea I'd ever had. I couldn't keep my eyes off you. I had never seen red hair on any girl before you. You were so pretty. I thought of that night many times while I was away."

"Orville Lewis, I didn't think you ever noticed me. All these years we could have been good friends. Why didn't you tell me how you felt before?" Missy asked.

"Shy, bashful or just plain dumb, I suppose. Even this morning I wanted to run when I saw you come into the garden," Orville smiled. "I'm glad I didn't do that."

"I'm glad you didn't either," Missy said as she reached for Orville's hand. "Orville, how do you really feel about me?"

"I don't know. Things are happening so fast." He leaned over and softly touched his lips to hers. "How do you feel, Missy?"

"Maybe we better see how Daddy is doing with the dishes. Would you like a little hot tea?"

Missy put the washed dishes away and made a pot of tea while Orville and Reverend Red sat in the parlor talking. "Missy tells me that she is having a hard time convincing you to come back to church and lead the singing. Why is that?"

"I don't know if it is the thing to do right now. I'm uncomfortable when I get around people since I lost my arm. I am having a hard time dealing with it."

"The way I see it, Orville, is that it is the only thing you can do. Everyone in this community knows that you lost your arm. Trying to hide or hide the fact will only make it worse. You have such a good voice and so much talent. I think the Lord wants you to use your talents for His glory and to bless others. Try to think about it that way."

After tea Orville said that he had to go. He thanked them for a fine evening. Missy walked out on the porch and said, "Daddy is right you know, about your singing."

"He may be, Missy. I'll think about it. Good night and thanks for everything."

Orville left with a full stomach and a lot to think about. He still wasn't sure about what to do, but decided he would go to church and the picnic on Sunday.

The rest of the week passed without Orville leaving home. Sunday morning he dressed in his finest clothes and walked his mother to church, carrying her picnic basket. The people greeted them but paid no mind to his missing arm.

Missy was dressed in her finest light green dress that Orville thought made her eyes look even greener. *Wow! What a beauty*, he thought to himself.

The entire community turned out and Reverend Red preached a homecoming sermon that had people wiping tears from their eyes. At the end of the service, Reverend Red had the four men who had returned from the war to stand by the door alongside him so each member of the congregation could shake their hands as they filed out the door. When the last person exited the church, Reverend Red shook their hands and thanked them for serving their country and the people of Lamb's Creek Community.

The women put their blankets and picnic baskets in the shade. Children ran and played tag or hide and seek while the men talked about their crops, cattle and farms, waiting for their wives to call them to eat. Orville helped Missy spread her blanket and unpack her food.

"Missy, you have enough here to feed half a dozen hungry men. You must have worked all night. Wonder how many roosters were cooked for this picnic?"

"I don't know but Daddy killed three. There will be a lot less crowing in the morning around here."

As Missy prepared a plate for Orville, Reverend Red walked up with Bill and Hiram. "Here are two more of our local heroes to join us for lunch. Get you a plate of Missy's cooking and find a place to sit before Orville eats it all."

Not much talking occurred until their hunger was abated and then Orville said, "Bill, Tater, I haven't had a chance to thank you for saving my life back at that army camp. I wouldn't be here now if it wasn't for you two. Thank you." Orville explained to Missy and the Reverend that Bill and Hiram stopped a man from beating him to death. He told them about being taken to the sick bay to see the camp doctor and how Miss Claire Allen nursed him back to health.

After hearing the story, Missy with tears in her eyes, also thanked the men for saving Orville and returning him home safely to her.

"We just done the same for him as he'd do for us," Bill commented. "Gotta watch out for our own."

Hiram spoke up, "Missy, you sure are pretty today. Never seen you look so good and this is the best cooking I've had in a long time. If Orville ain't smart enough to snap you up quick, he might just lose you to me. Thanks a lot Missy. It's time I got going. I'll be seeing you around."

After everyone had eaten and Orville and Missy were alone, they packed up the leftover food. Orville said, "That Hiram doesn't waste time, does he? Just spoke his intentions right out."

"Yes, Orville Lewis and you might ought to listen up. A girl can't just dangle forever. Do you have something that you want to ask me?"

"I'm not sure. You might be making a mistake with me. Are you sure you even want me to ask you a question?"

Missy was beginning to feel irritated with Orville and said, "I haven't heard anything said yet to know what you are talking about, Mr. Lewis. You know I could have little Taters same as I can have little Orvilles. He can't sing as well as you, but he is a handsome man. Don't you think?"

Orville gave a big sigh, rolled his eyes and grabbed Missy's hand in his. "Missy, you asked for it. I don't ever want to hear you say that you are sorry. So here it is, Missy Willis. Will you marry me and have little Orvilles? I do love you, Missy."

Missy said yes to Orville's proposal and they set the wedding for the following Saturday. Missy grew more excited as the time grew near and Orville grew more nervous.

"We haven't had a wedding here in Lamb's Creek since Samuel and Sari Lynn were married," Mrs. Lewis commented as she and a small group of women were talking in the store the day before the wedding. "I just hope my son doesn't run off before the wedding." The women laughed at the thought of it.

Orville thought of doing just that but thought better of the idea. *They would kill me and Hiram would be free to marry my Missy.* He shuddered at that thought. *I just have the jitters,* he thought to himself.

There was not enough room in the church building for the number of people that turned out for the wedding so many watched the ceremony through the windows. The service lasted about twenty minutes but seemed an eternity to Orville. He had no doubt he was doing the right thing marrying Missy but so many people and so much attention made him uneasy.

After the wedding and reception, Orville and Missy were presented as Mr. and Mrs. Orville Lewis. They had decided to live with Orville's mother until they could build a home of their own. The work on the new house started the week after the wedding. Over a dozen men and boys showed up at the site ready to help their pianist and music director build their new home. After the house was completed, the community gave them a house warming providing some much needed, and in most cases slightly used, items for housekeeping and stocking a pantry.

Once the building was finished, Bill called Eli and Samuel aside to tell them that he and Hiram were going to make a journey to check on his mother in Nashville. Bill told them they would return sometime in the future. "Been here too long," Bill said. "I need to see new places."

"I'm going along with him this time," Hiram added. "You know Bill is getting old and forgetful. He might need me to take care of him. Anyway, Orville done stole my girl, and I'll have to find me another one down the road."

Bill and Hiram left the next morning before the first rooster crowed.

EPILOGUE

As the years wore on, Lamb's Creek community grew. People continued to move into and settle the area. Babies were born. Additions were made to the church and store and a town hall was constructed. Roger Roads, Sara and Eli's son, married one of the newcomers, pursued a political career, was elected to Congress and moved to Washington, DC.

A fifty-year celebration was planned by and for the community. The day of the event, Eli, sixty years old, and Samuel, sixty-nine, sat on the front porch of Samuel and Sari Lynn's house reminiscing about the past.

"Folks have been coming in for this celebration for a week now," Eli exclaimed. "Some I don't even remember."

"I know," Samuel said. "It doesn't seem like fifty years since you, your parents and I drove our wagons into this little valley. It seems like just a short time ago. Do you recall that we were in a quandary about whether or not we should go on to Nashville and open a store or stay here?"

"I remember it all so well," Eli replied. "There's no doubt now,

Samuel, that we made the right decision. Look what came of it. It was slow getting started but then it seemed that overnight everyone wanted to live here. There must be over a hundred people now in Lamb's Creek, give or take a few."

"Eli, do you remember that oak over there where the women have their tables set up? You started to chop it down so we could build our store there."

"You stopped me just in time. Look how huge it is. I'm glad you didn't let me cut it down. Sara and I were talking about it last week. I remember you saying that one day we would use the shade of that tree to eat under. I couldn't imagine that back then," Eli said as he admired the scene. "Well, I better get back to the house and dress up a little. Sara says I might have to give a little speech before this celebration is over. Looks like you have company coming to see you anyway."

As Eli walked down the path to Samuel's humble home, a new fancy buggy pulled up.

"Is this where Dr. Samuel Lamb lives?" inquired the gentlemen as he stepped down from the buggy. "I have business to discuss with him."

"Right through this gate, mister, there on the porch," Eli answered.

The man was dressed in a finely tailored suit and Eli thought he looked like a big-city businessman. Eli watched as the man walked up to the steps and introduced himself to Samuel. "My name is Dr. Carl Biggs, are you Dr. Samuel Lamb?" Eli heard the man ask as he walked away.

"Yes, I am Samuel Lamb. Come on up and have a chair. Are

you here for the celebration?"

"No, I am here on business. I would like to make you a very lucrative proposition. The Board of Doctors at Vanderbilt Hospital sent me to make you an offer of fifty thousand dollars a year to join them at the hospital. One of our distinguished board members is Dr. William Kilpatrick. I'm sure you'll recall that Dr. Kilpatrick and you attended your studies and medical training together. Dr. Kilpatrick believes unequivocally that you are the man we need to head up our new mental health department. Now this is just a starting salary, Dr. Lamb. There's a furnished house waiting for you and your lovely wife. I personally think this is something that you cannot consider turning down. People of color, Mr. Lamb, don't get offers like this every day."

Samuel nodded his head thoughtfully.

Dr. Biggs cleared his throat and continued, "The individuals that come to our hospital are people of standing and means. They are the cream of the crop and are looking for treatment from medical experts. You won't be delivering babies or making house calls."

Samuel interrupted, "Now just a moment, Dr. Biggs, you haven't given me a chance to give you an answer. What do you mean no babies and no house calls? What do you mean by cream of the crop, Dr. Biggs? Look around you. Do you see the children running and playing over there as their mothers prepare for our celebration? I delivered them and they are the cream of the crop. They are my family and my friends and they don't see my lovely wife and me as 'people of color.' My foot was the very first to step on the soil of this valley. This valley is called Lamb's Creek

Community after me, Dr. Biggs. I am licensed in most every field of medicine, can go to any hospital and make more money than I could ever spend, but, Dr. Biggs, I choose to stay where my heart is. I am paid in some cash, whatever people can spare, but more valuable than a 'lucrative' salary as you mentioned is what I am able to give. What would they do if I up and moved away? Who would take care of them? I was born a slave, Dr. Biggs, but I was not a slave in my mind or heart. I was given my freedom papers, but that is not what made me free. A man is a slave only if he allows himself to be in his mind. Come in the house, I want to show you what is important to me."

Dr. Biggs followed Samuel into what he considered to be a meager home for a physician of such status in the medical community. It was a small house and Dr. Biggs had to admit to himself that it had a homey quaintness. He followed Samuel over to a few items hanging on a wall near a fireplace.

"These first three documents are self explanatory. They are doctorate degrees from three of the most highly acclaimed medical universities in the world, two here in the northeast and one in England. They should interest you. As for the money you offered, I could lecture at any one of these universities for a comparable amount of money. You have no doubt read some of my work in medical journals. The journals, like you and your board clamor for, are what I have to offer in the field of medicine. I have not been idle in my profession, Dr. Biggs."

Samuel now pointed to a small coin and said, "But that one little dime that you see hanging here means more to me than all the money in the world. It brings me back to my roots."

"Docta Biggs, I find dat dime when I be eight years ole and I punch a hole in it so I wouldn't get it mixed up with other dimes dat I might find. Dat dime made it possible to buy da next thing you see. It be da hide off a little black lamb, my first friend. It give me my second name, Lamb. I had just one name, Sammy, but it made me Sammy Lamb. Some mean man stole 'im and kill 'im, but I still gots his hide. It too means more than money. It brought me good luck and a friend for life, little Massa Roads. It brought bad luck to da man dat stole it.

"Da next thing, Docta Biggs, be my freedom paper dat my Massa Roads give me when I be nine. They ain't what make me free though. I always been free. I be two people, Docta, one dat lives in yo world and one dat lives in mine. Go back where you come from Docta Biggs and tell 'em I don't accept yo offer. Just don't try and explain. They wouldn't understand it either.

Dr. Carl Biggs couldn't believe what he had just witnessed. He looked dumbfounded at Samuel, perplexed by what he could never understand and embarrassed that he may have insulted the esteemed doctor. He turned and walked back to his new buggy and headed back where he came from.

Sari Lynn entered the room as Dr. Biggs climbed into his buggy. "Who was that, dear?" she asked Samuel.

"That's just someone that lost his way, sugar. I directed him back to where he needs to go." Samuel was still standing and looking at his mementos hanging on the wall. "I think I'm going into the sheep business, Sari Lynn."

"What in the world are you talking about Samuel Lamb?"

"Sorry, Sari Lynn, just one sheep, a little black lamb. I'll call him Blackie Two."

After the fifty-year celebration, Samuel did purchase a little black lamb. It quickly belonged to the whole community, treasured by all, a community mascot of sorts. Blackie Two followed Samuel on his house calls and everywhere he traversed.

Samuel thought a lot about time.

Have you ever noticed that everything goes in a cycle? Even I, Time, go around and around, watch my hands. A very smart man once stated, "There is nothing new under the sun. What is, has been before." Nothing stands still, not even me.

Lamb's Creek was no exception. The fifty-year celebration was a success and so was the hundredth. People will tell you time changes things. This is not true. People change things. The community became a city and no one remembered why it was called Lamb's Creek. They changed the name.

This is why I decided to tell this story. People are born, they live and die, but I go on and on and continue to observe.

The End

Photograph Copyright © 2011, Webster Miller

ABOUT THE AUTHOR

Donald Miller was born in a south Louisiana lumber mill settlement in the Atchafalaya Basin. He is a simple man of great spiritual conviction and wisdom. His first novel tells the fate of the families that struggled to build Lamb's Creek, a Tennessee community that spurned slavery and survived the bloodshed of the Civil War. Don lives in the hills of Tennessee with his wife, Dolores, and pup, Noggin, in an old tobacco barn they now call home.

For more information visit:
www.DonMillerWriter.com

Made in the USA
San Bernardino, CA
01 October 2014